THE KILLING JAR

Emily Slate Mystery Thriller
Book 18

ALEX SIGMORE

Dark Woods Press

THE KILLING JAR: EMILY SLATE MYSTERY THRILLER BOOK 18

1st Edition

Print ISBN 978-1-971270-22-7

Description

Some places are built to heal. Others are designed to hurt.

Special Agent Emily Slate has just been appointed to lead a new team within the FBI. It's a fresh start. A new boss. A new mandate. But no time to breathe.

A series of disturbing reports from a remote psychiatric facility land on her desk—patients suddenly cut off from family, strange staff turnover, and whispers of something far more sinister beneath the surface.

The deeper she and her team dig, the clearer it becomes: this isn't about mental health. It's about power, control, and silence. And someone inside will do whatever it takes to keep the truth buried—even if it means killing to protect it.

As the lines between sanity and conspiracy blur, Emily must navigate the shadows of an institution built on secrets… before she becomes its next patient.

Prologue

"Mom?"

Renata glances up, smiling at her youngest daughter. Where had she been just now? She'd gotten too lost in thought lately—too much on her mind. The bills, for one thing. The mold in the bathroom was another that, despite her repeated calls, the super still hadn't come to fix. And then there was the fact that Desiree was already failing one of her classes. Her teacher had said middle school would be more difficult for her. She'd made it through elementary okay, but middle school was a lot different. She was required to make her way to different classes all day and there was a lot more to keep up with. At least Ember was doing well enough. Maybe not a straight A student, but considering how much she helped out around the house and took care of her little sister, Renata was happy for anything above a C.

Just get through the school year, then you'll be able to relax.

It was a mantra she'd told herself repeatedly. Some days it was all she could do to make it to bedtime. It felt as if there was a huge weight bearing down on her all her waking hours. There was never enough money and Andre was barely pulling in minimum wage. Renata had been on disability since the accident two years ago which meant all she could do were office jobs these days, but without an associate's degree, there was a fat chance of that happening. No matter how much experience she had, she didn't meet the "standard" for employment at most places. And they could only limp along for another few months until they'd lose their apartment. And then what?

"*Mom*."

Renata turned to her youngest. "Yes, sorry. What?"

"I wanted to show you what I made," she said, holding up a pink sheet of construction paper. Drawn on it was probably the worst rendition of a horse Renata had ever seen. But it was the most beautiful drawing she could have ever received.

"For me?"

Desiree nodded. "Yep. Don't worry mama. Everything will work out."

Renata furrowed her brow. Desiree wasn't usually so introspective. Most of her attention was caught up on the next shiny new thing, no matter where it came from. It wasn't like her to notice other people's problems. Not that she wasn't a caring child, she just hadn't fully grown into her empathy yet. The fact that even *she* was beginning to notice was worrying.

"Thanks, honey," Renata said. "And thank you for the picture."

"You're welcome. I love you."

A funny feeling came over Renata. "I love you too." And as she said the words, the image of her daughter disappeared as if she were made of nothing but smoke. Renata looked at her hands, only to realize she was holding nothing more than a bedsheet between her fingers.

"Having the hallucinations again?"

Renata whipped her head around to the woman standing behind her. She was dressed all in white, with a strange little hat and two large men behind her, dressed similarly, minus the headgear.

Renata squeezed her eyes closed, trying to focus on the moment. Had her daughter even been real? Or was it this place that was her reality? Every time she was in one place, the other felt like a dream. Until she switched back again.

"I was… thinking about my daughter," Renata said, pushing herself off the floor to sit on the edge of the bed.

"You'll see her again soon," the woman said. Renata couldn't remember her name right off the top of her head. But it was something kind of funny. Her head hurt.

The woman took a seat beside her on the bed. "We'll get you better. It just takes time and treatment. That's why you're here right? To get better? And to help your family?"

Renata nodded. "There's mold… in the bathroom. The super—"

"I know," the woman—Renata recalled she was a nurse—said. She put her warm hand on Renata's, giving it a supportive squeeze. "You've told me. They don't have to worry about that anymore. Remember? Your family moved out of that apartment right after you came to stay with us."

"But Desiree's grades," she protested. "She's going to fail if I'm not there to—"

"Shh," the nurse replied. "It's okay. Your family is being well taken care of. You need to worry about you. About getting better so that you can see them again, right?"

Renata nodded, though she didn't remember any of that. Why couldn't she remember?

"Feel up to another treatment today?"

"I… I guess," Renata said. As she looked around her room some of the details came back. She'd been in this place for a few weeks…months? She'd come here because they could help make her better… wait, was that right? Or had she come here because she needed to help her family? To relieve them of the burden? She couldn't recall.

All she knew was she had been desperate. Things couldn't keep going like they had been.

Her room was tastefully decorated with a clean bed, a small table with a metal vase containing fresh flowers and there was even a TV on one of the walls, though she didn't remember ever switching it on. Outside rain pounded on the old window, which was built into the stone alcove at the end of the room. She remembered looking out and seeing the gardens beyond. It was a beautiful old building; it reminded her of a castle.

She'd come to stay in a fairytale.

"Would you like to walk or do you need some help?" the nurse asked.

"I… I can walk," Renata replied. "If you can remind me where to go."

The nurse smiled. "Of course." She nodded to one of the men who helped Renata stand and guided her to the hallway beyond her door. There were many other doors that looked just like hers, though she couldn't remember if she'd met anyone here or not. And if she had, who was to say they were any more real than her daughter had been a few moments ago?

Renata was sick, she needed help. That's what they kept telling her.

That's why she was here.

But as she made her way down the hallway, a deeper, more primal feeling stirred in her stomach. She thought she remembered people screaming. Of seeing other women, their eyes glazed-over and their jaws completely slack, drool hanging from one side. Had that been real, or just something her brain made up after having watched too many movies? When she tried to focus on the memories, they slipped through her fingers into the dark background of her mind.

Her daughters. Her husband.

She kept the images of them in her mind as she allowed herself to be guided in the correct direction. She was doing this for them. So she wouldn't be a burden. So Andre could take care of their needs for once. So she wasn't in the way any longer.

"Here we are," the nurse said, indicating the too-bright room to her right. Renata shielded her eyes as she was guided inside. "Just take a seat."

But as soon as she saw the chair, Renata recoiled, as if she'd been bitten by one of the rattlesnakes she found that time on her grandmother's farm. She'd come right up on them and it had been a miracle they hadn't struck. She didn't know why, but she knew sitting in that chair was *bad*. But she couldn't explain why.

Renata tried to back away, to get back to her room, or even away from this place, but found strong arms pinning her in place.

"No, no," she began to whine before the nurse appeared in front of her.

"Now, now, it's okay," she said. "You're safe here. You've done this a dozen times. We're trying to make you better."

That was a lie. She couldn't explain why, but Renata knew it in her soul as well as she knew her own daughter's birthdays. March 11th and November 16th. And that chair was *wrong*. She pulled away again, trying to get out of the man's grip, but he only tightened it.

"Renata, you want to get better, don't you? So you can go home to your family?" the nurse asked.

"Y—yes," she replied. "But… but…"

The nurse gave her a reassuring nod. "I know. It's scary. But it will only hurt for just a second, I promise. We have to do the treatment otherwise you'll never get better."

Conflict flooded Renata's brain. Was she telling the truth? Had Renata imagined something worse than was actually here? If she'd done it dozens of times it couldn't be *that* bad, right? And she did want to get better. She wanted to see her daughters' faces again. To see how proud they would be when they realized she was all better. That there was no longer anything wrong with her.

She relaxed in the grip of the man.

"That's better," the nurse said. "Come now, let's get you comfortable."

Renata made her way into the bright room and took a seat in the plush chair. It was more like a recliner that you would find in someone's living room rather than something you'd see in an examination room. But when she sat down, that unease bubbled up from her stomach into her throat and she found she had a hard time breathing.

"Deep breaths, slow," the nurse said. "Let's just take a second here, okay?"

"Okay," Renata squeaked. All she knew was she would rather be anywhere but here. She wanted to be back home. Or hell, even in the unemployment line, waiting for whatever meager payment she would get this month.

But all of that would be over once she was better. She'd be able to get a real job. Something stable. Which meant a permanent place to live. Maybe even a house one day. She just had to get through this.

"Great job," the nurse said. "Now just sit right there and I'll be back in a second."

One of the men stayed near the door, though he didn't look at Renata. He just stared straight forward. The other man left with the nurse.

She took three long, deep breaths, trying to slow her heartrate. She could do this. She had made it through so much, faced so many obstacles in her life. And maybe most of them had knocked her down, but she always found a way back up. And this was her chance. That much she *knew*. This was her one chance to make it all right.

Her mother had faced a choice like this once. A choice that would have pulled Renata, her brother and her cousins out of poverty forever, but mom hadn't taken it. She'd chickened out at the last minute. But Renata wasn't going to let that happen to her family. She'd been given this opportunity and she was going to make it count. She was going to change her family's life for the better.

No matter what it took.

"There now," the nurse said as she returned. "You look calmer already. Now you know how this goes. I'll give you something to help you relax a little more and then we'll begin."

Renata nodded as the nurse rolled up her sleeve. The thin cotton of the clothes she'd been provided rolled easily, exposing the dark skin of her arm.

The nurse pulled out a needle with a clear substance inside before swabbing Renata's arm with an alcohol swab. She pressed the needle to a vein just beneath the skin and a pinch later, Renata could feel the substance entering her bloodstream.

There was a snap somewhere in the back of her head, like the crack of lightning and all the memories came flooding back all at once. She tried to pull her arm away but the nurse had a strong grip on Renata's arm, keeping it from moving.

"Hold her, she's going," the nurse said as the glut of memories flooded Renata's brain. And in that moment she understood everything she'd forgotten.

As she began to thrash, the nurse removed the empty needle and Renata felt hands all over her, keeping her pinned to the chair.

"You can't do this to me!" she screamed. "This isn't what you promised!" Pain erupted from her arm and shot straight to her head, making it feel like her brain was going to explode. "You can't...."

But the words were cut off by her bloodcurdling scream that echoed through the halls.

Chapter One

FAILURE.

That's the word that keeps repeating in my head. I already know what they'll say: there was nothing you could have done, you aren't responsible for everything. No matter how much you try, Emily Slate does not control the universe.

But it still doesn't keep the word out of my brain.

Because somewhere, if I had been a little better, a little faster, a little smarter, maybe Janice wouldn't have died. Maybe I could have seen the pattern before anyone else, maybe I could have figured out Fletch's plan. It had been me all along. She died because of *me.*

"Slate! Are we boring you?"

I snap to attention, staring at the two people at the head of the conference table, Agents Vostov and Pendergast, my new bosses. Pendergast is a nerdy sort of man who always wears suspenders and a bushy moustache that looks too big on his thin frame. He's not the one I worry about. It's Agent Vostov, a woman who is probably younger than me with an intensity that reminds me of Camille. I still haven't seen the woman smile and she strikes me as the kind of person who if she were ever to take revenge on someone, she would take her time and enjoy it. She stares at me through her dark glasses, which match her hair, waiting for an answer.

"Not at all," I say, pretending like I've been listening this entire time. The rest of my team surrounds the table. Zara to my right, Liam to my left and past him, Nadia and Elliott. Nadia always has that effortless look of a movie star paired with the sweetest and most genuine personality and today is no exception. Elliott on the other hand, is the silent type, with deep set brown eyes and pronounced features, giving him an air of mysteriousness about him which I really think is just his dislike for conversation.

Everyone is staring at me, Zara giving me the eye in particular. We're in hour two of our initial introduction to our new team structure here and honestly, it's beginning to drag. While I'm grateful for the opportunity Agents Pendergast and Vostov have offered me here, I won't forget they were the ones ready to throw me to the wolves when they thought I was responsible for the bomb at the J. Edgar Hoover building. Until I'm sure I can trust them, I'll be watching my back.

Agent Pendergast stares at me a moment before turning back to the display on the screen at the end of the table. "As I was saying, this is a test program you'll be working under and has yet to be proven."

"What sort of program is this?" Zara asks, not bothering to wait for a pause in Pendergast's droning. "I've never seen anything like it."

"Essentially, it's a collator," he replies. "We take in massive amounts of data that is reported to the FBI and the program uses machine learning to parse that into actionable content."

"So it's an AI machine," she replies.

"No," Vostov says through her teeth. "This isn't just making shit up. These are real cases that fall outside the normal chain of communication and purview of the FBI."

"Why even put something like this together?" Liam asks. "The Department is already stretched thin as it is."

"Exactly," Vostov replies. "There are too many cases and not enough agents to handle them on a daily basis and priority must be delegated. That's where we come in. We take everything that isn't immediately actionable and try to find common threads."

"To what end?" Elliott asks. "What do you hope to accomplish?"

Pendergast clears his throat. "I'm sure you're all aware, the FBI has always had its fair share of scandals, especially with what happened regarding Deputy Director Cochran aka James Hunter." His eyes land on me for a brief moment. "We've been trying for over a year to repair that reputation, but too many people are being lost in the cracks. The idea behind this program is to help rebuild the public's trust in this institution by focusing on cases that may not be examined otherwise. Our thought is maybe only one in a hundred of the ones we put together will need to be actionable, but when that is the case, we want your team working them."

"I'm still not sure I understand," Nadia says, her long hair pulled back in a perfect ponytail. "We're a cleanup crew?"

"No," Vostov replies. "You're the agents who help the people who would never receive it otherwise. Based on our initial findings, the kinds of cases you'll end up with will be out of the ordinary, not your standard fare."

"I'm assuming you're not talking about hunting aliens," I say, barely masking my sarcasm.

Vostov shoots me a look that could cut through steel. "You are welcome to go back to your old job at any time, Agent Slate. Though, given everything that's happened, I'd be surprised if you'd be allowed much more than filing duties in the basement."

I scowl at her.

"We selected your team because you have a history of working with some less-than-ordinary cases. And you have an extremely high close rate versus your case load. But also because after everything that's happened, the Bureau was under a lot of pressure to make sure you were somewhere you wouldn't cause them any further trouble. And that happens to be here. If you feel a leash around your neck, good. Because until you can prove to us that you won't go rogue any longer, you're under a microscope."

"Wait a second," I say. "That was just me, it shouldn't—"

"*Don't*—" Vostov shoots back. "—insult my intelligence. Would you like me to name how each member of your team violated at least three federal laws *each*? Or may we continue with the presentation?"

I utter a frustrated breath. She's not wrong. After everything that's happened, I can't deny we're on thin ice. We've pushed our luck to the limit and I shouldn't be surprised we're getting a slap on the hand. But at the same time, I *hate* being constrained. And I hate that I've brought this on my friends as well. If it weren't for me, none of them, Liam included, would have ever been in this position.

"Thank you, Vostov says without waiting for an answer. "We know you're still getting used to being here, but you'll settle in quick. Oh, and don't bother spending a lot of time unpacking your new offices. This is still very much a test program. If it doesn't work, you'll find yourself right back where you started. Though I highly doubt any other division of the FBI will keep you together as a group."

She takes a seat without taking her eyes off me. Her message is crystal clear. *Don't fuck this up.* Otherwise we all go back to headquarters and are divided up. To be honest, she's not wrong. They would stuff me in a filing job so deep in the FBI I'd never see daylight again. Either that or they'd force me into early retirement. This place may be an opportunity, but it's also a lifeline. If it fails, we're done.

"Now that we have the basics out of the way, let me show you what your first case will be," Pendergast says, taking Vostov's place beside the screen. He clicks his remote and the image of an imposing gothic building takes up the screen. Along the bottom, the words *Lazar Mental Correctional Facility* are written. "Anyone familiar with this place?" Like Vostov, he doesn't wait for an answer. "It sits about two hours outside of DC, isolated except for a small town nearby. It was originally an insane asylum back from the early turn of the century until the 1950s. It then closed down and was reopened in the seventies as a women's Mental Correctional Facility which works hand in hand with the Federal Prison system."

Zara leans over to me, whispering. "Is it just me or does Vostov look like she could be an inmate?"

I chuckle but don't miss the flash of Vostov's gaze in our direction. The woman is so tightly wound it wouldn't take much more than a balloon popping to send her into low orbit.

"Here's where you come in," Pendergast continues. "We've received not one, but two calls from families attempting to reach their loved ones inside the facility and being met with silence."

"Don't the inmates have the right to visitation and communication?" Nadia asks.

He nods. "They do. The original complaints were that the facility was denying access."

"That seems more like an internal prison problem," Zara says. "Why not just report it and let the inspectors work it out? If the prison is in violation of federal law——"

Pendergast shakes his head. "It never got that far. Both families withdrew their complaints within twenty-four hours."

"That's... odd," Liam says.

"Indeed," Pendergast replies. "Even odder, when we looked into the families who contacted the FBI, we could find no record of anyone related to either family being interred at Lazar Mental Correctional Facility."

"Are you thinking they died while in custody?" Nadia asks.

"It's a possibility, though that's not uncommon. Unless

they died under mysterious or questionable circumstances. In which case someone may have erased their prison records."

"Could the families have contacted the wrong facility? Maybe the inmates have been moved to a different prison?" Elliott asks.

Pendergast shakes his head, but smiles as he does it, as if he was expecting the question. "No. They're not in the system… *anywhere*. As far as we can tell, they don't have any relatives in prison at all, state or federal."

We all exchange glances with each other.

"What does the facility say?" I ask.

"That's what you're going to find out," Vostov replies. "About ten years ago this facility had issues with patient abuse. It wasn't widespread and was eliminated quickly, but we don't want a repeat. This could also be nothing more than a clerical error. But the fact we have two different families claiming the same thing and then recanting makes me more than a little suspicious. If nothing else, I want you to go in there and make sure there's nothing fishy going on."

"Have you pulled the reports from the inspectors?" Zara asks.

"Agent Foley, that is precisely what *you* are here to do." Vostov glares at her. "Our system only identifies possible cases; it doesn't work them for us."

"Right," Zara replies, crossing her arms.

"Slate, I'll leave this to you to delegate. Check it out and see if we have something here. And keep me and Agent Pendergast updated with your progress. We're not going to be looking over your shoulder, but at the same time, you only have so much lead. Do we understand each other?"

I glower at the woman. "Yes, ma'am."

"Good. I look forward to seeing what you come back with."

Pendergast clears his throat again. "All the information is

being sent to your portal access. Take the weekend to settle in and get started on this first thing Monday."

He says that like it hasn't already been a whirlwind of a week. Seven days ago, I was in Italy tracking down Fletch and Theo with Zara and barely escaping with our lives. We spent the first half of the week just trying to get everything caught up with our paperwork to Caruthers, as well as clean out our old desks and move everything out here. At least I won't have to fight DC traffic in the mornings anymore, but working out of a nondescript office building in the suburbs isn't exactly ideal.

I head back to my "office" which is little more than a room with a window overlooking the parking lot where my car currently sits. Beyond that is nothing but more office buildings and trees as far as the eye can see.

"You okay?"

I turn to find Liam has followed me in from the meeting. I hadn't even realized he was right behind me. "What? Sure. Why?"

"You just seemed a little distracted," he says.

"Just… thinking about things," I say. If there's one thing that's been nice about this week it's being home with him and the dogs. I approach him and lower my voice. "Do you think this thing has any teeth? Or are they just trying to keep us busy?"

He shrugs. "If it wasn't something real I don't think they'd put five agents on it."

I pinch my brows together. "I guess. But I can't help but think this is all some kind of… daycare, for lack of a better word. They're just trying to keep us busy."

"For what purpose?" he asks.

"I don't know. Maybe they've changed their minds and are going to bring charges against me after all," I say. "And they need time to build a case."

"If that were true, you wouldn't still have your gun," he replies. "You'd be sitting at home with an ankle monitor on."

I sigh. "I guess you're right. I just can't help but feel like we're being pandered to here. I mean… what kind of case is this? Sounds like nothing more than a couple of mistaken identities to me."

"I guess we'll find out," he says and leans down, planting a kiss on my cheek. "Let's talk about it at home." He heads out before I can protest. I don't know why, but I can't help but be unsettled. As I plop down in my squeaky office chair behind my very standard and standard-issue desk, I can't shake these feelings that something else is going on with him.

Then again, I have been under a lot of stress this past week. Being arrested and interred isn't something that you just *get over*, even if you are eventually exonerated.

One thing is for sure, if Pendergast and Vostov don't see the kind of progress they want, the five of us are going to find ourselves spread to the four corners of the country, our futures filled with nothing but decades of grunt work.

Somehow, that seems worse than the internment.

Chapter Two

THE GUILT FOLLOWS ME ALL THE WAY HOME. I THOUGHT AFTER being banished to the desert for a month, then sneaking back into the city without being able to stay at my home or be with the people I love, that I'd find some solace this past week. And while it has been nice, I keep coming back to the question:

What if I'd done more?

"Careful or you'll pop a blood vessel."

I shoot Liam a quick snarl before going back to my brooding. Rocky and Timber lay on either side of me on the couch, somehow having nuzzled both their heads in my lap at once. They've been overly clingy since I got back, probably because they had no idea what was going on. One day I was here and the next I was gone for almost a month.

"This is the calmest I've seen them in weeks," Liam says, coming over to sit in the chair beside the couch.

"It's because your primary human abandoned you," I say to the boys, rubbing both their heads. "You had to deal with the backup."

"Uh, excuse me," he replies. "I am *not* the backup."

I shoot him a look, then glance at the dogs in my lap who haven't even cracked an eye open. Usually they're running all over the place, especially around feeding time. But ever since I've been back they've stayed right at my side.

"Okay, maybe I am," he says. "But I take offense to that name."

"Secondary?" I suggest.

"Somehow that sounds worse." Silence falls between us. Liam has cooked every night this week, even though I told him he didn't need to. He said he missed it, but I'm not sure that's the whole truth. He's been quieter than normal since I came back home and I haven't been able to get him to open up like normal. I can't help but wonder if he regrets helping me and putting his own career in jeopardy.

"Thinking about Janice again?" he asks, breaking the silence.

"Trying not to," I say. "I know it's not healthy. But I can't help it."

"Want to talk to someone about it?"

I scoff. "Like Frost? No, that man has listened to me enough. I don't think seeing a Bureau-appointed therapist would be a good idea right now. I don't exactly have the best reputation."

"No one blames you for what happened," he says, shifting slightly in his chair.

"Everyone *says* that, but I can see the truth in their eyes," I reply. "And in the way they act towards me. Towards all of us. It's like I've made us a bunch of pariahs." Before he can argue I hit him with it. I never have been one for subtlety. "Are you sorry you helped me?"

"What? Of course not."

"It could have cost you your career. It still might."

He leans forward and reaches for one of my hands. Finally, I give in. His hand is slightly rough, but warm to the touch. "Listen to me. I don't regret anything."

"But something *is* wrong. I can tell."

"I'm just getting used to not being a bachelor anymore,"

he says. "You were gone a long time. For a while I wasn't sure you'd be able to come back. And then there was all the undercover communications, the clandestine meetings… it was a lot."

"I know. And I'm sorry. If I'd known—"

He squeezes my hand. "I'm not saying it's your fault. Or that you're responsible. But it's going to take us some time to find our groove again."

I nod. He's right, of course. We both went through a major disruption. I'm honestly surprised he stuck around. Most guys would have taken a look at this train wreck and tucked tail. Still… I feel like there's something I'm missing.

"If we weren't starting this new position I'd say we should take a vacation," I finally say. "We need some time away. A reset."

"That sounds nice," he replies. "Vostov doesn't strike me as the type who grants vacations."

"I mean, I technically have weeks of it built up," I say. "I could force the issue. But I don't think doing that the first week of a new job is a great idea."

"Let's give it a month," he says.

"Yeah, if we still have our jobs by then."

Liam scoots to the edge of the chair, taking my hand in both of his. "Listen. I know you're trying to take on all this responsibility yourself. But you don't need to do that. We can each carry some of the load."

"But they're not looking to you or Elliott or Zara to make this work. They're looking to me."

"None of us are going to let you fall. You know that, right?"

I know they wouldn't… not on purpose. But if this is some kind of a setup by Vostov or Pendergast, where we're designed to fail so they can slap a "defective" label on us and lock us away forever, then I don't want Liam or anyone else anywhere close to that blowback.

He doesn't get it. I know he's trying to be supportive, but Liam isn't in my position. He can't understand, no matter how much he wants to.

"I think I'm going to take a bath, see if I can't get some of this stress out."

"Want me to—"

"No, I got it. Thanks." I head to the bathroom at the end of the hall, passing the room we've set up as a small office in the house. I can't see it, because it's in the top drawer of the desk in there, but I can feel Janice's letter to me as I pass the room. I've read it at least a dozen times since Liam brought it back from evidence. And every time I do, I only get angrier that I couldn't stop it. That the man who ordered it to happen is still awaiting trial and by all accounts will be for a long time. The justice system moves slowly for someone like Fletch. A powerful man with connections across the globe. Investigations have to be checked and double checked, evidence has to be cataloged and then the lawyers get involved.

And there is no doubt that Fletch has hired the very best. They will look for every little loophole or procedure to slow everything down further, to drain the state's resources and time, to drag things out until it's more beneficial to let him go than to continue prosecuting.

But that's not going to happen. He's not going anywhere and he will pay for everything he did. Including Janice.

As I draw the bath, my thoughts go back to Italy, where he confessed to me that it was some no-name grunt who got to her. Not an international assassin, or someone with a hundred kills under their belt. Nope. Just some nobody who was given a job and managed to get close enough to make it happen.

I think that's the worst part of it. That it was all so *normal*. It didn't take the cooperation of ten nation-states to take her down. And somehow it seems like it should have. She was a giant in the FBI, a formidable presence who at times seemed unstoppable. And no matter how badly I screwed up, she always had my back.

So where was I when someone was slipping something into her drink? Where was I when she was trying to track down the people responsible for all of this? I was off hiding like a coward.

But not anymore. I'm going to make sure that man pays for every single life he took, especially Janice's; I don't care if it was his hand or someone else's, he's the one responsible. And he can try to pull every dirty trick in the book; he's not getting away with it.

Liam's knock comes at the door. "Em, you okay?" I'm still sitting on the edge of the tub, the water cooling. I haven't even removed my shirt yet.

"Yeah," I say. "Just give me a few minutes."

His footsteps pad down the hall, followed by two pairs from the pups. He's not the only one who's needed to get used to a new routine. While I was away I'd gotten used to living on my own again, or at least, not living with a guy. Coming back has taken more adjustment than I'd anticipated. Probably because we've never really had time to fall into a regular routine. Usually there is always some crisis or another that either one or both of us are responding to.

That makes routine hard.

I empty half the tub and run it again, this time with hotter water as I get undressed. I slip in while it's still filling up, the scalding water feeling like it's going to burn my skin but I don't care. I want to feel the burn. Because it's how I feel inside. Like I'm going to erupt at any second. I just don't want to erupt at Liam or Zara or anyone else I care about.

No, there's only one person who deserves this level of wrath. And I need to save all my anger for him.

Chapter Three

When Zara opens her front door, a dark and foreboding apartment greets her. She allows herself to be enveloped in complete darkness until she hits the switch just inside. Half the place is still in boxes; except for the few items she uses on a regular basis. For a minute there it looked like she might never come back from New Mexico, but thankfully her stuff had arrived mostly intact.

As she moves through the empty apartment, she can't help but notice how noisy it is here. She can still hear some of the traffic from outside and the upstairs neighbors are at it again, thumping and stomping around like a bunch of Gorgs. Sounds that used to be nothing more than background noise now grate on her nerves.

She reaches her refrigerator only to find it mostly empty. She hasn't restocked since they'd gotten back, instead relying on a steady diet of Chinese and Italian. She'll have to order in again if she wants dinner. Opening the freezer, she finds the bottle of vodka she keeps inside and pulls it out, pouring herself a shot before knocking it back and surveying the apartment. What had once been a lively place now seems empty, despite it not being different at all.

No, what's different is she was betrayed by Theo, lost Janice, and almost lost her best friend. All at the same time.

She pours herself another shot.

"Maybe I should get a cat," she says to no one before knocking back the second drink. Her apartment has a pet policy but she can't remember what it is. Then again, Em might not want her to babysit the dogs anymore if she has a cat running around. Zara could get a dog too, but they need so much more care, and she wouldn't be around enough during the day. It wouldn't be fair.

"Guess it's just you and me," she says, taking the bottle with her to the couch.

It has been a rough two months. She chuckles. That's the understatement of the year. It's been an *insane* two months. And as much as she tried not to think about him, Theo had continued to occupy her thoughts. His betrayal was bad enough, but what was worse is she hadn't seen it coming.

Or had she?

She'd known something was off the past few months, something about working closely with him on all those cases. Maybe she'd just ignored it because she didn't want to face the truth, or maybe she thought she was overreacting, but something about him had seemed a little… *wrong.*

But damn, the sex had been *insane.*

Of course, now that it was all behind her, it was easy to see. In the moment she had assumed it was part of his eccentricity, or maybe his personality overall. Part of his appeal was his mysterious nature. She had been playing with fire and she knew it. But that was only because finding a stable relationship in this line of work was rare. What Em and Liam have is out of the ordinary and not common at all. But Zara's had more than her fair share of heartache and had just gotten tired of it all. After Raoul's "wet fish" attitude, Theo had seemed like a breath of fresh air. A fellow operative, albeit independent, working for the greater good. Someone who seemed to have integrity, skill, and would keep Zara on her toes.

She slumps into the couch, pushing herself as far into it as she can. Did she really think that a relationship with her was enough to change who he was at his core? She should have seen that he was only out for himself, that eventually he would betray everyone and everything around him to get what he wanted.

In that way he was a carbon copy of Sam.

Disgusted, Zara gets up and places the bottle back in the freezer. She goes to her computer and opens one of the RPGs she'd been playing through before their sabbatical to New Mexico. It's been a solid two months since she last really put some time into it, but she grabs the largest blanket she owns, wraps it around herself and sits in her chair, starting right back where she left off. She plays with the precision of a surgeon, attacking and dodging at the perfect times to vanquish the monsters in her way. Enough so that her other party members barely even had to raise a sword or staff.

It isn't until she runs into a dialogue scene that she can't skip that she realizes tears have fallen from her eyelids and dried on her cheeks. Theo isn't worth crying over. Not after his betrayal. He claimed he'd cared for Zara, but no one who truly cared for her would ever do that to her.

Again her thoughts return to Sam and she pushes them away. She would *not* think about him. She'd made herself a promise. Never again.

The dialogue scene ends, allowing her to make more progress, but it is slow and she isn't enjoying it. Instead she switches over to something with a little more punch. A battle simulator where she can just beat the snot out of character after character until she runs out of health. She makes it twelve rounds before some giant with green spikey hair finally takes her down.

Zara pushes herself away from the computer. This isn't

doing the trick. The intrusive thoughts just keep coming. She needs to find a way to self-regulate, otherwise she will start to spiral. What would Em do in this situation? Probably something stupid like going out for a run.

Zara groans. But if it stops her from thinking about all the times she's been disappointed in her life, she's willing to give it a shot. Not to mention she needs to get her head right for this new job they have coming up. She needs to be sharp and ready, and she *really* wants to get a look at that program Pendergast uses. See if it can really do what they claim it can do. Maybe Em was right and this was all nothing more than to placate them until the FBI could figure out what to do with them. Or maybe it *was* real, which if that was the case it would give them the opportunity to work some really unique cases. Whatever the situation, Zara didn't want to be caught off guard.

Grumbling to herself, she goes to her closet, then remembers her workout clothes are still in a box somewhere and stomps her way out to the living room, finding the box she needs and tears it open, tossing things left and right until she finds some sweatpants and a matching top.

"Stupid running," she says under her breath as she finds some tennis shoes and laces them up. Why did everything have to involve going outside to exert energy? Her games had always worked in the past. Not to mention it was dark as crap outside.

As she pulls her hair back into a ponytail and grabs a pair of earbuds and her key, she thinks about also taking some pepper spray just in case. But honestly, she's so keyed up that if anyone tries jumping her, she's pretty sure she'll just tear their face off.

Zara leaves her apartment, locking her door behind her and heads out into the dark, starting with a regular pace. Within minutes she is already panting, but it seems to be doing the trick. Theo's stupid face finally fades from her mind. But as she turns the corner and lets up, other thoughts begin to squeeze their way in.

Memories she hadn't thought about in years. Memories of her parents. Her brother. And the megaton bomb that went along with all of it. Zara pushes herself harder, forcing the memories away, running at a near sprint.

But they won't leave her alone. Before she knows it, she's run four miles away from her apartment without planning a route back. Part of her considers not stopping, just running out into the distance and hoping she can keep it all at bay. But she's been on this ride enough to know that they never go away, no matter what you do.

Hanging her head, she turns around and starts making her way back home.

Chapter Four

"You're not on the visitor schedule for the day," the guard says, staring at his monitor.

"I know," I reply. "This is in relation to a case. I just need to ask him a few questions." I hand over my badge so he can enter the information into the computer.

"Firearm and any other weapons." He slides a drawer open and I place my service weapon inside as he hands my badge back to me. "No physical contact with the inmate and stay at least five feet from the bars at all times."

"Trust me, the last thing I want to do is touch the man."

He nods. "I'll have someone escort you down. You have fifteen minutes until he's scheduled for his daily exercise."

"Understood," I say. "Thanks." I step back as the guard hits the button on his side which activates a loud buzzer and the door to my right opens. I enter an antechamber before another door opens in front of me, leading me into a small waiting area where a guard stands. Behind him, behind the glass, is the man I just spoke with.

"Agent Slate," the guard says. "This way."

I follow the man down a series of corridors, reaching another barrier every hundred feet or so which either must be activated by the guard waving at a security camera or by using one of the many keys on his keyring.

As we're walking, I pass Agent Pearson coming the other direction. He spots me but averts his eyes as we pass, not offering even a courtesy nod.

"You're popular," the guard comments.

"Always have been."

He takes us through a final secure door which leads into an area with six other doors. At the end of the hall, the last door opens to a small standing area that sits adjacent to a prison cell separated by bars.

And behind the bars, lying back with one arm behind his head and a book in his other hand, is Joaquin Fletch. He doesn't even look up when I enter, instead continues to read. Or pretend to.

His cell is larger than I would have expected. And filled with more amenities. He has a full bookshelf, as well as a widescreen television on one wall. There are even a set of dumbbells tucked under his bed, which has at least two types of blankets on it.

For all intents and purposes, his cell is the Shangri-La of prison cells.

"Comfy?" I ask.

"I was wondering when I might see you again," he replies.

"I'll be right outside the door if you need anything," the guard says. "Just knock." He leaves, closing the door behind us.

Fletch finally looks over the top of his book. "Ms. Agostini, looking lovely as ever."

I bristle. "You know that's not my name."

"Forgive me, it's the name I know you by," he replies, setting the book on his chest. "So it's how I think of you. Especially with your mouth on mine, that dress of yours inching up ever so—"

"Shut up," I say, though I can't help but go red in the face.

My undercover assignment to get information from Fletch's computer required some *uncomfortable* compromises. Clearly he's not about to let me forget them.

He sits up. "Oh, now, now, I'm particularly fond of that night. Sure you drugged me and stole from me, but for a few moments there, you and I had an undeniable spark."

"It's called acting. You were a means to an end. Nothing more."

"Perhaps we remember it differently. But I recall hand slipping down your back and you—"

"One more word and I come in there and beat you into silence," I growl.

He smiles before sitting up on the edge of his bed. He's dressed in standard orange coveralls and brown shoes. At least those haven't been given an upgrade too. "If you're not here to reminisce about our time together, then to what do I owe the pleasure?"

Why *did* I come here? I almost convinced myself last night that I could just let it all go. But there are still too many questions swirling around my head. Too many unknowns. And this man has the answers I need.

"Our last conversation ended abruptly with you ordering me dragged out into a field and shot. We still have a few things to discuss."

He chuckles. "Do we? Because unless you'd like to talk about the two of us, there's nothing to talk about."

I ignore the insinuation. He's just trying to get under my skin. "Why did you take the fall for Solitaire?"

He gives me the slightest smirk. "Why Ms. Agostini, I don't think I should be answering any questions without my lawyers present. Does the FBI know you're here? Is this a sanctioned visit?"

"What's Solitaire's plan? Why does he want me dead?"

He takes a deep breath and stands. He's a formidable man, even behind bars. Not many people could accuse

Joaquin Fletch of being ugly, which no doubt helped open doors for him that would have been closed to other people. But really it was his ruthlessness that allowed him to build the massive business he operated. One that we were alerted to via Theo, in which all of us, the FBI included, were duped into a scheme that cost three good agents their lives and left a trail of destruction in its wake.

"As I told you in Italy, Ms. Agostini, I don't have any more answers for you. You haven't earned them yet."

"Yeah?" I ask. "What does your daughter think of all this? Of her father being in an American prison for *life*."

He chuckles again. "You seem awfully sure of that. My daughter will be fine, don't worry about her. She has plenty of people watching over her. And she and I may be reunited sooner than you expect."

"There is a *mountain* of evidence against you. You're implicated in the death of Janice Simmons," I say. "Don't forget, I'm one of the key witnesses in your case."

"And I'm sure the Attorney General just *loves* the fact you're here, talking to me about it beforehand."

I scowl. "Everything here is being recorded," I say. "I have nothing to hide. Do you?"

He indicates his bookshelf. "I am as open as the books the prison has so generously gifted me." He approaches the bars of his cell, which requires me to take a step back so he can't reach me. "What are you really doing here, Emily? What do you really want?"

I grit my teeth as I try not to let him get to me, hating the way my name sounds on his tongue. I'd put off coming here for almost a full week, but last night in the tub, I realized I wasn't going to be able to move forward until I got some closure. Closure that this bastard continues to deny me.

"It's because of Janice, isn't it?" he asks, lowering his voice. "You're still angry."

"I'm not angry," I say. "I'm *livid*. And you will pay for what you did to her."

"As I told you, she did not die by my hand."

"Doesn't matter. It was your order. Your plan. And since you're claiming the title of *Solitaire* you can't pawn it off on someone higher up. That is… unless you were lying about that part."

The smile fades from his lips for a split second. "You know, I wish I could help you, Emily. But unfortunately you'll just have to wait to see how this all pans out. *If* it even goes to trial."

"You're *not* getting away with this," I tell him.

He gives me a brief shrug. "I guess we'll see."

He's so damn smug and arrogant, which really doesn't sit well with me. He shouldn't be feeling this confident being in the position he's in. And yet, he's acting like this is nothing more than a glorified vacation. I need to speak with the warden about his activities.

"Make sure you don't go anywhere too soon. I may have more questions," I say, knocking on the door.

"Oh, don't worry, I'll always be where you can find me," he says. "And look for a call from my lawyers soon. I can't wait to see how this lands with those new bosses of yours."

The door opens as I furrow my brow at the man. He knows more than he should—more than anyone in his position should. As the guard closes the door, I catch Fletch shooting me a quick wink.

"I need to see the warden," I tell the guard.

"I don't think he's in yet," the guard replies.

"I'll wait."

Half an hour later I'm sitting on a bench across from a small desk where a secretary types quickly on a laptop. A squat man in a suit carrying a briefcase spots me as he climbs the stairs, his face going dark.

"Sir, Agent Slate here to see you," his secretary tells Warden John Conrad as he takes a stack of messages from her.

"Does she have an appointment?" he asks, not even bothering to address me.

"No, sir. She was in to see an inmate this morning. Mr. Fletch."

Conrad sighs, then turns to me. "Come on, Slate. Let's get this over with." He leads me into his office.

"Thank you for seeing me, Warden," I say, closing the door behind us. "I have some concerns about Mr. Fletch's accommodations."

"Mr. Fletch has been given accommodations concurrent with the standard expectations of every inmate at this facility," he says, his tone telling me he's already bored with this conversation.

"Has he had any other visitors since he was brought here?" I ask.

Conrad sighs and places both hands on his desk. "What are you fishing for, Slate?"

"I'm not fishing," I tell him. "But Fletch has knowledge he shouldn't," I say.

"Such as?"

"Regarding my position in the FBI," I say.

He takes a seat, then motions around him. "You know you're not exactly a stranger around here. You're a known quantity, Slate. Which means people are going to talk about you. Word gets around quick in a place like this. It's a kind of currency. If I were you, I wouldn't expect any level of privacy when you come through these doors."

That's not a disturbing thought or anything. But I guess, given my closure rate, I shouldn't be surprised my name comes up a lot in the discussions around here.

"He also seemed highly confident he wouldn't be here very long."

Conrad chuckles without any humor in it. "Have you ever met a *guilty* criminal? They all think they're getting out of here… one day. They have to tell themselves that." He stands again, rounding his desk. "Look, Fletch is in maximum security. He's not going anywhere. Not until a judge tells me different. He doesn't even have a trial date set yet. But *you* being here isn't doing anyone any favors. It might appear like you were trying to coerce the man you're set to testify against."

"I know," I say. "It's just… he owes me answers."

"And you know someone like that will never pay up unless they're getting something in return."

He's right. I don't know what I expected when I came here. Maybe I thought I could get him to crack and admit he wasn't really Solitaire, as he's claimed ever since his arrest. Or that he would tell me who he ordered to kill Janice. Or maybe I just wanted to look him in the eye, standing behind those bars. Maybe I assumed I would feel a sense of satisfaction, knowing justice has been served. Except, it hasn't yet. And I can't guarantee that it will be. Fletch is as slippery as they come. I'll just be glad once the trial is over and he's under a life sentence.

Maybe then he'll feel like talking.

"Will there be anything else, Agent Slate?" Conrad asks, glaring at me.

"Have a good day, Warden," I finally say and turn to leave.

Chapter Five

I ended up not telling Liam about visiting Fletch. Not because I don't think he'd understand, but I just don't want someone else telling me I'm wasting my time, or putting myself in further jeopardy. I know the risks; I'm not stupid. But I've learned that sometimes you need to force someone's hand to actually get things done. And since I didn't receive a call from my superiors or Fletch's lawyers over the weekend, I'm feeling pretty confident as I head into the office for what will be our first official day in this brand-new unit.

"Nervous?" Liam asks, walking beside me as we make our way towards the offices. Despite my visit with Fletch not going how I wanted it, I came back home feeling lighter than I did before I left. Which meant I could actually relax around Liam and let down my guard. For a while there it felt like things had gone back to normal, but I can tell there's still something bothering him. Something he's holding back. I didn't want to pressure him into telling me; he'll do that when and if he's ready, but I admit it's put me slightly on edge. I guess that's to be expected; it's not like I'm being completely honest with him either.

"Afraid I'm going to assign you the grunt work?" I tease.

"I'm not saying you need to show any favoritism, just remember who drove you here."

I stop in the hallway, glaring at him. "Oh *really*? That's how it's going to be huh?"

He holds up both hands. "Just kidding. Maybe."

I chortle. "You just bought yourself a ticket to grunt town, hot shot."

"Yippee." The word comes out deadpan as I leave him standing in the hallway. I enter my office and log on, pulling the full file for the Lazar Mental Correctional Facility and schedule a meeting in twenty minutes. I take that time to scan the file, going over the pertinent details. It's just as Pendergast said—two complaints that were eventually retracted, transcripts of the calls and the performance reports from the facility, from the state inspector.

All in all… it looks pretty clean. And that worries me. If this ends up being nothing more than a waste of time…

I grab my materials and head to the conference room where I find Nadia and Elliott have already beat me there.

"Morning," I say. "Have a good weekend?"

"It was productive," Elliott replies. "I managed to create a new type of sourdough."

I pause, glancing up. "Sourdough?"

"It's an extremely complex type of bread," he explains. "And requires the utmost care."

I can't tell if he's kidding or not. Elliott has never been much of a jokester—actually I've *never* known him to make a joke. I turn my attention to Nadia who only shrugs. "I helped knead."

"That's a euphemism, isn't it?" Zara comes in and takes a seat across from Nadia. "Were you guys *baking* all weekend?"

"You don't seem to understand," Elliott says. "It's an extremely—"

Nadia lays her hand on his. "She's messing with you."

"Ah," Elliott says. "I should have been able to tell from the constant smirk. Though she wears it so often you couldn't fault me for thinking it was a permanent feature on her face."

Zara's mouth drops open. "I'm sorry, did you just try and *burn* me?"

"Consider yourself a crisp," he replies, dead serious.

Zara turns to me like she can't believe it. I don't miss the dark circles under her eyes. "Get a load of this guy."

I just shake my head. "I'm glad everyone is in a good mood," I say. "Because this should be relatively simple."

Liam rushes in and takes a seat across from Elliott, closing the door behind him. "Sorry. Was on a call."

Before I was kidding about the grunt work. But I might actually give it to him now for being late. "We were just getting started. Now—"

"Hey, Em, I was thinking," Zara says. "Before we get this train going, shouldn't we have like… a name or something for this operation?"

"A name?"

"Yeah, you know, like something we can call ourselves. Something cool, like *Raptor Squad*."

I glare at her. "Raptor Squad? Really?"

"I mean, it doesn't *have* to be that, but I wouldn't say no to it."

I look at the rest of the team. "Should we have a name?"

"It might simplify communications going forward," Elliott suggests.

Liam leans back in his seat. "I wouldn't mind something. Maybe Special Operations Division."

"Oh yeah, that's perfect, SOD," Zara says. "Hi there, I'm with *SOD*. We really get to the bottom of things."

"That's one vote for Raptor Squad," I say, glaring at her. "And one vote for SOD. Anyone else?"

"And no one say X-Files," Zara says.

Nadia shrugs. "The Justice League?"

"Not unless you want to be permanently associated with

comic books," Elliott replies. "It needs to be something enigmatic. Yet also easy and unique."

"As I said," Zara replies. "Raptor Squad. It's memorable."

"What do prehistoric predators have to do with anything?" Elliott asks. The two of them are really getting into it today.

"Okay, I feel we're getting off the rails here," I say. "Let's table the name discussion until later. Right now, let's focus on the job at hand. If we don't provide the FBI with a satisfactory conclusion to this case, a name will be moot." I motion to the folders in front of them. "As I was saying, I think this one should be straightforward. We'll start with the families. Liam, you're up. Get in contact with the Sawyers and the Eatons, see if you can't get to the bottom of the original complaints and why they recanted."

He gives me a quick nod.

"Nadia, you and Elliott pull the inspection reports on the facility. See if you can't get in contact with whoever performed the most recent on-site inspection. Note anything that looks out of the ordinary, even if it's nothing more than the filing was late."

"Got it," Nadia says.

"Zara and I will head to the facility and speak with the administration. Get eyes on the place and make sure they aren't restricting access. We'll also see what we can find about our mystery inmates and if they are actually there or not. And if they are, where they came from. As I'm sure you've all seen, there's no record of either a Renata Sawyer or Matilda Eaton anywhere in the prison system."

"Mingling at the funny farm, can't wait," Zara says.

"Don't call it that in front of them," I say. "I don't think that would be looked upon very kindly by the administration."

"Let's see what we find first," she replies. "Cause if they're hiding something, I'll call 'em whatever I want."

I shoot her my signature scowl then turn my attention to the rest of them. "Okay, that's it. Let's try and get this wrapped up by the end of the day. I'd really like a quick win to start us out."

Everyone agrees and begins to head off. "Hey, Z," I say, getting Zara's attention. "Everything okay?"

"Yeah, why?" she asks.

"Just...I'm just making sure you're feeling alright. You seem a little on edge."

She shakes her head. "Nope. All good. Are *you* doing okay?"

I pull her to the side of the room, out of earshot of the others. "I went to visit Fletch a couple days ago."

"Oh, Em."

"I know, I couldn't help it. It's that damn smug face of his. He still owes us answers. That and I hoped to see him cowering in his cell, a broken man."

"And?" she asks. "Was he?"

"No," I admit. "In fact, he was calm and collected. Like his incarceration was part of his plan all along."

She gives me an appraising look with a hint of pity. "You feel that way because he got in your head. Because he used you—*us* to attack the Bureau. Trust me, getting arrested was *not* part of his plan. His plan was to kill us and manipulate the FBI to his will."

"I guess," I say. "It was just... he knew things. He knew we were working in a new division."

A dark shadow comes across her face but disappears just as quickly. "Well... he was a broker. I guess information is his trade now. Still... that's not great."

"No," I say. "I spoke to the warden about it, but he didn't seem concerned."

She turns away, seeming to think for a moment before returning her attention to me. "Listen, don't let him get in your head again. He's in prison, you're not. You won. And yeah, I know the trial is still months away and all that, but in the end, *you* beat him. And despite everything else, that has to be eating him alive."

She's right. I *did* beat him. I need to give myself some credit. But that's hard, I'm not the kind of person to sing her own praises. "Is that how you feel about… you know?"

"That's different," she says. "We were in a relationship."

"I know," I say. "I'm just worried. It was a lot all at once."

She gives me a reassuring smile. "Don't worry about me. I'm fine," she says. "Let's focus on the case. It'll be nice to work on something official for once instead of sneaking around all over the place."

Isn't that the truth? We were undercover for so long I almost forgot what it felt like. "Yeah, okay," I say. "Thanks, Z."

"Hey, it's what I'm here for," she says. "And seriously. Don't discount Raptor Squad. You tell someone you're part of that, you're gonna get two reactions. One, people backing away because they know the rep. And two, people who are intrigued and want to know more. It's a win-win."

"Uh-huh, we'll see," I say. "Meet you at the car in five?"

"Only if I get to drive."

Chapter Six

THE BRISK MORNING AIR WHIPS AT MY HAIR AS ZARA DRIVES to the facility. The Lazar Mental Correctional Facility is an hour and a half outside of DC and sits nestled in the rural mountains of Virginia, near the town of Rochester. I only agreed to let her drive because I didn't feel like driving Liam's car and I wanted some extra time to go over the details of the case. While I don't feel like I'm unprepared for this, I want to make sure everything is completely by the book. With every-thing we've been through, with all the rules we've bent and broken over the past two months, I don't want to step one toe out of line, especially if it means my team will be split up and sent to the proverbial FBI gulags.

But as Zara drives, I can't help but notice she doesn't seem like her usual self. The radio isn't turned up to eleven, in fact it's so low I can barely hear it and she hardly says a word on the entire drive. It's clear she's grappling with something and I can't just let her deal with it alone.

"Okay," I finally say, closing the folder on my lap and placing it on her backseat. "Out with it."

"Out with what?" she asks.

"Whatever is going on with you. And don't tell me you're fine because we both know that's bullshit."

She huffs. "What do you want me to say?"

"I want you to tell me what's going on instead of keeping it bottled up. Or did you think I just missed the fact that you look like you barely slept?"

"I look perfectly fine; Charlotte Tilbury has the best concealer on the market and it works."

"Z. I'm serious. Talk to me."

"Fine," she says, fire in her voice. "You want me to admit that I fucked up? That I never should have introduced Theo to the FBI?"

I screw up my features. "What?"

"It's my fault, Em. If I hadn't insisted on bringing him in as an asset, none of it would have happened. Janice wouldn't be dead and we wouldn't be walking this tightrope."

"You don't really believe that do you?" I ask. "It's *not* your fault."

"If not for Theo, Fletch never would have gained access to the Bureau. He never would have been able to plant that bomb," she says. "It's *all* my fault."

"Look at me," I tell her. But she doesn't. "Zara."

She glances over but quickly averts her gaze. "This is *not* your fault. No one could have predicted what Theo would do. Least of all you. Even if you had a full dossier on him, you wouldn't have seen it coming. *I* didn't see it coming."

"You weren't sleeping with him," she replies. "You didn't purposefully keep yourself from learning about his past because you were scared that if you did, you'd get bored with him and dump him and then you'd be alone again anyway. Don't you get it, Em? I put the Bureau, you, me and *everyone* at risk because I was afraid that once I knew the truth about him, I might no longer want to be in a relationship with him. I put my own selfish needs above everyone else and it got people killed."

"The Bureau did a full background check on him. He was vetted. You wouldn't have found anything they didn't," I say.

"I might have," she replies. "I'm thorough."

"While that might be true," I say. "It doesn't mean you would have found anything that could have told you he was planning to betray us. Or that he was in Fletch's pocket. Even when we had Fletch's computer, there was nothing on there about Theo. The odds you would have found anything about that are infinitesimal at best."

She sighs. "I know you're trying to help," she says. "But I can't quit thinking about it."

"Listen to me," I tell her. "If you don't find a way to let this go, it's going to tear you up inside. Ask me how I know."

She shoots me a reproachful glance.

"Yeah. Do you know how many times I went back and forth in my head if I had only seen what Matt was doing. Who he was? Do you know how long I fought with myself about that?"

The edge of her mouth ticks up. "Yeah, because I was the one talking you down."

"Exactly," I say. "So I'm going to tell you what you told me. Accept it. Process it. And let it go. Because otherwise it's going to eat you up to the point where you won't be able to function. You'll be questioning every decision you make. And in a critical moment, it will cause you to make a mistake. I trust you. You're a good agent. And I don't want anyone else with me. But you need to forgive yourself."

She scoffs. "You're doing one hell of an impression of Frost."

"Maybe you should think about going to see him. As much as I hate to admit it, he helped."

She rolls her eyes. "I'm not sure he wants to open this Pandora's box. It's a mess in here," she says, making a circular motion to herself.

"All I'm saying is think about it."

She's quiet for a moment, the only sound is the wind coming through the windows and the rumble of the road. "Yeah," she finally says. "Maybe."

I take it as a positive sign that she turns her music up a few notches the rest of the way to the facility. Not at full blast like normal, but at least I can hear it.

We finally arrive at the facility. It's tucked deep in the woods of the Shenandoah Mountains, a long, winding drive leading up to the gates, which are flanked by stone columns on either side. Zara pulls up to the gate and addresses the camera by the little card scanner that sits atop a small column by the drive.

"Can I help you?" a voice says from the other end. There's a video monitor, but it only shows us; the camera sits just above the card scanner.

Zara pulls out her badge. "Special Agent Foley and Special Agent Slate from the FBI. We're here to inspect the facility."

"On what grounds?" the voice says on the other end.

"We're looking into complaints received at the FBI about some of your inmates," I say.

"Are you with the OIG?" the voice asks.

I shoot Zara a glance. Whoever this is, they're being thorough. "We're with an independent section within the FBI," I say. "Backed by the Department of Justice. Under the Federal Prison Oversight Act we have the authority to enter and inspect your facility at any time."

"One moment." The line goes dead.

"Wow, they really don't want to let us in," Zara says. "That's not suspicious at all."

She's not wrong. I didn't expect to receive this much push-back already. Though I suppose from their position, this is something of a surprise. It isn't like we told them we were coming, which was on purpose. We didn't want to give them time to cover their tracks, if there were any to cover.

Finally, the gates open without another word from the speaker unit. Zara pulls forward and we follow the drive further. The woods are denser on this side of the gates and we still can't see the facility.

"I guess a warm welcome was too much to ask," she says.

Already this has put me on guard. There's no telling what level of cooperation we'll receive once we're up there, but so far it's not looking promising.

As the road curves, we find ourselves facing a white van coming in the other direction. Its windows are covered in metal lattice bars but the man driving gives us a quick wave as we pass. I didn't see anyone in the back of the van, which means he must have been dropping off instead of picking up.

"How many inmates does this place hold?" Zara asks.

"I think a couple hundred," I say. "Why?"

She points ahead of us. "Cause it's big." Ahead of us a large stone building begins to emerge from the trees. It's made completely of gray limestone and looks almost like a kind of castle. A large central section dominates the building, rising at least four stories and capped by a sharp, tapered roof. On either side are two more pillar-like sections, only about three stories tall apiece. From that the rest of the building extends out on either side. The drive widens to three or four car lengths and splits off in three directions. One heads around the side of the building, another off into the woods to our left and the third towards the front, where a large roundabout circles a bed of freshly planted flowers which surround some pine trees.

"Front door?" Zara asks.

"That'd be my guess." She pulls up to the roundabout, and I note there is a small area here for parking and four spots that say "visitor." Zara pulls into one of those and kills the engine as we stare up at the building.

"So the objective is to get into the castle, kill the dragon and rescue the damsels, right?"

"I'm hoping we don't have to kill anyone," I say. "But we will if we have to."

"Best news I've heard all morning," she says, pulling out her firearm and cocking it.

I narrow my gaze at her.

"What? I'm just making sure I'm ready."

I guess some improvement is better than nothing. "Just try not to shoot them until we have probable cause."

"Mm-hm." We get out of the car and head to the main entrance, which is up two series of marble stairs that have fallen into disrepair. Green moss covers part of them and they're cracked or broken in other areas. And now that I get a good look at the place, what looked pristine and imposing from a distance now appears old and decrepit. Vines snake their way up the limestone, working their way into all the cracks and crevices of the building while other areas have been discolored by mold or other growths over time. I wouldn't say the place is falling apart, but it definitely could use some TLC.

As we reach the top of the last run of stairs, I catch sight of the building's cornerstone which says *1878*.

"Almost a hundred and fifty years old," I say.

"I wonder if my apartment building will still be around in a hundred and fifty years," Zara replies. "Doubtful, the way my landlord treats it, but you never know. Guy has to die at some point, right?"

I knock on the heavy wooden door before it opens with the sound of a buzzer. On the other side we're met with a large open area that splits off into three different directions, each of them with bars and a locked door. To our right is a small office. A guard emerges, followed by a woman in a white uniform, her blonde hair tied back tightly.

"Good morning," she says. "You must be the FBI agents."

She doesn't sound like the same voice we heard on the intercom, but I can't be sure. I give her a quick nod. "I'm Special Agent Slate. This is Special Agent Foley."

She holds out a hand for us to shake. "I'm Lena Booth. Head care provider here at Lazar. Most people just call me Nurse Booth." We both shake her hand. "I have to admit this is something of a surprise. We weren't informed you were coming."

"We're responding to complaints from two separate families," I tell her, getting right to business. "Do you have inmates by the names Sawyer and Eaton?" It's time to find out if Pendergast's suspicions are true. If Booth denies they were here, we may have to pull this place apart stone by stone.

Nurse Booth's lips form a straight line. "I'll have to check the records. We have over two hundred and ninety inmates here with dozens of transfers every week. Some we barely get to know before they're removed again."

"What sort of care do you provide here?" Zara asks.

"Mostly we work to find some level of stability for our patients," Booth says. "Usually that means finding the correct dosages of medications so that they are no longer a danger to themselves or others. Our goal here is to stabilize our patients so they can either serve their sentences or stand trial if need be."

"Then you don't actively work to improve their overall long-term health," I say.

"Unfortunately, no," she replies. "That's beyond our scope. As much as I would like to say that we do, often patients aren't here long enough for a lengthy therapy. But we do provide some education and training, where applicable. Whether that's general education or help with the patients' cases, we try to give them as many resources as we can."

I chance a quick look at the guard and find he's watching both me and Zara closely, but he looks away when he catches my eye. He's a big man and I think I catch the edge of a tattoo peeking out from the cuff of his sleeve but I can't tell what it is.

"And you don't take any patients who are not already incarcerated or have been indicted, is that correct?" I ask.

"Correct. We work one hundred percent with the federal government," she replies. "Everyone here has either already been convicted of a crime or is in the process of going to trial." She shoots an inquiring look between us. "I still don't understand. Isn't this something that could have been cleared up over a phone call?"

I give her a wan smile. "We like to be thorough. Could you check on those two names for us please?"

"Of course," she replies. "I'll be right back. One moment." She heads back into her office, leaving us with the guard.

I take the time to look at the entryway, noting the cameras at every angle, keeping an eye on the entire area. The corridors that split off all look like they're controlled by electronic locks on both sides. However, instead of plexiglass separating us from the corridors, there are just good, old-fashioned bars in every direction.

"Worked here long?" Zara asks the guard.

"Three years," he says.

"Good pay?"

He shrugs.

"Do any of the inmates have access to this area?"

"Only when they're being processed in and out," he says, nodding to another office directly across from Booth's. However, the door is closed and the screens are pulled over the windows so we can't see inside.

"Thanks for your patience," Booth says, coming out of the office with a file in her hand. "I've got both of them right here. Renata Sawyer and Matilda Eaton. Sawyer has been with us for five weeks, Eaton only three."

Zara and I exchange a glance. "They're here? Right now?"

She nods. "Yes, why?"

"Can I see those?" I ask, holding out my hand. From what we could find, there was no Sawyer or Eaton that fit either of their descriptions in the Federal Database. I take one file while Zara takes the other and I read the brief description inside.

Renata Sawyer. Arrested 11/19/24 for manslaughter. Subject attempted to stab victim with broken bottle. Incarcerated at Pimlo Women's Prison until 2/19/25 awaiting trial. Inmate began exhibiting concerning behaviors—suspected self-harm. Transferred to Lazar Correctional for evaluation and treatment 2/20/25.

I furrow my brow. Eaton's file reads similarly. Why wasn't this in the federal database? These are two violent criminals with clear psychiatric issues. I guess we can eliminate the possibility they died while in care here.

"Are you aware there is no mention of either of these cases in the Department of Justice database?" I ask.

Booth seems surprised. "No. I don't understand why they wouldn't be. They were both transferred in from Pimlo. Their records came with them. Maybe you should speak with Pimlo to make sure they're filing correctly."

"We'll do that," I say, handing the folders back to her. "May we see each of the patients?"

She pauses. "You want to see them? In person?"

I nod. "Now, preferably."

"Of course," she replies, visibly flustered. "I'll need to make the necessary arrangements. Give me a few moments. As I said, we weren't expecting you. We could have had everything ready—I'll be as quick as I can."

She retreats back into the office as Zara and I move out of earshot of the guard. "Thoughts?"

"Something isn't adding up," she says. "I mean, I guess they're not dead. But Pimlo had no record of either patient. I checked. Neither did any other Federal prison. There should have been something… arrest records, transport orders…. trial dates. Something. Whatever this is, I don't think it's a routine mix-up."

Unfortunately, I think she's right. It seems like our first case might not be so open and shut after all.

Chapter Seven

"If you're ready you can follow me," Nurse Booth says as she comes out of her office. She doesn't strike me as the kind of person who gets flustered. She exudes a quiet calm, fitting for her position as a nurse. But at the same time I get the sense that she isn't one to suffer fools or put up with any nonsense. She's been thrown by our appearance here, which is exactly what I wanted. But she's maintained her composure enough to tell me she's experienced with unexpected disruptions. Her bun is tight and perfectly maintained, keeping her long hair out of her eyes and giving her a professional appearance. I wouldn't put her age past forty or so, but her eyes reveal experience beyond those years. She's been doing this a long time, and it's going to take more than a couple of FBI agents showing up at her doorstep to throw her off her game.

"I've arranged for both inmates Sawyer and Eaton to be moved to the common areas in their respective wings," she says. "You can speak with them there. If you don't mind me asking, what is this all about?"

"We received complaints," I tell her. "Related to your two inmates. The families complained they couldn't get in touch with them and that they were being denied access."

"That's patently not true," Booth says. "We follow the strict guidelines set out by the government here. Visitations are Tuesdays, Thursdays and Saturdays. We don't restrict access and families can request contact at any time. All calls are monitored, of course, but that's standard procedure."

"Have either Sawyer or Eaton tried to reach out to their families?"

"I'd have to check with the nurses on duty in those departments," she says. "I don't handle cases individually." She motions that we follow her as another nurse and two more guards appear from one of the other hallways, using their keycards to open the doors. The other nurse takes residence in the office while the guards stand outside. The guard who we first met follows Zara as Booth leads us to the main door directly ahead of us.

"How many people do you have on staff here?"

"Thirty full-time health professionals," she says. "That includes our medical doctors. And we have between sixty and seventy security personnel at any given time."

"That's one guard for every four prisoners," I say.

She nods. "Something like that."

I glance back at the man following us. "Are all your guards male?"

"Most are. Only about twenty percent are female."

"Any issues with inmate abuse?" I ask.

She stops, turning to me. "Absolutely not. And if there were, it would be reported immediately. We don't condone or allow that sort of behavior here." She says it with such ferocity that I'm momentarily taken aback.

"Because there were reports about ten, fifteen years ago," I say. "Female inmates were complaining—"

"Those individuals were fired and removed from the system," she says quickly.

"I'm assuming you were here then. Were any charges ever brought?"

She turns and heads the other way, leading us back down another corridor.

"I'll take that as a no," I say. "Do you know if any of the offenders are still working as guards?"

"Look," she says, spinning on me quickly. "I didn't have anything to do with that. I was only first starting here when that happened and it was above my pay grade. If you want more details, you'll have to speak to our administrator. But as far as I know, the problem was resolved and the responsible parties were punished."

"And no complaints since." I watch her reaction carefully.

For a split second her gaze flits to the guard behind Zara. "No."

"Good to know."

She turns back, but not before I catch the steel in her gaze. "You'll speak with Sawyer first. She's closest. In the South wing." She opens the door with her keycard, while a guard on the other side of the main door holds out a container for our weapons. I deposit my sidearm and Zara does the same before we're allowed through the next doorway, which Booth again opens with her keycard.

"Are all your doors controlled electronically?" I ask.

"Yes," she replies. "We upgraded twelve years ago."

"What happens when the power goes out?" Zara asks.

"We have backup generators on site," Booth says. "Enough to power the full facility for seventy-two hours. But if you mean what happens to the doors when the power goes out, all the individual rooms immediately unlock, but all the common areas and everything that connects to the outside goes into full lockdown, sealing all areas of the facility. Only those with master keys can open the doors." She removes a small set of keys from her pocket.

"Isn't that dangerous?" I ask. "What happens if there's a fire?"

"We can't control every condition," she replies. "If all

areas were accessible, it wouldn't take more than a temporary outage or two to send inmates running into the woods. We have a twelve-foot fence at the perimeter of the property—you probably saw it on the way in—but I'd rather not take the chance, would you?"

We walk the rest of the way in silence, but the energy radiating off Booth is almost palpable. She's concerned, despite her calm demeanor.

It also doesn't escape my attention how close the guard continues to walk with us. I couldn't say for sure, but there is a good chance Zara can feel the guy's breath on the back of her neck. Whatever is going on here, I don't like how defensive Booth is acting. If she *isn't* hiding something, she's doing a fantastic job of making herself look suspicious.

"Here," Booth says, opening a final door into a small room with a couple of round tables with seats attached to the base. At the furthest table sits a woman in an orange jumpsuit, her hands cuffed and folded as another guard stands behind her. She has dark brown hair that falls in mats on either side of her face and her dark skin seems to be irritated with something, having broken out in a couple of places. From what I can tell, I would guess she's probably my age or a little older, but not much.

"Sawyer," Booth barks with an authoritative tone, causing the young woman to jump. "These Agents have some questions for you."

"Thank you," I say to Booth. "We can take it from here."

"All activities must be monitored," she replies, taking up a position by the door.

I weigh my options. I could fight her on it, but I don't have much of a leg to stand on. The person we came here to find is actually here, not dead in a morgue somewhere, and she's sitting right in front of us. Despite how much of a tool Booth is being, I don't have cause to force her out of the room.

I motion to Zara who nods, taking a seat at the table next

to the one where Renata Sawyer sits. I take a seat directly in front of her. "Renata? My name is Emily. I'm with the FBI. Is it okay if I ask you a few questions?"

She doesn't answer at first.

"Renata?"

"S-sure." She doesn't look up, though her voice cracks.

"Okay," I say, trying to be reassuring. "We're doing a wellness check. We received a call from your family who told us they couldn't get in contact with you here. Are you okay?"

She glances up, her eyes going directly to Booth before landing on the table again. "Yes. I'm fine."

"Do you not want to talk to your family?" I ask, though I don't like how she needed "permission" from Booth to speak.

"No. They—they don't understand."

"Don't understand what?" I ask.

She glances up to Booth again. "Renata," I say. "Look at me. What don't they understand?"

"How… how hard it is in here," she replies, though her gaze is going from me to Booth and back. "I—I just want to be left alone."

"Renata," I say, clearer and more authoritative. "Have you been hurt in here? Is anyone abusing you? Any other inmates? Or staff?"

"Now wait a minute—" Booth begins but Zara gets up and stops her.

"Don't," Zara says. "This is a federal investigation. The only reason you're still in here is because we're allowing you to be."

"This is outrageous," Booth yells. "I've already explained to you that no one in this facility is being abused."

"Is that true?" I ask Renata. "You can tell me the truth. If you're being hurt in here, tell me right now and we'll have you moved. You won't leave my sight until you're out of this place. Understood?"

Something like a tremble has crept up through the

woman's extremities and she glances at Booth again before swallowing hard. "No, I'm fine. I—I like it here."

"Just as I told you," Booth says. I hold up a hand for her to shut up for a moment.

"Renata, are you sure?" I ask. "We can get you the help you need. Your family is worried about you."

"We have received no calls or complaints," Booth says, interrupting again. "I checked our logs. I don't know where you're getting your information, Agent Slate, but it's clearly wrong."

I try to meet Renata's eyes, but she never looks up, only keeps her gaze pointed at the table between us. There is something else going on here, I *know* it. But without someone who is willing to say something, there's nothing I can do about it. She's not going to give us anything.

Finally, I get up. "Take us to see Eaton."

"I should have you removed," Booth replies, though she doesn't seem angry. She almost seems to be enjoying this confrontation. Like it's fueling her. "You've upset our inmate."

"I don't have to remind you we have the full authority of the federal government to be here," I say. "And until I'm satisfied that this facility is operating within the standards prescribed and upheld by The Federal Prison Bureau, then we're staying here as long as we need to." Renata may be afraid of Booth, but I'm not. And I'm not about to let her push me around. "Take us to see Matilda Eaton."

I catch a jerky movement from Renata as I say Eaton's name, but she doesn't say anything. Only allows herself to be led away by the officer behind her.

"I'll be making a full complaint to the Inspector General, Agent Slate. This sort of behavior is only making things worse," Booth says once they're gone.

"The sooner you give us what we want, the sooner we're out of your hair," Zara says.

Booth takes a deep breath, weighing her options.

"We don't need your presence," I add. "I'm sure anyone can escort us."

"If you're going to be slinging lies about us and the level of care we provide, then while you're here, you won't be leaving my sight," she replies before motioning to the guard to move out of the way. She leads us down a long corridor and through three more security checkpoints before we reach another common room. Though this one is a mirror image of the last, Booth's demeanor has changed dramatically. Whereas before she was on edge, she's turned downright hostile. Apparently, she doesn't like being accused of any possible infractions happening on her watch. But given this place's history, it isn't something we can ignore.

"Here," she says, pointing to the tables at the far end of the room. "Eaton will be here in a few minutes. Excuse me." She leaves us in the room with the guard.

Zara and I retreat to the far end of the room. "Thoughts?"

"If we piss her off enough, she could cause trouble for us. Especially if there's nothing wrong here." Zara pauses. "So far."

"I know," I whisper. "But you saw Sawyer's face. She was terrified."

"She's also in a *psych ward*," Zara points out. "These aren't the most stable people in the best of conditions."

It's a solid point. So far we can't point to anything being done here that's against the law or violating the inmates' rights. That would take a much more thorough investigation, and from what I can tell, we don't have probable cause for that. They're obviously not dead and seem to have full autonomy.

Still… something is amiss here. I can *feel* it.

Chapter Eight

Our meeting with Matilda "Tilly" Eaton went about as well as our meeting with Renata Sawyer. The woman seemed partially out of it, possibly from the drugs the ward has her on, but she didn't seem to indicate that she was being suppressed in any way. Like Sawyer, she wasn't interested in speaking with her family and even actively agreed that she should be in the ward. When I suggested that we move her, she vehemently disagreed and I didn't miss the smirk on Booth's face.

Once the meeting was over Booth had us escorted back to the front, where we retrieved our weapons and were essentially kicked out of the facility, with Booth's assurances that she'd be making a full round of complaints to the proper authorities for government overreach and harassment. And she did it all with an infuriatingly pleasant smile on her face.

Coming up empty, Zara and I were forced to drive the hour and a half back to the office hoping that one of our other team members had more luck.

"Did you see the way she reveled in kicking us out of there?" Zara asks as we pull into the parking lot. "I can't get that stupid smile of hers out of my head."

"She definitely enjoyed it," I say. Booth is clearly the kind of person who likes to taut moral authority over everyone around her, who delights in being "better" than everyone else. Not exactly the kind of person I would want as the head of a Mental Correctional Facility.

"Is it bad I want to take her down just for the hell of it?" Zara says. "That woman has to be guilty of something."

"Being an asshole isn't a crime," I say. "But we have to face facts. If there's nothing here, then we close the case and move on."

"Come on," she replies as we head into the building. "You don't really believe that, do you?"

"Of course not," I say. "But without the evidence to support any kind of corruption, what can we do?"

"Keep digging?" Zara asks. "Everyone has skeletons if you go deep enough."

She has a point. But I don't think our job description extends to tearing someone's life apart just because they were being obtuse. Though I really don't look forward to going back to Pendergast and Vostov with our heads hung low, letting them know the program was a failure and had identified a false positive. I thought I'd wanted a quick resolution to this case, but something about this feels wrong. Too clean, like someone is putting their thumb on the scale.

I stick my head inside Nadia's office, giving her door a quick knock to let her know we're back. She glances up. "Oh, hey," she says. "Productive trip?"

"Not really," I say. "Did you and Elliott find anything?"

She gives me a quick shrug. "Not much. Were they actually there?"

"Let's get together in the conference room in five," I say. "We can go over everything we have." I glance at Liam's office which sits directly across from Nadia's. "Is he back yet?"

Nadia shakes her head. "Haven't seen him."

I pull out my phone as I head to the small kitchenette

that's part of our office. No messages or calls from Liam. He must still be with the families. After spending three hours in the car and our morning at the Facility, I need something to keep me awake.

I swear, Pendergast and Vostov couldn't have chosen a more pedestrian office. This place is like an insurance head-quarters, a set of seven individual offices which have a conference room and small kitchen attached. Beyond that is an area where normally there would be a set of cubicles, however, that area is completely open with nothing but a few tables right now. This place doesn't make me feel like we're on the cutting edge of the Bureau's resources here. In fact it's the opposite. It's like we've been relegated to some dark corner where we can be quietly forgotten.

I get into the kitchen and turn on the coffee maker, which looks like it was made in the '80s. It takes a few minutes, but I manage to brew a halfway decent pot of coffee and pour myself a mug, grateful for anything that will help keep me awake for the rest of the day. I can't get the smug look on Booth's face as we left the Facility out of my head. Like Zara, I want to find a way to knock her down a peg or two, but so far it doesn't seem like we're even going to have anything to continue the investigation.

I sigh and head into the conference room where I'm joined by Nadia, Elliott and Zara a few moments later. Zara and I give them the *CliffsNotes* version of our morning, including our meetings with both of the women that the government apparently has no record of receiving.

"We should probably look deeper into the transfer records and find out where they came from," Nadia says.

"Booth mentioned they were both transfers from Pimlo. I don't know why they aren't in the system if that's the case."

"I'll do some digging," Nadia says.

"She was clearly lying," Zara replies. "I've already checked all the transfer records in the entire system. Plus, you didn't meet this woman. If there's a more unpleasant person on the face of this planet I'd be surprised." She glances at me. "We just need to find the chain of custody for both of them, right?"

"I'd like the original arrest records as well," I say. "Booth had them on hand… but…"

"But what?" she asks.

"I don't know," I say. "Something doesn't feel right."

"Unfortunately, we can't prosecute off our feelings," Elliott replies, prompting a reproachful glare from both me and Zara.

He clears his throat, turning to his own work. "Our morning was just as uneventful. We pulled all the inspection records for the facility going back five years. No reports of any incidents of any kind," he says. "The facility is in full compliance and is being inspected monthly."

"*Nothing?*" I say, exasperated.

He shakes his head.

"Sorry, Em," Nadia says. "We pored over everything."

I fold down until my head reaches the table, my hair falling to either side of me. I feel a hand rub my back. "Would it make you feel better if I plant some evidence on Booth?" Zara asks.

"Maybe," I reply, my voice muffled.

"Though there was one discrepancy," Elliott says and I pull my head off the table long enough to meet his gaze. "All the inspection reports came from one inspector."

"So?" I ask.

"It's not unheard of," he says. "But this inspector has never missed an inspection, nor has he ever assigned it to someone else. For the past five years it has been him and him alone."

"Is he keeping up with his certifications?" I ask. "Maintaining his clearance?"

Elliott nods. "It didn't seem significant, but given your... reaction, I thought anything might help."

"Thanks anyway," I say. "Did you speak with the inspector personally?"

Nadia shakes her head. "Couldn't get in touch with him. But we left him messages to call us back."

"Maybe Liam found something," Zara suggests.

I pull myself all the way up off the table. "I'm sure if he did, he would have let us know by now. More than likely he's just trying to get full statements from the families before coming back with the bad news."

"What bad news?" We look up to see Pendergast poking his head in the room. "Making any progress?"

I let out a long breath. "Let's talk," I say.

"Well," Pendergast says, folding his hands in front of him. "This is disappointing."

We're sitting in his office which has been tastefully decorated. There are a few commendations on the wall and probably more than a hundred books on the shelves behind him. Unlike the rest of us, he and Vostov have been here long enough to unpack and get themselves situated. Actually, I don't even know how long they have been here, just that they were already here when we arrived.

Vostov stands to the side, leaning up against one of his bookshelves, her arms crossed as she glares at me.

"Are you sure about this program?" I ask him. "Maybe it's delivering false positives."

He glances to Vostov then back to me. "No, the program is solid. But...I guess this was to be expected. Not every case we identify will be actionable. If you couldn't find any evidence of foul play and the two women in question were alive, well and being cared for in the system, then I'm not sure there's much more we can do."

"We're still waiting to hear back from Agent Coll," I say. "I assigned him to speak with the families."

"But the evidence says there's nothing here," Vostov says.

"Yes, and my gut says the opposite," I say. "But I can't prove anything. Booth has that place wrapped around her finger and on paper everything looks above board."

A look passes between Vostov and Pendergast. "Very well, Agent Slate," he says. "Once Agent Coll is back, make your full report and submit it. Then we'll move on to another case."

"This isn't a failure," I say. "But we can't act on something without evidence."

"This is exactly why we brought you in," Vostov says. "Why we saved you. These cases aren't going to be easy. They won't be open and shut and they won't always follow the standard pattern. We needed you because you have enough experience to see past all that."

"What are you asking me to do? Investigate without cause? I can't do that."

"We're asking you to think outside of the box," Pendergast replies. He clears his throat, glancing at Vostov again. "Given everything that's happened, we can't rely on the Bureau at the moment. There have been too many conciliations, too many altercations. And we still can't be sure the Bureau's systems aren't compromised. What Fletch has done to this organization—he's damaged it beyond belief. We could have come back from the Hunter scandal, but this… it's something different. Agent Vostov and I… we're part of a handful of agents who are exploring new ways the agency can operate without relying on traditional intelligence. This is one of those ways. But if it doesn't work—"

"It means going back to a broken system," Vostov says. "A compromised system."

"People already don't trust the government," Pendergast says. "Which makes enforcing the law difficult. It means fighting the very people we're trying to protect."

"I respect what you're trying to do," I say. "But I can't turn a nothingburger into a full-fledged case with nothing to go on but a couple of phone calls. Wouldn't that just continue to undermine the public's trust?"

"I told you this was a waste of time," Vostov says.

Pendergast doesn't take his eyes off me. "If you truly believe there's nothing here," he says. "Then make your report. We'll move on. But the reason we chose you is because we know you'll make the right call. No matter what's in your way."

I furrow my brow. What is he saying?

"Okay," I say tentatively as I stand. "Well… then expect my report tomorrow." I give them each one last look before heading back over to my office.

"How bad was it?" Zara asks, intercepting me on the way.

"I got the distinct impression that failure isn't an option here," I reply. "But…"

"But what?"

"I don't know," I say. "They're being cagey. I think they were telling me to find out what's going on here, no matter what."

Zara raises an eyebrow. "They want you to go off-book?"

I shrug. "It's like talking to a cryptogram with those two, I'm not even sure *they* know what they're saying."

"Em, we just got off some pretty serious charges," she replies. "I don't think breaking protocol again is the best idea."

"That makes two of us," I say, glancing behind me to find Vostov standing at the end of the hall, watching us walk away.

Chapter Nine

THE DOGS CIRCLE ME AT LEAST FIFTEEN TIMES BEFORE I finally manage to get their food bowls down. Timber never used to do this; he would sit and wait for his food, but with the addition of Rocky into the family he's become a little looser with the rules.

Of course it doesn't help that I let him get away with it. Both of them. I figure they've both had enough stress in life a few bends here and there won't ruin them forever. Plus, Timber is getting older. And I have a standing rule that older dogs get pretty much whatever they want whenever they want it. That doesn't mean he still can't sprint at twenty miles per hour whenever he wants to, he just doesn't do it all the time anymore.

In the middle of feeding, both their heads pop up a second before I hear keys in the door. Liam comes in, causing the dogs a moment of panic between finishing their dinners and running to him. Timber elects to eat furiously while Rocky abandons his food, runs up to Liam, gives him a few frantic sniffs and a lick before darting back to his bowl before his brother can take over.

"Hey," I say as Liam plants a kiss right on my lips. "Where have you been? I had to get a ride from Zara back."

"Sorry," he replies. "I spent half the day in the car. One of those families is in Stokesdale and that's like two hours out of the way."

"Right," I say. "I didn't think about all the driving you'd have to do."

"That'll teach me to open my big mouth," he says, dropping his bag into one of the stools beside the bar. Timber has finally finished his food and goes up to Liam, performing the same dance Rocky did.

"How was your day?" he asks.

"Weird," I say. "What did the families say? Did you get anything?"

He gives me *the look* before heading into the kitchen. "Did you eat yet? I could whip something up."

"Liam," I say.

He pauses as he reaches for a plate from one of the cabinets. "Unfortunately, neither family was very talkative."

"Seriously?" I ask. "What about the complaints?"

"The first family I visited, the Sawyers, denied it in the beginning. It's just the husband and his two daughters. Eventually though, once I pressed him, he admitted they called and tried to get in contact with his wife but was denied access. When I asked him why he withdrew the complaint, he said it was because he didn't want to cause trouble for Renata. He was afraid if he kept pressing that it might mean she'd have some of her privileges taken away."

"But that's—"

"I know," he says. "I told him that was illegal and he had the right to speak with his wife but he kept insisting he thought it was a bad idea. He said he wished he would have never made that call."

"What the hell," I say. "And the others? The Eatons?"

"Couldn't even get them to talk," he says. "They wouldn't

let me in the door. Just said there was no problem and asked that I please leave them alone."

I sit at the kitchen table, dumbfounded. "So both families make a complaint. They suspect something is going on enough to make formal calls to the authorities, but then both go back on it. Meanwhile the people they're calling about don't want to have any contact with them and seem perfectly happy to sit in a mental facility."

"Then you did find them," he says. "I guess Pendergast's theory was off."

"That's the other thing," I say. "After our meeting today, he pulled me into his office, with that vulture Vostov watching over my shoulder."

"What did they want to talk about?"

"They seemed insistent that something was going on, and that I needed to 'think outside the box', whatever the hell that means."

Liam brews himself a pot of tea. "Why are they so determined to find something on this case?" he asks.

"I don't know," I say. "But something about it doesn't fit right to me. That was the other thing, we couldn't find any transfer orders for either inmate. Zara and Nadia are going back over it now. But at present we can't figure out *how* they got there."

"There has to be a paper trail somewhere," he says.

"I agree. But the way this is going it will be nothing more than a clerical error somewhere down the line. Just two people who got lost in the system."

Liam finishes brewing his tea as the dogs make their way to the living room and settle in their beds, chewing on some of their post-dinner toys. I admit, it's nice to be back here and fall into some sense of normalcy again, especially after everything that's been going on. But at the same time, I don't have a good feeling in my gut about all this.

Liam takes a seat with me at the table. "What do you think is going on?"

"I think someone is hiding something. But what that is, I have no idea. You should have seen this *nurse* we met today. The kind of person who is always perfectly pleasant on the outside, but still slinging underhanded insults despite the fact we were just there to do our jobs."

"And you spoke to each inmate?"

I shake my head. "Not enough. We couldn't get them alone. But they seemed afraid of her… or at least clammed up around her. I would love to get them alone, see if their stories change any. But I don't see that happening. Especially since all the inspection reports are clean."

"What do you think Pendergast's endgame is?" he asks.

"No clue. Maybe they're feeling the pressure from above to make this thing work. But the way they're going about it is just… weird," I say. "I don't know." I rub my hands down my face. "At least with Fletch, I knew who I was fighting."

"Maybe you don't need to be fighting anyone," he says. "Maybe it's not as complicated as it seems."

"You think there's nothing here," I say.

"I didn't say that. I just don't want you so distracted by 'enemies' that you miss the big picture."

"Which is?"

"That not everything is a conspiracy. Sometimes things just happen. Coincidences do happen." He takes a tentative sip of his tea.

"Not in my experience," I say. "Things happen because people want them to. Or they don't. Or they're trying to hide something. We deal with some really awful people, Liam. I can't just hope that this case or that one is nothing more than a series of happenstance and everything is cheery in the background." I get up and stare out the window.

"Em, you've been under a lot of pressure lately," he says. "And you're still coming down from it. After everything that happened, everything with Janice and the Bureau you need to give yourself some time to acclimate."

"How am I supposed to do that?" I ask, spinning on him. "This job is a never-ending series of disasters, one on top of another. How am I supposed to *regulate* during that? I can't just take things day by day. I *feel* it when victims are abused, when people are suffering. It's why I can't just shut things off. Those feelings don't go away when I walk through that door." I point to our front door. "They live in here, *all the time*. And I can't do anything about it." Tears begin to prickle at the corners of my eyes and I turn away before he can see them fall.

I feel him come up behind me and wrap me in a hug. "I know," he says gently. "It's your empathy that makes you so good at what you do. But you need to save some room for Emily in there. Otherwise you'll lose yourself in the despair."

I place one hand over his, feeling his warmth envelop me. I've missed this. Missed this feeling of home with him, of safety. I've been operating in survival mode for so long I've barely taken a minute to just stop and breathe. I pull in the scent of his tea—chamomile, the sound of the dogs chewing and the soft melodies of the radio. I close my eyes and take in five deep breaths.

"Can I be honest with you?" I ask.

"Always."

"I'm afraid."

He pauses. "Of what?"

"I'm afraid that I've damaged us. That I've been away too long, or all of this is too much." I make a brief motion to nothing in particular, but I think he gets what I'm saying.

"You don't need to worry about us," he says.

"No, I think I do," I say. "Something has been going on with you ever since I got back. I can see it in your eyes, Liam. I feel like I've broken something between us." The tears fall despite my best efforts.

He gently turns me around to face him. "Hey," he says. "You're not losing me, okay?"

"I don't want you to stay out of some sense of duty or pity," I say. "Because I know you. I know you'd do that, even if it wasn't what you really wanted."

"Don't do that," he says. "Don't tell me what I want. If I wasn't willing to be part of this, to work on this with you, I would have been gone a long time ago. I know what this relationship requires, and I don't have any illusions about the sacrifices we both need to make." He takes a deep breath. "If I wanted a normal life, I wouldn't have enrolled in the Bureau. I'm willing to accept the risks… if you are."

I bury my head into his shoulder. "I am," I say.

"Good," he says. "Because you can't get rid of me that easily. You don't have to carry this alone. I'm always here."

"I know," I say into his shoulder again. "I… I did something I shouldn't have."

I feel him go stiff for a moment. "Whatever it is, I'll understand."

"I went to see Fletch over the weekend."

He takes a step back, still holding my shoulders. "Why?"

"Because that son of a bitch owes me," I say. "He owes Janice. I thought maybe I could maneuver him into telling me something about it all. Or to reveal who Solitaire really is."

"Em, that could jeopardize—"

"I know," I say. "Zara already voiced that concern. But I can't just let him get away with it. He has to pay for what he did to her."

"He *is* paying. He's in prison," Liam says.

I shake my head. "You didn't see his cell. It's more like a hotel room. He's got nicer bedding than we do."

"Listen," he says. "Fletch will have his day in court. And you'll be there to testify against him. And then he's going to prison for a long, long time. He attacked the FBI, killed at least three agents, maybe more. He's not going anywhere."

Despite his assurances, I'm not as confident. Fletch is a slippery bastard. And until he's in max security with a dozen life sentences on his head I won't be satisfied. Too often I've seen how something "certain" turns out not to be that way at all.

"It's going to be okay," he says. But even as he says it, I can still feel his hesitation. He's holding something back. And despite his assurances, I can't shake the feeling like something is wrong.

"Are you sure everything is okay?" I ask. "With you?"

"Me?" He brushes it off. "Of course. I'm fine. Why?"

"You just seem like something's bothering you."

"You don't need to worry about me," he says. He heads off and makes us a quick dinner before we head to bed. But the whole time I can't help but wonder why he continues to lie to me. I trust Liam, I trust him as much as I trust Zara; but I can't deny my instincts. I know when someone isn't being honest with me.

But at the end of the day, I'm too tired for a fight. I don't have it in me after today. What bothers me isn't that he's lying, but that he doesn't feel like he can tell me, whatever it is.

As I lie in bed, staring at the ceiling as Liam falls asleep beside me and the dogs tetrised somewhere around our legs, my thoughts go back to what Pendergast said.

We know you'll make the right call.

We needed you.

What was he trying to tell me? Everything about this case seems reasonable on the surface. There are discrepancies, but nothing that would raise a red flag. And yet...something is dead wrong here. Pendergast almost seemed desperate this afternoon. Desperate for me to understand without coming right out and saying it...whatever it was.

Maybe he's on the right track after all. And maybe it's time for me to do something desperate in return.

Chapter Ten

"WHAT'S GOING ON?" LIAM ASKS AS HE TURNS OVER IN BED. I'm in the closet, pulling on my leggings and a running jacket.

"I'm going out for an early run," I say.

He picks up his phone. "It's not even five," he replies.

"I couldn't sleep," I say. "Go back to bed. I'll be back soon." I lean down and kiss him on the forehead. Timber stirs and looks up, whining. I settle him and tell him to go back to sleep before I slip out of the bedroom.

Grabbing my car keys, my weapon, and my badge, I head out to my car and get the engine running. It's cool enough I can see my breath inside the car but it warms up quickly. I back out and head through the neighborhood, noting most of the homes are still dark. There's an errant light on in one house or another, but for the most part it's quiet out.

If I had the willpower, I would get up at this time every day to get started. But this is a special occasion.

It takes about thirty minutes to reach my destination, and by the time I do, the sun is just barely beginning to peek out from behind the trees. This street is as quiet as mine was, if not more, the only difference is a line of trash cans lines the street, a garbage vehicle rumbling down the road and upturning each can into its back like a giant trash monster who can never be sated.

About ten minutes after the truck comes by, I see the person I'm looking for. He comes out through a side door, grabbing the newspaper lying there at his feet. He then makes his way down the driveway in his bathrobe to grab his trash can. I pull up his image from the case file on my phone just to make sure I have the right person.

But there's no doubt about it. It's him.

I get out of the car just as he starts pulling his can back towards the house.

"Mr. Frey," I call out.

He turns, startled. The man has long dark hair that falls to his shoulders, and a full beard and moustache though those have begun to go gray. His eyes are bloodshot like he hasn't gotten much sleep and he instinctively takes a step back, releasing his hold on his trash can.

"Who are you?"

I hold up my badge. "I'm Special Agent Slate with the FBI. My colleague Agent Kane tried contacting you yesterday."

"Yeah," he says, clearly caught off guard. "I was out. What's this about?"

"Just a few questions about your work with the Lazar Mental Health Facility in Rochester."

"Look, I include everything in my reports," he says, backing up towards his house. "If you want information, look there and don't bother me at home."

"Then perhaps you can help me with a discrepancy we've found with the Facility," I say before he can reach his door. "We have found two inmates who don't seem to have transfer records for where they came from. Their families alerted us to tell us they were denied contact. And yet, when we look at your reports, nothing seems amiss."

The man winces, something having struck a chord with him somewhere. "I don't know what you're talking about."

"You should," I say, getting closer. "You're the person who determines the facility's fitness and compliance. Tell me, how would they even get two additional inmates? We were told they transferred from Pimlo, but as far as my colleagues can find, no such transfer orders exist."

"That's not my concern," he says, backing up further. "Inmate processing is up to the Facility. I just make sure they're not in violation of the law."

"Holding two people against their will is very much against the law, wouldn't you agree?" I ask. I'm going out on a limb here, but I've struck something with Frey and I don't want to let it go. "And if you don't know they're there, how can you be sure they're not being mistreated?"

He hesitates. "I don't answer to you—" he begins, but I cut him off.

"Lazar is a federal detention center, and falls under the purview of the FBI. So in a way, you very much answer to me, especially if they're hiding something in there. I need to know how and why those two women were transferred in, and you're going to tell me."

He looks to the left and right, the lights on in the houses on either side of him. "Okay, fine. Just… not out here. Come on." He motions for me to follow him inside.

I don't expect he'll try to jump me; his beer belly tells me he wouldn't be much of a threat if he did, but still I'm cautious heading into his house. As soon as I'm inside I'm hit with the smell of bacon and grease. Beer cans litter his table and there is clutter everywhere. Frey tosses the newspaper on the kitchen counter before going to the kitchen and placing some errant dishes in the sink.

"Live alone?" I ask.

"I got divorced three years ago," he replies. "Not that it matters."

"Tell me about Lazar," I say. "What isn't in your reports?"

"Everything *is* in there," he insists. "I don't know what you want me to tell you."

"Let's start with the fact that every month, the facility has a perfect rating," I say. "Statistically that isn't possible. I don't care if it's the best facility in the world, eventually, somewhere, someone is going to fuck up. Yet every month you give them a glowing recommendation, which I'm sure keeps the top brass happy. But you can't tell me you're not glossing over things when you're in there."

He places his hands on the counter, hanging his head before looking back at me. "Well, what can I say? They have excellent quality control."

"And the inmates who have no record of being transferred in? Did you even know about them? Sawyer and Eaton?"

He shakes his head.

"How many other people are there who don't have official records? How many people may be being mistreated because you don't even know about them?"

He slams his fists on his countertop, as if coming to a realization. "Fine. It's going to come out anyway."

"What is?" I ask.

"You don't know what it's like," he says. "Going in those places. Seeing those people day in and day out. Seeing how the system mistreats people who have been incarcerated, how they're treated as less than human."

"Is that what's happening at Lazar?" I ask.

He winces again. "I… couldn't tell you what's going on at Lazar."

"But you signed off on the inspection reports," I say.

He sighs and sits on one of the stools in his kitchen. "Look around. Do I look like I'm living life to the fullest here? My ex-wife takes most of what I bring home and I haven't seen my kid in months. She tells me he doesn't even want to see me anymore, which I'm sure is because she keeps telling him what an asshole I am behind my back. Do you know what it's like coming home to an empty house, day after day, with nothing to look forward to? After spending your days inside some of the hardest and cruelest places you can imagine? It isn't just what guards do to prisoners in there, it's what the prisoners do to each other."

"What do they do?" I ask, softening my tone.

"Worse than you could ever imagine. Trust me. So when an opportunity came along, I took it. If for no other reason than to get some goddamned relief for once."

"What kind of opportunity?"

He takes a deep breath. "The warden at Lazar approached me last year. He said if I was willing to fudge the reports, he would make sure I got a certain… bonus every month. It was just supposed to be a little score pumping, that's it. At least, that's how it started."

"But it didn't end there," I say.

He opens a nearby cabinet and pulls out mostly empty bottle of whiskey, pouring the rest of it into a nearby mug and drinking it all down in one gulp. "I guess he looked in my eyes and saw weakness. And he exploited it."

"You say that like you didn't have a choice in the matter," I fire back.

"Yeah, I had a choice all right," he says. "A choice not to have to walk through that godforsaken place every month and still get paid for it. In fact, paid better than I ever was before. So I could afford something nice for once. Just once. I'm sure in the FBI you all get fancy vacations and enough money to live on, but not everyone gets to be that way. I'm drowning in credit card debt. I've got two mortgages on this house. So when someone offers me a hand up, yeah, I'm gonna take it."

"And violate your oath in the process," I say. "You know you'll lose your job for this. And you'll face federal charges."

"It doesn't matter," he says. "I knew it was never going to

be forever." He looks out the window to the driveway. "Weird that it was today, though. Of all days."

"Why, what's today?" I ask.

"My son's birthday," he replies.

"Mr. Frey, I'm going to have to place you under arrest for falsifying federal records," I say. "And I'm going to need a signed testimony of what the warden told you. If what you're saying is true then there's been a massive coverup at Lazar."

He nods. "Sure. Sure."

I grab my phone to call it in, but before I can, Frey grabs a knife from his knife block. I pull my weapon, dropping the phone but before I can do anything, he draws the knife quickly across his neck, spilling blood all over his shirt.

"Shitshit*shit*," I say, rushing over to him as he collapses on the ground, a gurgling sound coming from the opening in his neck. Putting pressure on it I can tell the wound is already deep and he's losing too much blood. "Why?" I demand, but all he can do is look into my eyes as I watch the life fading from his. It's almost like he's looking at me with relief. Blood squelches through my fingers as his carotid pumps it from his heart up through the wound and outside his body. He barely has seconds.

It's all I can do to try and save his life, knowing it's futile anyway, but I keep trying, looking for anything that could keep pressure on the wound better. But by the time I turn back to him, his eyes are closed and he's no longer struggling to breathe.

"Dammit," I say, finally removing my hands from the wound. They're covered in blood, along with my hoodie, arms and everything else around us.

I can't believe I actually found a crack in this system, something that proved something more was going on at Lazar, and my witness just committed suicide right in front of me.

What a mess.

Chapter Eleven

It's past eight by the time I finally manage to get the blood off my hands. Frey's house has turned into a full-blown circus, complete with police vehicles, an ambulance and the local news showing up. Neighbors stand on their laws, trying to look over the crowds or past the police tape to figure out what's going on.

After a lengthy discussion with the two detectives who responded to my 911 call, they finally admitted that I wasn't going to be treated as a suspect and allowed me to check in with the medical staff to get myself cleaned up. I'm just getting the last bits of dried blood out from between my fingernails when Liam pulls up.

"Are you okay?" he asks, ducking under the police tape and showing the officer there his badge.

I nod. "Yeah, this… isn't mine." I indicate the blood all over my hoodie.

He wraps me in a hug. "You scared the hell out of me. When I heard the call come over the system an FBI agent was involved—"

"I know, I say. "I'm sorry. I didn't think—I wasn't sure this would be anything. It was a Hail Mary."

"What's a—never mind," he replies. "Some morning run, huh?"

I glance at the house. "Yeah. I keep going over it in my head. Looking back, I think he made up his mind to do it the second we went into his house."

"Wait a second," he says, taking a seat beside me on the bumper of the ambulance. "Start at the beginning. Whose house is this?"

I nod and go through the whole conversation with Frey. "When Elliott told us yesterday that only one inspector had been signing off on Lazar it stuck in my brain. That's not uncommon, especially if inspectors run regular routes, but there was just something about it that I didn't like. And the fact that Nadia said they had tried at least a dozen times to get in contact with him and hadn't made any progress… I thought he might be intentionally ducking us."

"He knew his days were numbered," Liam says.

"I just don't understand," I say. "Why didn't he run? Get out of town or… something other than this?"

"Maybe he couldn't face the possibility of looking over his shoulder for the rest of his life."

Yeah, I suppose I can understand that. Liam wraps an arm around my shoulder, pulling me close. "I'm just glad you're okay."

Another familiar car comes tearing down the road, screeching to a stop in front of an officer. He's about to pull his weapon when the occupant jumps out, her badge already in her hand. "FBI," she yells. "Where is she?" She looks past the officer and spots me, ducking under his outstretched arm and running up to the ambulance. "Jesus fuck, Em! What happened?"

"Z, I'm fine," I say.

She looks at Liam, who only shrugs. I give her the quick version of what went down. Her eyes widen as I go through the whole story. "So then he admitted it. To taking a bribe."

I nod. "Except now we can't exactly use his testimony," I say. "I didn't record anything and I doubt he's left a paper trail."

"You never know," Zara says, taking another look at the house. "Is CSI in there?"

"Yeah, they just got here about twenty minutes ago."

"I need access to that house," she says. "I want to go through his financials. See if I can find proof to back up the claims. If so, then we'll have them nailed. Because you'll never guess what I found out last night."

"What?"

"There are no transfer orders for either Sawyer or Eaton," she replies. "They don't exist. That's why Pimlo doesn't have them. The only criminal records I can find for the two women are those paper versions Booth handed us."

"Are you saying that they made up their criminal records?"

"I can't prove it yet, but I think I'm close," she says. "It's still possible they came from some obscure prison somewhere else or that the orders were lost somewhere in the shuffle, but given what you just learned, I'm thinking that's very unlikely."

"What's the endgame here?" Liam asks. "Why go to all this trouble? Bribing the inspector, falsifying criminal records. What's going on behind those walls?"

"I don't know," I say. "But I think we need to regroup and get everyone on the same page."

Two hours later I make my way back into the office, freshly showered and no longer smelling of blood. I had to hand over my hoodie to the LEOs and I don't expect to get it back. Frey's suicide investigation will take some time and they'll be doing a lot of legwork to put the pieces together.

Meanwhile, his death has already hit the local news, which means that if anyone at Lazar is paying attention, they'll know their golden calf just went the way of the Dodo. Which may put them on the back foot, especially if we try to get back in there again. Which is exactly what I want to do.

I make my way into the conference room to find Nadia and Elliott already there, along with Pendergast. Vostov, Zara and Liam are nowhere to be seen.

"Agent," Pendergast nods as I enter. "Glad to see you're okay."

"That's two of us," I say. "It's been a morning. Where's Agent Vostov?"

"On assignment," he says. "As soon as the rest of your team members join us we can get started."

I exchange a few words with Nadia and Elliott; both express concern at what happened this morning. I'm anxious for Zara to share what she learned from looking into the prisoner records, but as the clock ticks by, I find myself getting more and more annoyed with the fact they haven't shown up yet.

"Excuse me," I say. "Let me find what's keeping them." Pendergast gives me a quick motion of his head before opening his phone and scrolling.

I head back down the hallway, ducking my head in Zara's office to find it empty with the lights off. It's only three more doors to Liam's office, but the door is closed. I knock once and open it to find Zara sitting across from Liam, both of them turning to us with surprise on their faces.

"Hey," I say. "Meeting. Remember?"

Liam checks his watch. "Shit. Sorry, we got caught up."

"Sorry, Em," Zara says and quickly gets up, heading past me down the hall. I'm momentarily struck by the odd interruption. Zara and Liam aren't strangers by any means, but it's not often that they have closed-door meetings without me.

"Is everything okay?" I ask Liam.

"Yeah, just lost track of time," he says, gathering his laptop. "Pendergast already in there?"

"Everyone else is," I say, hesitant. Do I confront him about this now? I know neither Liam or Zara would ever do anything to hurt me, yet at the same time something about this feels wrong. Like I've interrupted something I shouldn't have. Something that wasn't for me.

I don't like the pit that's developed in my stomach.

Liam flashes me a quick smile. "Okay, great. Let's get to it." He plants a quick kiss on my cheek that I'm slow to reciprocate. Could he have been talking to her about whatever has been bothering him? Or is it something else entirely?

I mentally wipe my brain. This kind of thinking isn't going to do me any good. I trust Liam and I trust Zara. I'm not going to sit here and double guess their motives or their actions. If it's something I need to know about, they'll tell me. Until then, I have a job to do.

Once we're all in the conference room, I ask Zara to give everyone a rundown of what she found via the records for Sawyer or Eaton.

"I did full background checks on both women," Zara says. "First off, they both have arrest records, but they are for minor offenses. Trespassing, minor possession, stuff like that. And they aren't recent. These are from five, ten years ago. Nothing that would lead to incarceration. And certainly nothing that would warrant being placed in a mental correctional facility."

"Are you saying someone has falsified the documentation required to hold them?" Elliott asks.

"I believe so, but I still can't a hundred percent prove it yet." She glances at me. "But with what Em found this morning..."

"As you all know, I was involved in an incident this morning which resulted in a man tragically taking his own life," I say. "That man was Jeremiah Frey, the federal inspector for Lazar." I turn to Nadia. "He got your messages, by the way, but chose not to respond. Before he took his own life, he confessed to me he'd been taking bribes from Lazar—specifically from the warden there—in order to give them a better rating for their monthly inspections. He also revealed to me it had been some time since he'd actually visited Lazar, meaning we don't know *what* is going on behind those walls."

"The local police still have possession of Frey's computer and electronics," Zara says. "As soon as those are accessible, I want to see if I can find any evidence of these bribes. At least back up the story."

"Interesting," Pendergast says. "It looks like your instincts were right after all. The question now is how do you proceed?"

"Frey's death is already all over the news," I say. "I don't think we can wait. We need to go back to Lazar and force them to shut down operations until a time in which a new independent inspection team can provide an unbiased look at what is going on in there. Given the facility's history, it's not unreasonable to assume there may be rights violations taking place. Especially if the warden was looking to keep Frey's mouth shut."

"The problem," Liam jumps in, "Is that we can't prove this… yet. With Frey's death, his confession goes out the window. Until Zara can find something that backs up his claims, all we have is a working theory."

"Which will be difficult to pin on the warden," Pendergast says.

"He must suspect something is coming," Elliott says. "Perhaps like Frey, he'll confess once he's confronted."

"I don't think it's going to be that easy," I say. "But as I see it, we have two separate issues here. One, the facility is operating unchecked. And two, they have at least two inmates who should not be there. I think it's in our best interest to find out why Sawyer and Eaton have been interred and if they should be removed. And I think the only way to do that is to return to the facility."

"What's the strategy?" Pendergast asks.

"We go in under the guise as quality control. Let them know their inspector has unfortunately passed and that we found some questionable material in his possession. Inform them that all activities are to be suspended until time when a full investigation can take place. Get the warden's cooperation and try to find any evidence to support our theory."

"Seems reasonable," Pendergast replies. He turns to Nadia and Elliott. "Start putting together a new inspection team. And I want full background checks on every member. No one slipping through the cracks like Frey."

"We'll get right on it," Nadia says.

"And Coll, stay on the LEOs. Let them know we need access to their scene and the effects as soon as possible. Put whatever pressure on them you deem necessary."

"Got it," Liam replies.

"And you two," Pendergast says, pointing at me and Zara. "Try not to piss them off so much that they freeze us out completely. The less of a fight this is, the better chance we have of finding out what the hell is going on in there."

Chapter Twelve

"DOES PENDERGAST REMIND YOU OF THE MONOPOLY MAN?"
Zara asks as we head back to Lazar Correctional. It's another
long drive on the back roads of Virginia with little more than
trees and more trees to keep us company.

"Not really," I say. "He's too tall."

"Yeah, but if you like, squished him down and gave him a
monocle," she says. "And a top hat."

"I think if you did that to anyone they'd look like the
Monopoly Man," I reply.

"I guess. He just seems to fit that kind of profile."

"Plus, the Monopoly Man doesn't wear a monocle," I say.
"That's a myth."

"Of course he does," she says, pulling out her phone.
"Wait a second… what the hell?" She shows me a picture of
the cartoon figure on her screen. "I could have sworn he had
one."

"It's that Mandela Effect thing," I say. "Collective misre-
membering."

"Oh, I don't like that at all," she says. "I'm the one who's
supposed to have all the weird useless trivia taking up all the
space in her brain."

"Afraid I'm muscling in on your territory?" I smile.

She snaps her fingers. "I guess the only thing to do is get even *nerdier* about things. I can't have you beating me."

She definitely seems like she's in a better mood today. I have the urge to ask her about her discussion with Liam this morning, but I decide to skip it. "We need a plan for Booth. I don't want to confront that woman again."

"We'll just say we need to speak to the warden," Zara says. "Simple."

"You don't think she'll be running interference for him? There's no way she's not involved in whatever this is. She wouldn't let us see either inmate without being present, despite telling us she doesn't handle either of their cases personally."

"That's a good point," Zara says. "But if she's in charge of things there, how are we supposed to circumvent her? Jump the fence and scale the walls?"

The thought did cross my mind. "We'll just have to make sure we don't engage. Someone like that gets a rise out of pissing other people off. If we stay cool and collected, I think maybe we can just bypass her."

"Excuse me but have you *met* me?" she asks. "*Cool* is not exactly in my vocabulary. Unless you're talking about my taste in music."

"Make it your defining feature for the next hour," I say. "You heard Pendergast. We need to keep this as clean as possible."

She shifts in her seat. "Easy for him to say. He sits behind a desk all day."

Half an hour later we pull up to the same gate, but this time I'm driving, so it's me who shows her badge to the screen.

"This facility is for authorized personnel only," the voice on the other side says. It doesn't sound like Booth. "Do you have an appointment?"

"No," I admit. "We're here to see the warden. It's an urgent matter regarding the operation of this facility."

"I can't just let you in with—"

"Listen, as I'm sure you already know, the FBI operates under the DOJ, the same DOJ which regulates how this prison is run. Now either let us in, or face a call from the Attorney General."

"One moment, please." A second later the gate opens.

"Get ready for it," I mumble to Zara as we pull through and head down the long and winding drive for a second time.

"What are the odds they lock us in? What if Sawyer and Eaton are undercover FBI agents who never got back out? And now they're brainwashed to believe they're prisoners?"

I've only just gotten back into my martial arts training after being lax on it for so long, but I can guarantee one thing: no one is taking me by force. And I pity the person who even tries. "Maybe we should ask them for their clearance codes next time we see them," I tease back.

As we pull up to the building once more, my heart drops. Nurse Booth is already standing outside the facility, her hands folded together and a pleasant enough smile on her face, watching us the entire way. I should have guessed she'd be here waiting for us given our last encounter. It was too much to hope today was her day off. Which means we're going to have a hard time scrounging for any evidence with her watching us like a hawk. We may need to pivot.

"Fuck," I whisper as I pull into the parking spot and kill the engine.

"Want me to put her in a headlock? You'll be able to get by. I'm pretty sure I can subdue her without too much fuss."

"As much as I wish I could tell you to go ahead, I don't think that would be very conducive." I get out of the car and give the woman across from us a wan smile.

"Agents," she says. "How nice to see you both again so soon. How can we help you today?"

"We need to speak with Warden Pearce," I say.

"Is there something wrong?" she asks, still wearing that infuriating smile of hers.

"We just need to have a discussion with him." We scale the steps to meet her. "Immediately."

"Of course, Agent Slate," she replies. "You of all people would be the perfect person to judge the seriousness of an event."

I exchange a look with Zara. What the hell does *that* mean?

"This way," Booth says. "You'll of course need to go through our new security procedures."

"New?" I ask.

"Yes," she says. "Just implemented. But don't worry. They shouldn't take long."

We follow her inside where we're met by three guards now instead of one. "Come with me," the first one says, leading us into the room adjacent to the office that had been closed before. "I need all your weapons, ID, anything metal or potentially harmful," he says.

"We just had to provide our weapons yesterday," I say.

He holds out a bin for our effects like I didn't even speak. I sigh and pull everything from my pockets, placing it all in the bins. Zara does the same.

"You'll need to fill these out," he says, handing us both clipboards with forms on them. They're official visitor forms for law enforcement personnel and they are *lengthy*.

"We don't have time for this," I say, handing the form back to him.

"Sorry, new procedure. Either fill it out, or you can turn around."

Grumbling, I quickly scribble my answers on the form as another guard comes into the room. As soon as we're done, the first guard hands them to his colleague. "Contact the local FBI office, let's verify their identities."

"*What?*" Zara says.

"Should only take a few minutes," he says.

"You realize we were here *yesterday,*" I say. "You've already given us access once."

He nods. "And we experienced an incident yesterday evening. A patient somehow became in possession of a ball-point pen. Used it to stab another inmate who is now in our infirmary."

"You don't think we would seriously leave a potential weapon for an inmate, do you?" I ask.

He nods. "It *was* in one of the corridors you were escorted through." Upon seeing my face he softens, but only slightly. "These are just new procedures to protect everyone. Maybe you dropped it by accident. The point is we don't know."

"I don't even own a pen," Zara says. "We wouldn't be so careless as to drop one along the way."

"That doesn't matter," he replies. "Orders from the Warden. We've moved into full lockdown protocol. Which means if you want to get in, this is the process."

"This is ridiculous," I say. "How long will this take?"

He gives me a smile. "Not long."

An hour later we're still waiting in the adjacent room while Lazar's security goes through whatever bullshit motions they think they need to justify this to themselves.

"You know they're stalling us, right?" Zara asks. "They probably planted that pen themselves."

"Yeah, I know. But they could be a little less obvious about it," I reply. I pace the room for what has to be the hundredth time. Without my phone I have no idea how much time has actually passed, but it feels like half a lifetime. Which I'll take to mean has been about an hour.

"Do you think they're even going to let us in there?" she asks. "We might have to come back with a warrant."

"I don't know," I reply. "I'll give it another—"

But before I can finish, the door opens to reveal Nurse Booth and two of her guards. "Good news, we've completed all our security checks. If you'll follow me."

"Finally," Zara says as we both follow her back into the hallway. We're taken through the security checkpoint to the right, the one we didn't go through yesterday, Nurse Booth opening the doors using her keycard again. "I apologize for the wait, but we're all still getting used to these new procedures. Patient safety is our top priority."

"Did you check the camera feeds?" I ask. "Surely they would have caught whoever left the pen out in the open like that."

"Unfortunately the camera that checks that corridor was having trouble yesterday," she says, her voice completely even, as if she had been expecting the question. "But it's been fixed now. No more problems."

"Uh-huh," I say.

Zara leans into me so Booth can't hear. "I was halfway joking before," Zara says. "But if Sawyer and Eaton actually do end up being undercover cops who got caught up in this woman's insanity, I won't be the least bit surprised."

We follow her through a series of security doors until we reach an elevator. Another guard meets us there and I note the elevator is only operated by a physical key, not the keycards. It takes us up to the third floor where we get off and head down a long, wood-paneled corridor. At the end are two large doors with glass inset into them, allowing us to see a man inside, working on a laptop. Behind him is a large window which looks out on the front of the property.

Booth approaches the doors, though there's a small area off to the right where a secretary sits and is taken up mostly by large filing cabinets. She motions to the secretary. "Our FBI guests are here to see the warden."

The secretary nods and picks up her phone, speaking into it quickly. "You may go on in. He's expecting you."

I wonder if Pearce will say anything about putting us through all these hoops. Or was this whole thing planned by him?

Booth knocks on the door and the man beyond gives a small beckoning wave.

"Sir, Agents Slate and Foley with the FBI to see you," she says.

The man looks up. He's mostly gray up top and has a long, angular face. He wears a suit though his jacket hangs on the coatrack next to his desk and his tie is slightly loosened at the neck. "Ah," he says, standing. "Thank you, Lena." Finally, he addresses us. "I'm sorry for all the delays; we've had quite the eventful twenty-four hours here." He holds out a hand and I give it a tentative shake, as does Zara.

"That will be all." Booth nods and heads back out, leaving us alone with the Warden.

"Thank you for seeing us," I say. "But was all this really necessary?"

"We take security breaches here very seriously," Pearce says, taking a seat again. "I understand you both visited us yesterday as well and were given ample access to the property. Well, unfortunately, that may have caused some of our issues. I instructed my team to give you some leeway yesterday because you are with the FBI, but when I saw what it could lead to, I realized I shouldn't have been so generous."

"You understand what you're accusing us of?" Zara asks. "Two decorated FBI agents."

"Hold on," he says. "We're not accusing you of anything. All I can say is we had a protocol breach yesterday. After reviewing our procedures, the only anomaly was your visit.

Now, I don't think you intentionally did anything. But mistakes do happen. We're all human, after all."

"Don't you have visitors who come here all the time?" I ask.

"We're currently reviewing our visitor policy," he replies. "We may need to take extra precautions from here on out. And our visitors don't have access to the same areas you toured."

"Look, Warden Pearce, let me get right to it," I say, noting there is nowhere for Zara or me to sit, so we're forced to stand. "Do you know a Jerimiah Frey?"

"Ah," he says. "I thought that might be what this little visit was about. I understand he passed away this morning. Tragic. He was such a friendly face around here."

"When was the last time you saw Mr. Frey?" I ask.

"Probably his last inspection," Pearce says. "Though I can't recall when that was. I'd have to look it up. Why?"

I don't miss the quick glance from Zara. "We have reason to believe his investigations may have been compromised in some way."

"Compromised? How?" Pearce asks, seemingly shocked. Though I can't tell if it's just an act or if he's really surprised.

"We're still looking into that," Zara replies.

"In the meantime, you'll need to halt all professional care here at the facility until an independent team can come in and give this place its approval."

"We can't just pull the plug," he says. "This isn't a factory. It's more like an airplane. Or in our case, two hundred airplanes. If we shut everything down, quite a few of those will plummet to the ground and crash. Some of these patients could die if they go off their medication."

"Barring any life-saving medication," I say, having heard this spiel before. "All services are to be put on hold. Everything goes into lockdown and we're going to need each of your employees to submit to an interview process."

"But that will take weeks," he protests. "We have a facility to run here, Agent."

"If we find out this facility has been compromised, then with all due respect, Warden, no you don't. And unless we can find the source of this breach, then we will take this place apart brick by brick until we do." The man's reaction lands somewhere between frustration and anger. "Like you, we take security breaches very seriously."

He sits back in his chair, regarding me for a moment. "Yes. Of course. You're absolutely right. I'm sorry, I don't know what I was thinking. I'll order Booth to wind everything down until the inspection team can arrive and begin their work. In the meantime, what more do you need from me?"

"We need all records of Frey's activities here at the facility," I say. "Along with all your security footage from his last visit."

"That will take some time," he says. "But we'll get right on it. Have you informed the Oversight Board?"

"Our team is working on that at the moment," Zara says.

He nods once, then a few more times, though it is more to himself than us. "Excellent. I want you to know my people will cooperate in any way we can."

"That's good to hear," I say, though I'm somewhat surprised by his heel turn. Still, I'm not going to argue the point. "Though I would suggest that you not subject the new inspection team to such... rigorous security measures."

"Hopefully by the time they arrive we'll have the situation contained," he says. "It's only one pen, but in an abundance of caution... you understand."

"Mm-hm," I say, shaking his hand again quickly. "We'll be in touch within the next few days."

"I look forward to it."

Chapter Thirteen

AN HOUR LATER, ZARA AND I ARE BACK IN THE CAR, WITH everything that was "held" for us, headed back to the office.

"I swear I am going to bean that woman the next chance I get," Zara says. "Her and her troop of flying monkeys."

"I know how you feel," I say. I just hope Booth enjoyed her little power trip, because that's the last time she's ever going to have one up on us.

"Just the… I don't even know the word for it," Zara says.

"Audacity?"

"Yes, audacity," she repeats. "A ballpoint pen? Please. Not to mention Pearce didn't seem the least bit bothered that we were treated like common criminals." She holds up her phone. "And you can bet your ass the second we get back to the office I'm stripping this thing down. I don't trust them for a second. There could be a rogue program on here, some kind of tracker or who knows what else. I'm stripping your phone too."

I sigh. Great. I'll have to switch *again*. But that's not what really bothers me. "I don't trust Pearce's little show in there," I say. "I got the distinct feeling he was telling us what we wanted to hear just to get rid of us."

"You think Frey was telling the truth? That Pearce paid him off?"

"I don't think someone would kill themselves unless it was a serious offense," I say. "And Pearce is definitely hiding something. I think we need to get that new inspection team in there as soon as possible."

Zara pulls out her phone. "No bars. I'll have to wait until we're back before I can call Nadia to see where they are. Plus, even if I could make a call on this thing it could give them a preliminary heads-up."

It's not surprising. The roads leading away from the facility are tucked deep within the mountains where cell coverage is spotty. Once we get a little closer we should regain cell service.

"God, that *woman*," Zara says. "I feel like we could go after her for making false statements, impeding an officer, obstruction of justice... you name it."

"It's going to be hard to prove," I say. But to even risk such a move requires a massive amount of confidence. Which means she's confident she can't be touched. In a way, she reminds me of Fletch.

"You know she's going to try and deny it, or hide behind whatever BS they made up, but I want the inspection team to seize *all* their video. Not just of us. I mean, if they think they can get away with that kind of crap with two FBI agents, imagine what they're doing to the inmates."

"It won't matter. In the next few days we'll get eyes inside there and figure out what's really going on," I say.

"Do you think we should have asked Pearce about Sawyer and Eaton?"

"No, I think he would have just deflected," I say. "Whatever they're hiding in there is a group effort. I'm sure of it."

We spend the next ten minutes in silence as I go over everything bit by bit. Booth clearly wanted to push us to our limits, but in the end it didn't matter. We persevered and got what we wanted. I keep thinking about Pearce's reaction to my accusation about Frey. What came off as surprise may not have been about what Frey was up to, but that we knew about it. He could have seen Frey's death on the news this morning and concluded that all his troubles were over. He hadn't expected Frey to give me a confession. Dead or not, it's given us an opening.

But that also tells me that finding this paper trail Zara believes exists is going to be difficult, if not impossible. He probably paid Frey in cash, or possibly with other methods. "You know, I was thinking we should probably look into Frey's travel history," I say. "See if he's taken any vacations lately. Anything outside of his normal range."

"Yeah," Zara replies. "That's a good idea. As soon as I'm sure we're not being monitored I'll add it to the list."

A silence stretches between us for a moment before she turns back to me. "You know, maybe we should—"

Her words are cut off by a cacophony of screaming metal, the explosion of airbags, of a jolt that lands like a punch to my side as the car is lifted from the ground. I lose the sense of gravity as I go weightless, the only thing holding me to my seat being my seatbelt. I have the good sense to let my body go completely slack instead of tensing up as the car falls back to Earth and slams into the ground before rolling over on its roof and back again. It's all I can do to close my eyes and focus on staying as loose in my body as possible. Most injuries from car crashes occur because people tense up. Though I don't have time to think about anything else other than airbags currently pressing into me and the sensation of being thrown through a washing machine.

Finally, the car comes to a stop, though it takes me a second to realize it. I'm upside down, a white airbag in my face and another beside my head. My ears are ringing and there's something wet and sticky on my face.

"Z?" I ask but don't even hear the words in my ears, I can

only feel them through my jaw. My vision is obscured by the airbag taking up most of my periphery but as it deflates and I push it out of the way, I take stock of myself. I don't feel any immediate injuries, but shock could be obscuring damage somewhere that I won't notice immediately.

First thing's first. I need to assess, then make sure Zara is okay. My hair hangs around my face as I reach up for my seatbelt which still has me pinned to the seat. As I do, a sharp pain surges across my shoulder. I reach up with my other arm and find my jacket and shirt have been torn away all the way down to the skin and I'm bleeding, which is probably what's all over my face. The pain from the injury isn't too bad but I need to move quickly before the adrenaline begins to wear off and I get stuck.

Fumbling with the seatbelt, I finally manage to unhook it, which causes me to fall to the roof of the car, hitting my head and sending a new blinding pain through my whole body. "Z!" I call out again but still can barely hear myself speak. I become aware of a hissing, kind of like static and the *tick tick* of a turn signal that hasn't been turned off.

"Em?"

I crawl to the passenger seat to find Zara pinned like I was, but her door is completely missing, exposing plants and trees beyond the car. We're no longer on the road, we must have been thrown into the ditch or beyond.

"I'm here," I say. "Are you okay?"

"I—I don't know," she answers.

I run my hands over her face, finding no injuries there before moving on to check her arms and legs. I can't see the lower part of her body due to her airbag, but her arms seem to be fine. "Hold your hands over your head, I'm going to unlock your seatbelt. Get ready."

"Ready," she says, a little steadier.

I unlock the belt and she falls, almost into me, but manages to catch herself better than I did. Her legs come out from under the airbag and I'm relieved to see the bottom half of her is still there and seems to be in working order.

"Can you crawl out?"

She nods and shuffles across the roof until she pulls herself out of the car. I follow and it's only then I realize I'm smelling a mixture of gasoline and oil that's permeated the air. Zara crawls a little further before pushing herself up. She's unsteady at first, but manages to right herself against a tree.

I pull myself into a squat, closing my eyes for a second and trying to do another assessment. The burning from my shoulder is worse, but there's something else. Pain in my hand. I look down to see one of my fingers is at a strange angle, which sends another surge of adrenaline through me.

"Shit," I say, noting the ring finger is bent at an angle to the rest of them. I pull on it hard and pop it back into place, the sound almost like a crunch.

"You okay?" Zara asks.

I don't dare try to bend the finger. It's already beginning to swell. I point to the injury on my shoulder. "How bad is this?"

She comes over and pulls the remaining bits of my jacket and shirt away. "Doesn't look too deep. But it will need stitches."

I finally turn around and examine the car. It's pulverized on one side, the indentation clear that someone t-boned us and knocked us off the road. I glance up to the embankment about twelve feet away. But we're down on the other side and can't see the road from here. "It was intentional," I say.

"Are you sure?"

"Better to be safe than sorry," I reply. I go for my weapon, but my holster is empty. It's lost somewhere in the wreck. "Do you still have yours?"

Zara pads herself like she's looking for a lost pair of keys before reaching into her coat and pulling her weapon. "I'll be right back."

"You're not going up there alone," I tell her.

"You're injured," she replies. "Sit there and let your body calm down. I'll just be a second."

Before I can argue she's working her way up the embankment. I move to go after her but the whole forest begins to spin and I stumble back until I'm sitting back on the ground, holding my head with my good hand. The vertigo passes quickly but there's still no sign of her.

"Z?" I call out to no answer. "Zara!"

She appears at the head of the embankment a moment later and comes back over. "Are you okay?"

"Just a little dizzy," I say. "What's up there?"

She pulls her face into a frown. "The other car is gone. Just some bits of plastic and glass. That's it."

"No sign of anyone?" I ask.

She shakes her head. That only reinforces my thought that it had to have been intentional. There's no way this was a random accident. "Do you still have your phone?"

"No bars," she says. "Remember?"

"Ugh," I say. "What about the car radio?"

"Yeah," she says. "Lemme see if I can fish one of them out," she replies. "I may need to get out of this ditch to pick up anything though."

"Just don't stay around that car too long," I say. "I smelled gas crawling out."

"Em," she says, glaring at me. "This isn't a movie. It isn't going to explode. It's a Chevy. Just relax there for a second and I'll be back."

I nod as she heads back to the vehicle and returns moments later with the radio. As she's calling in the wreck, I try to think back. Did I even see the other car? It came out of nowhere and was gone just as quickly. And then I remember Zara's comment about our phones being bugged. If someone was watching our GPS position they would have known right where to find us.

The only problem now is I need to prove it.

Chapter Fourteen

By the time we get to the hospital, Liam, Nadia and Elliott are already there waiting for us. We're only given a few words before the paramedics wheel me into one of the examination rooms and Zara into another. We both rode in the same ambulance from the scene of the wreck. The local police had arrived but no one from our office had made it out there by the time they insisted they take us away. I tried to tell Zara to stay but she insisted on coming with me, and the paramedics wanted her checked out as well just to be sure.

As I lay on the examination table and a nurse cuts away the clothes around my shoulder I can't help but think of Nurse Booth and how she seemed to walk around that place almost with a swagger—like she wasn't worried one bit about us being there, investigating them or what we might find. Which makes me even more suspicious that she was somehow behind that wreck. The doctor and nurses ask me a bunch of questions that I automatically answer, all while going back to everything that's happened today. There is definitely a larger agenda at work here, someone pulling levers behind the scenes. First Frey offs himself right in front of me, and now Zara and I are almost killed in a wreck that was probably meant to look like nothing more than an accident. Nothing about this is usual or ordinary and as they begin to stitch me back together, I'm forced to admit that Pendergast and Vostov were right after all.

"How are you feeling?"

I glance up to see Liam has pulled the curtain back and is grinning at me with a bag of chips in one hand and a bottle of water in the other. I take a look at my left shoulder, which is now a zipper of black stitches that extends from front to back.

"Okay, I guess. They said it was mostly superficial. Nothing broken, nothing severed. Apparently I'm going to make it after all."

He grins. "I never had any doubt."

"Where's Zara? They didn't bring her in with me."

"She's in the waiting room, talking to Pendergast," he says. "They just sent a CSI team out to the crash site."

"But she's okay?" I ask.

He nods. "Barely a scratch on her. You took the brunt of the hit, it seems."

My finger has been wrapped and put into a splint. It's already swollen so much it feels like my skin is going to pop. There's a small ice packet beside me that I've neglected to use. I pick up the ice packet and place it on my finger, wincing at the cold.

"They said it's going to be a few weeks before I can really use it again," I say.

"Good thing you have nine more." He hands over the bag of chips, already open for me. I grab a few and stuff them in my mouth—I've been starving ever since they brought me in here. "Zara gave us a rundown of what happened at the facility. Nadia and Elliott are working on assigning a new inspection team as we speak."

"Something weird is going on over there," I say in between crunches of chips. "And I would bet my life that Booth had something to do with the crash."

Liam reaches over and pushes a stray bit of hair out of my face. It's a surprisingly tender movement, one that catches me off guard. "We're investigating all the possibilities."

"Are *you* okay?" I ask.

"Just… yeah, I'm fine," he replies but I feel that distance again. That pulling away.

"You can tell me," I say. "I won't break."

"It's nothing that can't wait," he says. "You've just been through a traumatic accident and that's on top of what happened this morning. You need some downtime. Let me take you home and get you on the couch."

"I can't do that," I say. "We have to figure out how we're going to nail Booth's ass to the wall and make sure those inmates are protected. Pendergast was right. They are covering something up in there."

"Em, it's nearly six in the evening," he says. "It can wait until tomorrow. You need some rest. Otherwise, you're going to burn yourself out before you can even do anything."

There it is. I can see it in the way his eyes drop when I keep pushing. Like he's getting tired of this fight, of trying to convince me to slow down. And to be honest, I don't exactly blame him. I'm not sure I could keep putting up with me when I keep insisting to never take a break, to never stop until I'm satisfied. Because the true problem is I am *never* satisfied. I can't ever take the win. If it's not infiltrating an international criminal to get leverage on someone, it's working a murder case when I should be hiding out and lying low.

I've come to accept that about myself; that I'll never be still. And that I may push too hard and people may not be able to deal with that. But ever since I've met Liam he's always been there for me in one way or another. But everyone has their limits. And maybe he's starting to question whether he can keep this up for much longer. Maybe he believed that it was all only temporary, that once I took down Hunter and discovered the mystery behind my aunt that I'd slow down.

Instead I threw myself headfirst into what turned out to be an international crime syndicate, and it almost cost us everything. And now, I've barely been back a week and already I've been in a wreck that was probably intended to kill me *and* I've witnessed a man kill himself before my very eyes.

This is exactly what Vostov was talking about. We aren't normal agents. Most FBI agents go home to their families at the end of the day. They take vacations. They leave the job at the office when they're done. And I just can't do that. And as I look into his eyes I can see a longing there, maybe a desire for some normalcy. For things not to be so crazy all the time.

I'm just not sure I can do that. But I can slow down, at least for one night.

"You're right," I say. "A night on the couch will do me good." Despite the fact the whole time I'll be antsy as hell. I need to meet him halfway, to show him I'm willing to compromise. I can't lose him; I've come to rely on him too much. But at the same time, I can't be selfish. Maybe I'm not the best person for him. And if that's the case, I can't try to change who I am to fit his needs.

"Let me go talk to the doctor, see when you can get out of here," he says, handing me the bottle of water too. I feel like something has fundamentally shifted and in the moment I have to focus just so I don't tear up.

"Thanks," I say. "And can you send Zara in?"

"Sure," he says. "Back in a minute."

He heads out while I down half the water and finish the chips, which now taste like ash on my tongue. Have I ruined Liam? Or am I still in the process of ruining him?

"Hey," Zara says, coming in a minute later. "You okay? Liam said—"

"Are *you* okay?" I ask before she can get any further. "No concussion or anything?"

"Nope, they said it was all that physical training in the gym. My big-ass muscles acted like a cushion and absorbed the entire blow."

I give her a glare.

"Okay, no, it was the airbags," she says. "But I'm fine. How are *you*?"

"Physically I'm fine. My finger will be sore for a few weeks. But that's not really what worries me."

She takes a seat on the edge of my bed. "What's wrong?"

"I feel like Liam and I are drifting apart," I say. "He's been acting more distant ever since our names were cleared. But I can't really blame him. I mean, we were in New Mexico for over a month and then when we came back he couldn't even be seen with me. Then there was the bomb at the FBI and we went off to Italy and—"

"Em, stop," she says, holding up a hand. "Liam loves you. He knows you've been through it. You both have. You just need to give him some time and space to acclimate. It's a lot for anyone to handle. And if you start freaking out, you might push him away for real."

"Then he hasn't said anything to you," I say. "Like, in passing."

She chuckles. "No. We don't exactly talk about that kind of thing."

"What about that meeting the other day?" I ask. "You guys looked like you were deep in conversation about something."

She averts her eyes for a moment and my lizard brain does something I never thought it would do: it shoots a spike of anxiety through me because for one split second I think that maybe something *is* wrong and she's just not telling me. "I was talking to him about Theo," she finally says. "I didn't want to tell you because I'm fucking embarrassed about it, okay? I'm just trying to figure out what's wrong with me."

"What do you mean?" I ask. "There's nothing wrong with you."

She gives me a mirthless laugh. "Yeah, tell that to the line of ex-boyfriends that I've left in my wake."

"Just because they're not the right fit doesn't mean it was because there's something *wrong*," I say. "The right guy is going to be lucky to have you. I mean, look at it this way. The reason none of those other relationships worked out was because there was something wrong with *them*. Theo was a traitor for fuck's sake. Can you imagine if you guys had been married or something?"

"But I should have seen it," she says. "I should have been able to tell."

"Listen," I say. "One of the best things about you is you are open and honest. All the time. You tell it just how it is. Not everyone does that and sometimes people will take advantage of it. But that doesn't mean you should stop being you." Pot, meet kettle. How come it's so much easier to give out advice than to follow it myself? I guess because in my situation I don't want who I am to drive Liam—or anyone else for that matter—away. "But... I understand how that feels. It hurts when we find out the people we love aren't who they say they were."

"Yeah," she says.

Liam pops his head back into the room. "Good news. They're getting you checked out now. Shouldn't be more than fifteen minutes." He's gone just as quickly.

"Go home. Get some rest," Zara says, getting up.

"What are you going to do?"

"I'm going to go through our cell phones," she says. "See if I can find some evidence we were being monitored. CSI should be pulling them from the wreck now. I would have grabbed them before we left but I didn't want to leave you alone and they could have been anywhere in that mess out there." She pulls the broken pieces of the vehicle out of her jacket pocket. "And I need to drop this stuff by the lab. See if they can't start working on a make and model of the car that hit us."

"Can I help?" I ask, motioning to get up but she puts a hand on my good shoulder and gently pushes me back down.

"No, you can go home, psycho. I promise I'll keep you updated with my progress."

"But without a phone—"

"I'll send updates to Liam. Tell him to give his phone to you until we can get new ones assigned."

Ugh, that is going to be torture. Do they really expect me to just sit there on the couch and what… watch TV?

"Okay, fine," I say. "But I want hourly updates."

She leans in for a gentle hug. "You'll get them when you get them." Before I can protest she's up and out the door. "Byeeeee."

"Zara!" I yell after her but she's already gone. I throw the blanket off and lift myself up only for a throbbing pain to erupt from my shoulder. The nurse comes in a moment later, fussing over me.

"Not too fast, Agent Slate," she says. "We don't want you to pass out. Let me get you a wheelchair."

"I'm *not* waiting on a wheelchair," I say. "I'm fine." I've been in much worse situations than this and I won't be babied. "Just give me what's left of my stuff so I can get out of here."

The nurse throws her hands up like I've just stomped on her last nerve before leaving me. As soon as I stand up, the blood rushes to my head and I'm back on the bed steadying myself when Liam returns.

"Ready?" he asks.

"More than ever," I say before holding out a hand. "Can I get a little help?"

"Always," he replies.

Chapter Fifteen

T RUE TO HIS WORD, L IAM TAKES ME BACK HOME, GETS ME SET up on the couch where I'm joined by not one but *both* dogs who fight for position between my legs and somehow both end up smashed together and pushing me halfway back off. Liam prepares a proper meal, bringing it to me like it's my last one. Without my phone I'm completely cut off and bored out of my mind. I circle through the streaming services over and over again for a full hour without finding anything.

"I miss Blockbuster," I say as I scroll through the same app for the fifth time.

"What?"

"Blockbuster, did you ever do that?" I ask. "Dad used to take me. It was like an event. Driving over there, anticipating they'd have the movie you wanted to see and getting so excited when you could grab the final copy."

"Oh… yeah," he says. "We had one of those in Stillwater. But Dad was more of a sports guy. We didn't watch very many movies. I don't recall that we ever went in."

"Really?" I ask. "That's so sad. It was kind of like a whole experience. You'd go in, pick the movie you wanted, maybe a few extras. And you had to physically pick it up. But they kept all the discs behind the counter. Still, you'd take the box up there and they'd hand you the rental copy and you'd get a few packets of popcorn and other snacks and come back home to watch it. Maybe it wasn't as convenient, but you really had to commit. There was no backing out because heaven forbid your parents waste money on a rental. But by the time I was ten or eleven all the stores had closed. Everything had moved to streaming by then." I glare at the TV with its unlimited options of what to watch. "Anything has to be better than this."

"Yeah, I was kind of aware of it," he says. "Just never really did it. A few of my friends would rent games sometimes." He takes a seat across from me. "Convenience is a double-edged sword. Just how stir-crazy are you right now?"

I huff and turn the TV off before tossing the remote to the side chair. "About a nine. Is it that obvious?"

"Zara is going to find the culprit," he says. "In the meantime, just try and take it easy."

"You don't understand," I say. "I'm not wired to take it easy. Taking it easy is stressful for me. I need to *do* something."

He purses his lips and looks past me before getting up and going over to the bookshelf that's built into the wall on the other side of the fireplace. He pulls five books from the shelf, gathers them up and brings them over to me, setting them on the table between us.

"What… you expect me to read?"

"You love reading," he says. "How many times do you complain about never having enough time to read all the books on your TBR? Here's your chance."

I glance at the pile, books I've collected over the years that have sat unused on my shelf, books that I'd forgotten about but was at one time very interested in reading. Some of them feel like they were from a different Emily, a woman who could still enjoy small comforts in life. A more naïve woman who hadn't yet faced the hard reality of the world.

The first book on top features a young woman with a sword standing in front of a purple dragon that's blowing fire. The one under that features a skull on the front with flowers knives all around it. It really does feel like a different woman picked these books out all those years ago.

"Or you can sit there and be miserable," Liam says, a slight edge in his voice. "At least this will be a distraction."

"Fine," I say, picking up the dragon book. "I guess it's better than nothing."

"Great," he says. "I have an errand to run, so I'll be back in an hour or so."

An errand? At this time of night? "It's almost eight o'clock," I say.

He leans over and kisses the top of my head, causing both dogs to look up. "I won't be very long. Enjoy your book."

I hesitate because I want to ask him where he's going, but at the same time I don't want to be too overbearing. Maybe dealing with me all day has been too much for him and he just wants an hour or so alone. I guess that's not an unreasonable request. Plus, if he wanted me to know what he was doing, he would tell me. Still, I can't help but feel that prickle of anxiety at the fact this is even happening.

"Okay," I say. "Be careful."

———

A soft glow warms my face, causing me to barely crack my eyes open. Sunlight streams in through the window across from me, landing right in my eyes and I shift so I'm not looking directly at the sun. But as I move my entire body protests, feeling like it's breaking out of some kind of full-body cast. Everything is sore. My legs, my abdomen, but most of all my arms and shoulders. And my finger is practically throbbing. The dogs are still between my legs, though Timber is on his back with all four legs in the air while

Rocky is all the way at the end of the couch curled into a tight ball.

I pull myself up on the couch so I'm sitting up and spot the book I was reading last night on the ground. I must have fallen asleep reading. My mug of decaf is cold on the table beside me. As I look around the room, Liam is nowhere to be found.

Carefully and slowly I extricate myself from the tangle of animals at my feet. It takes longer than I would like to admit and I carefully stretch before fully standing. Thankfully there's no vertigo this morning and I don't feel nearly as unsteady as I did yesterday. I take the mug to the kitchen and place it in the sink. There's a note on the counter from Liam.

Didn't want to wake you. Back soon. <3

What time did he come back last night? *Did* he even come back? Ugh, I hate where my mind goes with this. I'm not the kind of person who suspects the people she loves. But he has been acting very weird lately and I can't help but think it's because of me.

As I make my way into the bathroom both dogs finally stir and follow me in. A quick tooth brushing later I head out to the back porch and let them out to run around. It's a little chilly this morning and the oversized sweatshirt I'm in is barely doing the trick. I have to back up into the door frame until they're both done and back inside the house. Brewing a fresh pot of coffee I'm still wrestling with whether Liam really didn't want to bother me or if something else is wrong. I can't remember a time when he didn't at least let me know he was leaving if we weren't leaving together. Maybe *that's* being over-bearing though. Am I coming off as too clingy after all this madness?

Once I have my mug warming my hands I resolve not to think about it any longer. I can't change what all has happened and I can't force someone to be a person they're not. If Liam needs to tell me something, I'll have to wait until he's ready. And until then, I still have a job to do.

The doctors suggested I take at least a few days off from work to recover, but they obviously don't know me. I have a case to work and victims to protect.

The shower is an arduous experience. But I manage it well enough, though I completely soak the bandages around my finger and I'm forced to change them one-handed. The good news is everything else seems okay, so I can go without using a finger for a while. At least I can still drive. Much like the shower, dressing takes about twice as long as it should, but I manage it with both the dogs watching me intently.

"You're good boys," I tell them. "But I'm okay. You don't have to worry about your ol' mom." Timber tilts his head while Rocky watches me with the intensity he normally reserves for squirrels. They know something is going on—I never sleep all night on the couch so no doubt they can feel something is different in the air.

As I'm gathering up my keys and badge, the door opens to reveal Liam.

"Hey," he says, surprised. "What are you doing? I thought you were taking the day off." He reaches down and rubs both dogs as they swarm him at the door.

"We've got a case," I tell him. "And I feel fine. Just a little sore."

"Are you sure?" It's then when I notice the bag in his hand, the name of my favorite breakfast spot emblazoned across it.

God, I'm an idiot. He was out getting me breakfast.

"Did you eat anything?" The look on my face tells him everything he needs to know. "Sit down. Get some fuel in you first. Then I'll drive you to work."

"Really?" I ask. "You're not going to insist I spend another day on the couch reading?"

"I know a losing battle when I see one." He grins. "But I'm glad you're feeling better."

I take a seat at the counter while he pulls out a full breakfast for me, cinnamon waffles and a heaping pile of eggs with bacon. Inside is a breakfast sandwich for him. He chuckles as he does.

"What?"

"Just the fact that you didn't even slow down. I could have helped you with a shower and wrapping that back up." He indicates my finger.

"I thought you'd gone into work," I say.

"The note was very explicit," he replies, holding it up.

"Um… no it wasn't," I shoot back. "It just says back soon. That could be an hour or five. Especially if you thought I was knocked out for the day."

"I have to admit I'd hoped those drugs would have kept you out for a few more hours," he replies. "But you're like an antelope or something. You just burn them right off."

"Very funny," I say as I stuff my mouth full of waffles. As I eat, I realize I was a lot hungrier than I'd let myself admit.

As we're throwing playful jabs back and forth, Liam's phone vibrates on the counter, interrupting what feels like a lone bit of normalcy that we've been sorely missing. He grabs it. "Coll here." His eyes go wide and he hands it to me. "It's Zara."

I grab the phone. "What's wrong?"

"Em, we have a problem," she says. "Our phones are missing."

Chapter Sixteen

It only takes us about thirty minutes to get over to the office since most of the morning traffic has already come and gone by the time we get out the door. When we arrive I'm still longing for the taste of the waffle I didn't get a chance to finish. Zara offered to come to us, but I don't want any special attention just because I was in a car wreck. Plus, she seems perfectly fine and she was right there beside me.

She meets us at the elevator to our floor, surprising me.

"Hey," she says. "So CSI couldn't find any trace of either phone. I even went out there first thing myself this morning. Someone must have grabbed them." She is speaking with an intensity I haven't seen from her in a while.

"Are you sure they couldn't just be lost in the woods somewhere?" Liam asks. "The car flipped. They could have been thrown from the vehicle."

"The car flipped *three* times," she corrects. "And yeah, I took that into account. But even broken cell phones emit a low-level electronic frequency that can be picked up by our equipment. If they had been turned off and batteries removed then no, but as far as I know both our phones were on before the wreck."

I nod in agreement as we make our way down the hallway. "Who else had access to the scene?'

"The first responders, the local police… I don't know who else. The tow company?"

"Have you reached out to them?" I ask.

"Waiting to hear back from the LEOs now. But Em, I don't like the implications here. First we're taken out by a wreck and then the evidence that might have led us back to the culprit is missing?"

It really does throw a wrench into things. Without those phones we're going to have a hard time proving that someone was actually tracking us and this wasn't some freak incident. "Speaking of which, where are we on the inspection teams?"

"That's the other thing," she says. "But I'll let Nadia give you the bad news." She leads us into Nadia's office where she's working diligently. Elliott is in the far corner of the room on his phone, speaking at a low volume.

"Hey," Nadia says as we come in. "How are you feeling?"

"No worse for wear," I say, holding up my hand. "But my typing is going to be stunted for a few weeks."

"That's what we have dictation for," she replies. "We assembled a new inspection team and they arrived at Lazar this morning, but they were turned away." Nadia isn't prone to frowning, but she's wearing one now like it's her job.

"Turned away? Why?"

"They were told they hadn't filed the proper paperwork to gain access. Something about following proper procedure."

Elliott covers one end of his phone. "They're claiming we need a warrant. That anything else is pure harassment."

I turn back to Nadia. "Is that true? It's a federal facility and Warden Pearce agreed to allow us access yesterday."

"Well, apparently today he's changed his tune," she says. She rummages in a drawer and pulls out a piece of paper, handing it over. Liam and I read it simultaneously. "They're claiming the inspection would violate the prisoner's constitutional rights?"

She nods. "Seems to be the path they've chosen."

"This is ridiculous," I say. "They have to know this won't hold up."

"Nevertheless, it does require us to take a lot of extra steps to gain access. Which means everything slows down."

"It also gives them time to clean up whatever they're doing in there while no one is looking," Zara adds.

My thoughts go back to Nurse Booth and all the hoops she had me and Zara jump through just to talk to the Warden. I should have suspected they wouldn't have made it this easy for us. No wonder the Warden's sudden change of heart yesterday seemed so strange. He just wanted us out of there so he could lock it down.

"How long until we can get people in there?" I ask.

She shrugs. "We're working on it. Maybe a few more days? A judge will have to review the facts. And you know as well as any of us that we don't have very much here that's concrete other than a couple of retracted complaints."

Shit. She's right. It's not like we have any evidence of wrongdoing. In fact, Booth and Pearce could claim that it was our visit that caused a disruption in the first place if they keep up with that ridiculous "lost pen" story. That and our other "witness" decided to cut his own throat. I feel bad for Frey, I really do, but his actions have potentially put other people in danger. And without him, all we have are a bunch of accusations and suppositions. We need hard evidence.

"They're probably afraid if we get in there that we'll find out they were behind the wreck too," Zara says. "I'd bet my left boob that Booth sent someone down there to get our phones before CSI arrived. There was a period of about two hours between when we left and they arrived."

"Have you talked to Pendergast or Vostov?" I ask Nadia.

"Not yet," she says. "Elliott is trying to get us a solid time-frame on the warrant. There's also the possibility we find some way around this, but I wouldn't hold my breath."

"If that place wasn't such a fortress I'd say we just run a truck through the front gates and go in ourselves," Zara adds. "Fuckers."

"We can't just wait for the judicial process," I say. "By then Booth will have that place cleaned and spotless for the new inspection team. We need some way of getting eyes in there *today*."

Elliott hangs up, slipping his phone in his pocket. "Unfortunately it doesn't look like that will happen. Judge Conner is out of chambers today and can't even review a request until tomorrow."

"What about another judge?" I ask.

"That's what I've just been arguing. But the clerk is adamant and…" He holds up his fingers in air quotes. "…the system doesn't bow to the whims of the FBI."

"Ugh," I say, steadying myself on Nadia's desk.

"We need something concrete to push this through," Liam replies. "Do you want to talk to Pendergast?"

"God, no," I say. "And tell him what? We're out of options? No, we need to figure this out. There's a way around this." I snap my fingers on my good hand. "What about trying the families again? I know you said they weren't open to talking, but we have a dead man on our hands now. Maybe they'll have changed their tunes."

He shakes his head. "You can try, but I did everything I could to get those people to talk to me and they were zipped tight."

"I don't see that we have any other option, do you?" I look at the rest of my team. No one else is coming up with any suggestions. "Okay. Liam, you and I will take a crack at the families." I turn to Zara. "Keep working on locating those phones. I don't care who you have to talk to. Maybe one of the first responders picked them up by accident. But they're out there somewhere. If we can prove Booth or someone else at Lazar was behind the crash, screw the warrant. We're going in with the SWAT team."

"Got it," she says, reaching into her pocket. She pulls out a phone and hands it over. "Your new standard issue. I took the liberty of transferring as much as I could from the cloud."

"Thanks," I say. "Z, you and Elliott keep after the judge. Maybe if you pester the clerk enough he'll push it to someone else just to get you off his back."

"Or he'll put us in purgatory and we won't see the court for a week," Elliott replies.

"Tread lightly," I reply. "But carry a big stick." I slap Liam in the chest. "Let's get moving. You still have the addresses?"

"Em," he says, causing me to pause. I can hear it in his voice. The concern I'm pushing myself too hard. That it's too much too soon. But it was just a jammed finger and minor shoulder injury. I'm fine. I fix my gaze on his, *willing* him to understand. To not make a big deal about this. Especially in front of everyone else. "Never mind. Let's get going."

Chapter Seventeen

"WHAT'S THE ADDRESS?" I ASK. LIAM INSISTED ON DRIVING, which was probably a good thing in hindsight. My shoulder is throbbing, all this movement is pushing blood through my system and causing it to swell. Not to mention the constant ache in my finger. But all in all, I have to consider myself very lucky. Thankfully standard issue FBI vehicles are usually well equipped in the safety department. Yet, I can't help but think about how Zara managed to make it virtually unscathed and I had to go to the hospital—*again*. The whole reason I train as hard as I do is to keep me out of that place. And yet I seem to keep finding myself there.

"Uh, I had it written there in the file," he says. "Something Mondale Avenue, I think?"

"Yeah, it's here in the corner," I say. "But I was looking online at their socials—at least the one the dad's posted and they are *not* from the same house. Look." I show him my phone with the man—Andre's—social media account pulled up. It's ninety percent pictures and videos of him and his kids, but the yard and the house in the background don't match the one on Liam's report.

"That's… not the house I visited," he says. "Maybe a family member?"

"Maybe," I say. "But it's odd *all* the pictures and videos are from there," I say. Using my new phone, courtesy of Zara's fastidiousness, I do a property search on the house we're headed to. 1178 Mondale Ave. It's a modest two-story home in a middle-class neighborhood. Nothing special as far as I can tell, about as average as they get. But when I look at the property records I pause.

"The house was purchased six weeks ago," I say. "Records show the purchase price was twenty grand *over* the asking."

"Is that strange?" he asks.

"Clearly you haven't been looking at real estate," I say. "It's a complete buyer's market out there. They could have gotten any other house for a lot cheaper. So why pay more for this one? What does the husband do?"

"Delivery driver, I think," he says. "At least that's what I had from his employment records."

I pull open the file, rifling through the pages. Sure enough, Andre Sawyer is a delivery driver for a local company that also handles moving. He's been employed with them for sixteen years. "And the wife?" I ask more for myself than Liam.

"She was an administrative assistant for a local distributor before she had an accident," Liam says. "Some kind of hip injury that made it hard for her to sit for long periods of time. She was on disability before she was arrested."

"And yet we still don't have the arrest record that put her in Lazar," I say, closing the file. "Tell me about her accident."

"I couldn't find much," he says. "The company only reported that there was an incident that happened on the job, and she qualified for disability because of it, but wasn't able to work anymore."

"She qualified for disability… but if something happened

on the job shouldn't she have qualified for worker's comp too?"

"Like I said," Liam replies. "I didn't get a lot of answers from people. No one wanted to talk about it."

"That's a luxury they no longer have," I say as he pulls up to the address. An old Corolla sits in the driveway of the home. From the outside it looks almost identical to the listing from the realtor's website. Andre doesn't seem to have changed much since they moved in. With it being the middle of a weekday, I'm actually surprised that he's here. I half expected us to arrive and then need to track him down at his job.

We get out and I feel a stronger twinge in my shoulder. I'm going to need to ice it later tonight. And apparently now I'm on a painkiller regimen, but I'm holding off on those for as long as possible. Painkillers tend to make me groggy and hazy. That's the last thing I need.

As we make our way up the driveway, I catch movement at the window. "He's watching," I say. "Was he on edge when you were here last?"

"Barely opened the door," Liam replies.

"Maybe you just needed to smile," I mutter under my breath as we reach the door. I give it a solid knock and take a few steps back.

There is a long pause and I'm just about to knock again when I hear the deadbolt and the door cracks open, still on the chain. "Yeah?" I can barely see the man beyond, the house is dark, though his green eyes stare back at us with a deep intensity.

"Mr. Sawyer?" I ask. "I'm Special Agent Emily Slate, with the FBI. You already know my colleague Agent Coll." Liam nods at the man.

"I don't have anything to say to you people," he replies before moving to close the door.

"Mr. Sawyer we're not going away," I say before he can slam it shut. "Until I get a satisfactory answer."

He glares at me. "I already told him. There's nothing to talk about. I made a mistake, okay? I never should have made that call. Now leave me alone." He closes the door and throws the bolt again.

"See?" Liam asks.

The pain in my arm is growing worse and it's only darkening my mood. "Okay. He wants to play hard, we'll play hard." I head off the porch and around the side of the house towards the garage.

"Where are you going?" he asks. Making my way past the vehicle I enter the side yard and all the way around to the back of the house, where I find a modest patio and some furniture on a concrete pad. Nothing has been changed from the realtor's pictures. There's a swing set out here as well but it has some dirt caked on the sides of the plastic and leaves have collected in the seats and at the bottom of the slide.

"Em," Liam calls after me. I walk up to the back entry which is nothing more than a sliding glass door that looks directly into the home's kitchen. Inside I see Andre Sawyer staring at the front of his house, a bottle of vodka in his hand. I tap on the glass and the man just about falls out of his seat, knocking over the stool he was sitting on and tipping over the bottle, sending vodka everywhere.

"God *dammit*," he yells before righting himself and coming up to the glass. "This is harassment! I'll call the police!"

"Go ahead," I say. "You can make a full report about how we wouldn't leave you alone. You'll go down to the station, make your statements, they'll probably want to talk to your daughters. And who knows, maybe they'll even look into your property records."

At that his eyes go wide.

"Or you can let us in and we'll talk," I say. "We'll even

help you clean that up." I motion to the shattered bottle behind him.

He turns and looks at his dark kitchen, then back at me, as if he were weighing his options. My bet is there is something he doesn't want anyone else to find out about why he bought this house. There's something there, and I plan on finding out exactly what. But first we need to get inside.

"Fine," he finally says. "But I ain't saying nothing."

I shrug. "Your choice. Let's get that taken care of." When he opens the glass door I'm immediately hit by the smell of alcohol, but I can't figure out if it's coming from him or the spill. Regardless, Liam and I come in and the three of us work in silence to clean up the mess. Once I'm sure there's no more glass anywhere, I'm the first one to speak.

"Are your daughters at school?"

He nods.

"Good. Wouldn't want them to get cut on any of this. Do you often drink in the middle of the day, Mr. Sawyer?"

"Now wait a minute," he says. "If you're gonna come in here and accuse me of being a bad father, you can just—"

I hold up my hands. "I'm not accusing you of anything. It just seems to me like you're under a lot of stress."

"Of course I'm under stress! You people won't leave me alone. I feel like I'm being terrorized in my own home."

"From two visits?"

He nods feverishly. "From the FBI? You bet your ass. Wouldn't you be on edge?"

"Let's... just take the temperature down a little," I say. "How about we all go sit down?"

The man shakes his head. "Fine. But like I said, I ain't saying anything."

Liam gives me a "what are you gonna do" look but I'm not willing to take no so quickly. Sawyer is under a lot of pressure here and I don't think it has to do with a couple of visits from the FBI.

"How have you been holding up, handling the kids on your own?" I ask as the three of us take a seat.

"It's fine, been no trouble," he replies. "The girls have been good. Desiree… she's—" He almost says something before waving it away. "No. I'm not talking."

He strikes me as the kind of man who says he doesn't want to talk, but holds a deep desire to do so regardless. It's like he's holding something close to him that it's slowly killing him. But he doesn't know how to let it go.

"Still," I say. "It must be tough without your wife here. I'm sure they miss her."

"Look, you can play all the mind games you want," he replies. "But you're wasting your time."

I lean forward, placing my elbows on my knees. "Then I'll get right to the point," I say. "We know something is going on at Lazar Correctional. And we think your wife is in the middle of it. I had a man slice his own throat in front of me rather than tell me the truth about what they're doing in there. As the spouse of one of the women being treated inside, I would think you'd be more concerned."

Sawyer swallows hard. "Jesus. He…" He reaches for his own throat.

I nod. "He was the inspector for the facility. He hadn't been there in *months*. Since before your wife was transferred in. In fact, as far as we can tell, no inspectors of any kind have been in there since your wife was transferred in."

He runs a hand down his face before wiping his brow with his sleeve. Part of that is the alcohol I'm sure, but it's not hot in here at all.

"Want to tell us what you know?" Liam asks. "Or do we keep playing games?"

"Listen, there's nothing to tell," he says. "She's… she'll be coming back soon and she'll be better then."

"Why exactly is your wife in Lazar?" I ask. "Because we

can't seem to find an arrest record, or transfer orders that put her there."

His fingers are practically digging into the arms of the chair he's sitting in. He looks as if he's about to rip them right off the supports.

I soften my tone. "Mr. Sawyer, we're not here to get you into trouble. We are trying to help you *and* your wife. But we can't do that unless we know the details of how and why she's in there. At one point you were concerned enough to make a complaint to the FBI. What changed? Why retract your statement?"

He wipes his brow again and I can tell we're close. It's right on the tip of his tongue. "I can't… I can't talk about it. It would ruin everything."

"How's that?" I ask.

"You don't understand," he says. "My family is at risk here. I can't say nothin'."

"Have you been threatened by someone at Lazar?" I ask leaning forward. "That's a crime. And if that's the case, we can protect you and your family from any blowback you think—"

"*No!*" he yells then gets up, pacing the room. "If I tell you, it'll all be for nothing. Everything falls apart." He wrings his hands together. "It's part of the deal."

"Then you have an agreement with them?" I ask. He winces, telling me I've hit pay dirt. "Did they pay you…" I look around. "The house. They bought it for you, didn't they?"

He closes his eyes and hangs his head.

"Was it on the condition that you didn't speak about what transpired?" I ask.

He sits down again and hangs his head between his knees. "Oh, God," he mutters.

"Mr. Sawyer," I say gently. "Are you being blackmailed into silence?"

"We just wanted a better life," he says. "Do you know what it's like day in and day out, working ten to fifteen-hour shifts and never getting anywhere? Following all the rules and never being able to save a dime? Watching it all be whisked away by greedy landlords or rising grocery prices or the cost of gas? Looking back on your whole life and seeing you ain't accomplished nothing?" He looks up. "I couldn't have that for my daughters. They deserve a better life. They deserve to grow up in a home with grass out front. Where they don't have to worry about being shot on their way home from school."

"What happened?" I ask.

"There was an incident—at Renata's work. She had an episode. She's… bipolar. But she's always managed to control it with medication. But with the cost of drugs… we just couldn't afford it anymore. And she threw hot coffee on another co-worker. They restrained her, injuring her in the process. They pressed charges; she was fired, of course. We thought the cops would show up to take her in, but they never did. Instead, we got a visit from someone who said they worked for Lazar."

I exchange a quick glance with Liam.

"Said that they could offer us a deal. If Renata admitted herself without protest, not only would they take care of the assault charge, but they'd also help us out… financially. Sort of a compensation. The catch was she would be under treatment for at least a year." He sighs. "We couldn't say no. Neither of us could afford a good lawyer and if she went to jail it meant I'd have to support the girls on my job alone. And it ain't paying much these days.

"Lazar offered to get us this house, move us out of the trailer. Provide us with a stipend for as long as Renata was in treatment. We saw it as a win-win. She could get better and in the meantime, we'd have a better place to live."

"So what happened?" Liam asks.

"At first it was great." Andre wrings his hands together again. "We got regular updates, went to visit her and I talked to her almost every day. It seemed like she was getting better. But then a few weeks ago, they wouldn't let me see her anymore. The calls stopped. I tried going to them to complain, but they just pointed out the NDA I signed. Nowhere on there did it promise contact with the patient."

"When did you call the FBI?" I ask.

"A few days later," he says. "I was getting so frustrated. I figured the only reason they wouldn't let me talk to her was because something had gone wrong. I was afraid. But I swear, not more than half an hour after making that call some big guy showed up at my front door. Made it clear. If I didn't call back and tell them it was all a mistake, not only would I lose the house, but I'd lose my daughters too."

"Do you know who this man was?" I ask.

He shakes his head. "Just looked like he could bench a mack truck," Andre replies. "He was also armed. I'm not a weak guy by any means, but I could tell this man would have no problem putting me in the ground. So I called and retracted my complaint."

"Have you heard from Lazar since then?"

I can already see the answer written on his face. "I just want to know what's going on with my wife. But now that you know… they'll come for me. I know it. They'll probably kill me."

"We can move you to protective custody," I say. "You and your daughters. Until we get this all figured out."

"Who originally approached you from Lazar?" Liam asks. "Who offered the deal?"

"Some guy named Wilson," he says. "I never saw him after the day they took Renata with them. He seemed to be in charge of it all though. And there was a woman with him, kind of stern, but I never got her name."

"Blonde hair, pulled back tight? Late thirties, maybe forty? Stern look on her face?" I ask.

"Yeah," he says. "I think so. She seemed permanently pissed off about something."

"The good news is I can assure you your wife is okay for the moment," I tell him. "We visited Lazar a few days ago and were able to speak with her."

"You did?" he asks, perking up. "Did she say anything? How did she look?"

"To be honest, tired. And worn down. We think something very wrong is going on in Lazar, but with your testimony—"

"Wait a second," he says. "I didn't say nothin about no testimony." He's on edge again, defensive.

"Mr. Sawyer, your wife may be being held against her will," I say. "You're the first person we've spoken with who could potentially get her out of that situation. With your statement on record—"

"Nuh-uh," he says. "My statement don't mean shit unless you got something to back it up. I've seen all those cop shows, I know how this works. If I talk, all I'll be doing is putting a target on my family's back. Protective custody or not, they'll come for me."

I try to maintain my composure. We finally have a credible witness we could use and he isn't willing to help secure his wife's freedom? Lazar has really put the fear of God in him. "Please, Mr. Sawyer, if Lazar is doing something illegal to your wife, we need to get her out of there."

"Say you do," he says. "What happens to the assault charge? Does it just come back? Don't you get it? If I break my deal with them, everything goes back to how it was. We'll be in the gutter again without a dime to our names." He shakes his head. "No, Renata wouldn't want that. Not for Desiree and Ember."

"Mr Sawyer—" I begin again, but feel Liam's hand on my uninjured shoulder.

"Thank you for your time," Liam says. "If you change your mind, please let us know immediately. And if we make any progress, we'll be sure to let you know as well."

Andre nods a few times as we get up and head for the door. He doesn't say anything else as we leave, only holds his head in his hands.

"Why did you do that?" I ask as soon as we're back outside. "He needs to cooperate."

"You were pushing him too hard," Liam says. "He's not ready. He needs time to think about it."

"But we don't *have* time—"

"I know," he says gently. "But I think you're taking this too personally. You're letting your emotions override your better judgement. Think about it. If you kept pushing, he could end up denying everything he told us. Give him some time to digest it all. Maybe he'll come around." He rounds the car and opens the door for me even though I didn't need him to.

"And if he doesn't?" I ask.

"Then at least we know Lazar is involved in bribes and coercion," he replies. "Maybe we can find something that corroborates his theory."

I huff as Liam closes the door and rounds the car to the other side. I hate that he's right. Maybe I am taking this too personally. But it's kind of hard not to when someone just tried to kill me.

"Plus," Liam adds. "We still have one more family you need to harass."

I glare at him under hooded eyes, but he just puts the car into drive and smiles as we pull away from the curb.

Chapter Eighteen

Where Andre Sawyer was at least willing to talk to us, we don't manage to make any headway with Matilda Eaton's family. I pull out every trick in the book but our brief talk with them manages to be little more than a series of "yes" and "no" spoken on their front porch. However, I notice their house is very similar to the Sawyer's and looks to be relatively new for them which leads me to conclude Matilda Eaton was in a similar situation and was "admitted" in order to prevent a worse fate, the family then paid off to stay quiet.

What I can't understand is why Lazar would go to all this trouble to obtain two additional "inmates" when they have hundreds to choose from. What is it about Renata Sawyer and Matilda Eaton that makes them special? That makes them worth risking all this? Maybe Warden Pearce and Nurse Booth think they're untouchable and haven't considered the consequences. But it seems like it would be a lot easier and a lot less noticeable to use current inmates than to pull in two additional women to the prison.

Regardless, now we know the arrest records they showed us were both falsified. And it explains why we can't find any transfer orders for either inmate. Because they have only ever been residents of Lazar and nowhere else. Maybe that's the reason they pulled in these women. Inmates transfer in and out of Lazar on a daily basis. And if they're conducting some sort of research, they would need a couple of "inmates" who were sure to be there over an extended period of time. Andre Sawyer said he expected the treatment to take a year, far longer than the normal inmate stays at the facility.

It's a shaky explanation, but right now, it's the only one I have.

By the time we get back to the office it's late afternoon and I'm starving, having skipped lunch while we were trying to interview the families. Liam promises to order something as I head back to my office to try and make heads or tails of the situation. I pass Zara's dark office, wondering if she's making any progress on her end.

I barely sit down at my desk and stretch out my arm and shoulder before Nadia pokes her head in.

"Oh, good. You're back. Got a sec?"

"Is it urgent?" I ask.

"I think you'll be interested," she says. "We may have a lead on that car that hit you." She comes in and hands over a file.

"I thought you were supposed to be convincing the judge to expedite the warrant," I say, taking the file.

She gives me a terse smile.

"Shit. Don't tell me. Thrown to the back of the line."

She shrugs. "We tried. Apparently the clerk wasn't in the mood. Maybe he had a bad weekend."

Fuck. Just what we needed. More delays.

"In the meantime, Elliott and I spent the day tracking down your mystery vehicle. I was able to make some progress with the lab and the debris Zara pulled from the site. Based on the breakage pattern, the scuffs on your vehicle and the treads at the scene, we managed to narrow down the field considerably. And doing a little sleuthing I discovered the culprit was most likely a 2022 Hyundai Santa Cruz, in white."

I read through the file, looking at all the details from the lab, including the collision report from my vehicle they towed back to the impound yard. "How sure are you?"

"Ninety percent as of eleven this morning," she says. "But now I'd say a hundred."

I glance up.

"Once we had a positive ID on the car, I spent some time trying to track it down, speaking with mechanic shops in the area of the crash. Whoever hit you would be looking at some major body work to get the vehicle repaired. In fact, I'm surprised they were able to drive away from the scene."

"Let me guess, no luck at the mechanic shops?"

"No. But we did have better luck at a local impound yard only about thirty minutes from Lazar." She reaches over and flips to the relevant page in her report. "Found it slated for crushing."

"You're kidding me," I say, staring at the page. "Nadia. Holy shit."

She smiles. "I know, right?"

"Were you able to procure the vehicle?"

"Yep, it's being transferred to our custody as we speak. But the man running the impound yard was a little… hmm. Squirrely."

I arch an eyebrow.

"Elliott and I went down there to ID the car personally," she says. "But when I started asking him about who brought it in, he got quiet real fast."

"I'm sure whoever dropped it off paid him to move it through the system quickly and not ask questions," I say, noting the address she has listed for the impound yard. "Did he say *when* it was brought in?"

"Couldn't remember," she replies. "Conveniently. But it's a good thing we got there when we did. It was only one or two cars from being crushed. Whoever took you off the road didn't want any evidence left behind."

Great. So we can add a coverup and conspiracy to our list of charges when we finally nail these people.

"There's something else," Nadia says. "I went through the entire report from CSI. They didn't come back with anything from the other vehicle." I glance up, frowning. "The only reason we were able to connect the Santa Cruz as being the car that hit you was because of the pieces of the wreck Zara grabbed on site. Em…someone *cleaned* that crime scene before our people got there. Not just your phones. But *everything*."

"How is that possible?" I ask. "There were responders on site the entire time after the ambulance arrived."

She purses her lips and holds out her hands in a supplicating gesture. Like she knows the answer but doesn't want to say it aloud.

I know it too. Because it means that someone with the local sheriff's department must have been the one to canvas the scene between the time when Zara and I left in the ambulance and when our people arrived on site. This thing goes deeper than I think any of us want to admit. And if it is Lazar —and I suspect it is—it means they have really pulled out all the stops to make sure we stay as far away from their facility as possible.

"This is fantastic work, Nadia. Thank you," I say. "You and Elliott both."

I catch something flash across her face. It's there only a microsecond, but I see it nonetheless. It's something I usually only see in suspects when they're in the interrogation room. "What is it?"

"What?" A flush of red flashes across her cheeks.

Usually when a suspect does that it means they're holding something back. And generally I take that as an invitation to go after them. But Nadia isn't a suspect. She's my friend. And as Liam recently reminded me, I can't keep pushing all the time. "Nothing," I say. "Really appreciate your legwork on this."

She purses her lips again, looking frustrated with herself.

"You look like you want to say something," I add. I can't just let her sit here and stew in her own mind. But my words only bring more consternation crossing her face. She's having an internal battle, and I'm not sure which side is winning.

"Nadia, whatever it is, you can tell me," I say trying to be as gentle as I can. "We're a team here."

"I know," she says. "I just… I feel like a lot of this is my fault."

"A lot of what?"

She motions around the room. "This situation. Us being here. Losing our positions and transferring out here. I keep thinking maybe if I hadn't done all that stuff… if I had just followed the rulebook and let things play out, maybe it would have all worked out."

Ah. "You're upset you got caught up in the crossfire," I say. "I guess this isn't what you bargained for when you joined the FBI."

"It's not that," she says, trying to keep her tone light, but I can tell there is more there. "Believe me, I am so glad you were found not to be responsible and we managed to find the real culprit. But Emily… it could have easily gone the other way. We could all be in federal prison right now if things had turned out the slightest bit different."

I lean forward, pain radiating through my shoulder. "I know. And I'm so sorry I've put your future at risk. Trust me, I don't take any of this lightly. This assignment… it was the best I could hope for. But I realize that doesn't make up for what I've taken from you. And Elliott."

She gives me a slight smile. "It's not all bad. I think we are doing some good here. I just… I'm not sure what the future holds. But please, don't think I'm blaming you. If not for you,

Elliott and I might not be... well... you know. It's just been weighing on my mind."

"I promise you I will do everything I possibly can to rectify this," I say. "All of it. Whatever Fletch has planned, whatever his endgame is... I'm going to find it. And expose him and everyone else involved. And I will make sure I make you whole again. Okay?" I reach out with my hand and she takes it, giving it a squeeze.

"Okay," she says, nodding.

I guess I shouldn't be surprised at her reaction. This has been a big change for all of us. I know Zara would never say anything, but no doubt she's feeling it too. And Liam definitely is, otherwise he wouldn't be acting so weird at home. My actions have had some dire consequences, and I need to make good on my promise. I need to fix this. All of it.

"I did enjoy going out on site though," she says. "That part was fun."

"Why do you think I always assign it to myself?" I ask, grinning. "Speaking of, have you shown any of this to Zara yet?" I motion to the file.

"Not yet. I haven't seen her since this morning. She seemed like she was on a mission to find your phones, come hell or high water."

Which means she is probably knee deep in some scheme to track down the phones without anyone being the wiser. Given how well Nadia and Elliott have done, I wouldn't be surprised to see her walk in here any minute with both phones in her hands.

"I need to let her know that the LEOs could be involved in a coverup," I say. "Just for her own safety." I pull out my phone and quick-dial her number but it goes straight to voice-mail. I leave her a brief message, but also send her a series of quick texts as well.

"Hey," Liam says, popping his head in the door. "How does Chinese sound?"

Nadia's face lights up, as does mine. "Sounds perfect."

Chapter Nineteen

"HOLY SHIT, CHLOE, LONG TIME NO SEE."

Zara struts into the garage, flashing her signature smile at the man sitting at the desk on the far end of the room. The place is little more than cinder block on all sides, the walls full of gadgets, gizmos, wires and old circuit boards. It looks like a computer nerd's dream. A table sits off to the right holding a bunch of half-finished projects, each a little wackier than the next. Two of the machines have wings, and a third looks like it could be a submersible.

"Hey Hud, how are ya," Zara asks, putting on her signature accent she always uses with this persona.

"Be better if I got to see your pretty face more often," he says, pushing himself up. Hudson "Hud" O'Rourke is one of the many players in the black market known for providing "questionable" tech services to anyone with the cash on hand. Zara has used him multiple times in the past for jobs, most recently one of her last jobs with Theo. He's always been a reliable vendor for her, and she hopes this time will be no different.

"Maybe you just need to get out more," she says. "Look, I need a drone."

He lurches away from the chair. Hud is missing a leg from his time in the military, but he's got a prosthetic that he wears, though it slows him down and gives him a considerable limp. He's about as grizzled as they get, boasting a gut and a beard that looks rough enough to sharpen a pencil. "Then get on down to the drone store and buy you one," he says, grinning.

"A *special* drone," Zara says. "One that the FAA won't pick up."

"Ah, now you're talking," he says, moving over to one of his shelves. "What's the job? Payload delivery?"

"Surveillance," she says. "I need it light, quiet and maneuverable."

"Got just the thing," he says. "But prices been going up. You seen the cost of copper these days?"

Zara rolls her eyes. "Yeah, yeah. Just put it on my account. Show me what you got."

He grins, showing a missing tooth. "That's what I like to hear." He pulls out a rolling shelf on one of the units along the wall which opens to reveal a set of three small drones inside, all sitting on foam pads.

"Got this unit right here, complete with telephoto lens up to twenty meters with precision accuracy," he says. "Battery'll last you about two hours. Range is half a mile."

"That's it?" Zara asks. "I was hoping to be further away."

Hud points to the next one in the drawer. "This one has a longer range, about two miles, *but* the camera isn't as good. Maybe looking at only a five-x magnification with the sort of clarity I'm assuming you're looking for." He grins at her. "Doing some spying for a cheating husband?"

"I don't pay you to get in my business. What about this one?" She motions to the third.

"Has about ten-x magnification," he says. "And looking at maybe a mile range, but that's pushing it. I'd be a little closer if I were you. *But,* this one is quiet as a whisper. No one will ever know it's there."

"Battery life?" she asks.

"About an hour and a half. That long enough?"

If Zara has her way, it better be. "Yeah. Wrap it up for me. I'm on the clock."

An hour later Zara is perched in the middle of the woods on a rocky outcrop, just outside the fence of Lazar Correctional Facility. She can't see the building from here, but based on her satellite images, she knows exactly where it is in relation to her current position.

The phones are a lost cause. That much was evident the moment she realized they weren't in the wreck any longer. They have probably been long destroyed by now. Which means she needs to change tact.

Since Lazar seems intent on shutting them out and Nadia told her this morning that a swift resolution wasn't forthcoming on the warrant, Zara has decided to take matters into her own hands. After all, she owes Emily that much. Especially after lying to her face about her discussion with Liam. Not that she can tell Em about it, but at the same time, she feels horrible. She needs to do something to make it right, at least in the short term. So if she can get eyes inside of Lazar and figure out what the hell they're doing in there, at least maybe they can make some progress on this case.

She hovers over the small drone, making sure all the settings are right before switching the unit on. She picks up the control unit, complete with a liquid LED color screen built into the middle and turns on the device.

The drone cycles up and its tiny blades spin faster than her eyes can see as it lifts off the pad and hovers five inches in the air. Hud was right, this thing is whisper quiet. Zara checks the screen to make sure she has good resolution, then turns on the record button. She's already set the device to automatically record and upload everything that appears on screen to her personal cloud. That way if the drone is lost somewhere she doesn't have to worry about tracking it down to get the footage.

She watches herself on the screen for a moment before the drone launches high into the air, above the tree line. The image pans to the east as the drone takes off, moving at a swift fifteen miles per hour as it approaches the facility, the large stone structure just barely visible beyond the trees. As she gets closer, Zara drops the altitude so she's just above the tallest trees. She doesn't want to get hung up in any branches, but she also doesn't want to announce her presence. First item on the list is to identify all the surveillance. Once she's mapped it, she should be able to move about freely.

Zara drops the drone into the clearing as the woods open to the area around the building itself. She goes to work surveilling the perimeter, looking for all the cameras, calculating their scan radius before moving on to the next. She keeps the drone away from being spotted. After about fifteen minutes, she's got a good idea of the situation. Most of the cameras are on the gates, the doors… anything that leads to outside the perimeter. But beyond that, there's not a lot of surveillance she can see. A few guards make their patrols around outside, but she assumes most of the eyes will be indoors.

A cursory inspection of the roof of the building reveals a few air shafts, but none of them are large enough for the drone to pass through without clipping the blades. If she could get into the air shafts she could no doubt map the entire facility within an hour. Still, she's not completely out of options.

Carefully navigating around the building, Zara points the drone at every window she comes across, making sure to stay high enough to be outside of anyone's eyeline that might happen to look out and catch it. Many of the windows are dark, and quite a few others show nothing more than prisoners in their cells or in common areas. All the windows to those areas are high and out of reach of the general population, as she would expect.

And it's the higher floors she's really interested in. Maneuvering around camera sight lines and waiting for guard patrols to pass, Zara follows the height of the building up to the second floor where she begins a cursory search of every window. Checking the battery, she sees she has about twenty minutes left before she'll have to recall it for a second charge.

She falls into a rhythm… checking a window, getting the footage before moving on to the next. And with each one her mind continues to drift back. Not only to what she's potentially done to her relationship with Emily, but to all those thoughts that continue to invade her brain at all hours of the night. It's like as soon as she started thinking about him, he won't leave her alone anymore. Still… she'd rather think about Sam than Theo. The lesser of two evils.

Zara is about to call it and return the drone when she flies by the last window on the second floor. This one looks into an examination room of some kind, and as she slows the machine, the camera picks up the image of a woman on one of the beds. Zooming in, Zara holds her breath as she realizes who it is.

Renata Sawyer. The same woman they talked to not more than two days ago. Except now she looks considerably worse. Her face is pale and sweaty, her breathing erratic and she's physically restrained to the bed she's in. Zara even gets sight on the machines she's hooked up to, getting a clear image of her vitals.

Her heart rate is completely erratic, and her blood pressure is fluctuating rapidly. Whatever is happening to her is not good. And there doesn't seem to be anyone around who cares. She's completely alone in that room. Her vitals are critical.

They need to get in there. Right now. She pulls out her

phone to call Em, but there are no bars. Yet there *is* a text message that came through and she must not have noticed.

LEOs potentially involved in coverup. Watch your ass.

That's not good. If Lazar has the local police in their pocket, it means they may have a lot more eyes around than she took into account initially. She needs to get the drone back and get this info to the team. Maybe they can use the evidence of Renata's condition as an emergency writ to gain access to the property. She flies the drone away, pushing it at full speed as it flies above the trees again on its way back to the docking station.

What could they be doing to her in there? And how long does she have? Zara is no doctor, but given the vitals she could see, she wouldn't be surprised if Renata didn't have very long. Whatever is happening, it's clear that a standard of care is not being provided. That in itself will be enough to get Renata out of there and into a real care facility. Assuming they can get to her in time.

As the drone drops down into the trees on its way back home, Zara sees herself on the monitor again. But as the drone approaches closer, she catches something that stills her completely. A dark shape behind her, moving through the woods. *Fast.*

Her first thought is *bear.* Zara turns and draws her weapon as the drone drops into its docking station. But before she can get off a shot she's knocked off her feet to the wet ground of the forest. The smell of dead leaves and dirt permeates her senses. She scrambles to get her footing, to find her weapon, but something slams against her head.

She barely has time to react before everything goes black.

Chapter Twenty

I STARE AT THE BLANK SCREEN OF MY PHONE, FROWNING.

"What's wrong?" Liam asks as he sets my breakfast in front of me.

"Nothing," I say, putting the phone away. "I just haven't heard from Zara since yesterday. She usually doesn't take this long to respond."

He draws his features. "Maybe she's just knee-deep tracking down those phones." There's something odd about the way Liam says it, and it doesn't leave a good feeling in my stomach. Usually he isn't one to sidestep my concerns.

"You don't think something's happened, do you?"

"I doubt it," he says. "If there's someone out there who can handle herself, it's Zara."

I tap my fork on the edge of my plate, wondering how far I should push this. But I have to keep remembering that Liam is my boyfriend and he doesn't deserve me interrogating him. Maybe he's right. Sometimes Z gets so involved in stuff she forgets to look up. She'll let me know if she makes any headway. Still, I don't like how secretive she's been acting lately.

Last night I think I managed to make some headway with Nadia and Elliott. Some part of me had suspected they hadn't been completely happy with this arrangement—I don't think any of us are—but I feel like they took more of the brunt than the rest of us. Before they joined our division at the FBI they were both on the fast track to good careers. And I may have inadvertently derailed them from that goal.

But as Liam reminded me last night, I'm not responsible for their actions. No one forced their hands when Zara and I were in dire straits. Yet I can't help feeling like we somehow guilted them into making compromises they wouldn't other-wise make.

What I really need is Janice to sit here and tell me I'm being an idiot. That had they not helped us, I would probably still be sitting in a federal prison and who knows where Liam and Zara would have ended up. Some days I really miss her counsel, which makes what happened that much worse. She was always completely honest with me, never pulled her punches and never sugarcoated things. I could always get the truth from Janice. And I really wish I had her here now.

Because in all honesty, I don't know how this is all going. I feel like we're all guinea pigs in Pendergast's experiment and if we don't come through in a major way, it's all over. Maybe that's not the truth, but that's what it feels like. Which is why I'm so determined to figure out what is going on behind Lazar's walls.

And right now, I only have one way in. Which is to prove they were the ones behind the wreck.

"Shoulder okay?" Liam asks as he takes a few bites from his breakfast burrito.

"More sore today," I say. I was tossing all night because I couldn't get comfortable. I still refuse to take the painkillers, which means I feel every micromovement in my arm. When I twitch my thumb I can feel it all the way through to my breastbone.

"Maybe you should at least take one of those anti-inflam-matory meds," he says. "To help it heal quicker."

I stuff my mouth full, clearing my plate. "Maybe," I say through my eggs and turkey bacon. "C'mon, let's get moving. I want to be there early."

He finishes his burrito and we toss the dogs a treat each before heading out. Again I'm forced to let Liam drive since my reaction time with my shoulder won't be up to snuff for another week or two. As soon as some of the pain recedes, I plan on starting a stretching program that I'll work into my weekly training.

My finger is another story. It's completely swollen up to the point where I can't even bend it, but I was told that's completely normal and it will go back to the way it was in a few weeks to a few months. But I need to start working it as soon as I can.

The worst part is I can't make a proper fist. Normally that wouldn't be a big deal, but in this line of work, sometimes a fist is the last line of defense any of us have.

"What's the gameplan when we get there?" Liam asks as we head down the highway.

"Start soft, then go as hard as we need to go," I say. "But we're not leaving without an answer." If there's one thing this case has shown me, it's that I need to strike while the iron is hot. We should have made a move on Lazar while we were in there, rather than just assuming we'd be able to access it again later. I'm not about to let that happen again. That's what I get for following protocol.

Ten minutes later, Liam pulls off the main highway to an access road which winds around into an industrial part of town. About a mile down the road I see the sign for *Keller Impound and Salvage*. Making sure my badge is already out and on display, I nod to Liam as he pulls into the lot.

The salvage yard is a large fenced-off property with chain-link surrounding a full acre of land. Barbed wire runs around the top of the fence and there's a gate in the front, but it's already open by the time we arrive. Off to the left as we pull in is a mobile home up on cinder blocks with a couple of parking spots in the dirt.

"Looks like we're the first ones here," Liam says.

"While I'm in there," I say. "Take a look around. See if you can't find any cameras or something that might point to this area."

"You'll be okay in there by yourself?"

I huff. "I'm not some fragile flower," I say, holding up my hand that's still bandaged. "I got this."

He nods, his expression blank. "Good hunting."

I thank him and get out of the car, my boots squelching in the dirt and mud beneath my feet. Nothing in the lot is paved, nor is any of the rest of the property. Abandoned cars stacked three high litter the area, with bits of grass growing around each small tower. Beyond the building and the stacks, rows and rows of vehicles sit in various states of being stripped. Beyond that is a large machine painted yellow and a huge crane with a claw at the very end. None of the machines are on, but I'm assuming that's what the yard uses to crush vehicles.

I make my way to the trailer, climbing the wood steps to the porch, though I take a second to scrape the mud off my boots on the side of the stairs. I knock on the door to what's marked as the "office" with the door itself rattling as I do.

"Come on in," a spry voice says from the other side. I open the door and have to cover my mouth for a hot second, the smell of smoke inside so thick that I think I'm going to choke.

"Mornin," a man says at the far end of the trailer. He's at a desk with an old computer and a mug of coffee sits off to the side. He's dressed in a blue button up shirt and dark gray jeans and wears a pair of gold chains with a cross around his neck. "What can I do for ya?"

"Agent Emily Slate," I say, showing him my badge. "Are you Mr. Keller?"

"That's me," he replies. "You with that girl I spoke with yesterday?"

"If you're referring to Agent Kane, then yes," I say, slightly flustered by his description of Nadia. "I wanted to ask you some follow up questions about that White Santa Cruz that came in."

He gets up, shaking his head. "Now I've already released that vehicle to the FBI," he says. "Already told your friend all about it too. I don't know what else I can do."

"How about giving me a description of the man who brought it in," I say. "That's a good place to start."

"Lady, do you know how many vehicles we get in here a day? People are burnin' through cars like they were cigarettes or somethin'. I can't hardly keep up. And I sure don't remember everyone who brings somethin' in. I already gave your friend all the paperwork I had on the vehicle. You people cost me about five grand in good parts. Who's gonna reimburse me for that?" He stands to his full height, I'm sure thinking he's being intimidating. But all I see is a whiny kid upset that someone came and took his toy away.

"Vehicles that are impounded as part of a federal investigation aren't eligible for reimbursement," I say. "If you didn't want to lose money, you should have been more careful about who you buy from."

Keller narrows his eyes at me. "Well. You're a fiery one, aren't ya?"

I hold up my bandaged hand. "I was the one who was in the accident involving the Santa Cruz. It ran me and my friend off the road, nearly killing us. So you can understand I'm upset."

"Okay, okay," he says holding out both hands. "Don't get yerself in a tizzy. Look, I told the other girl that the guy didn't give me a name. He just wanted it gone, okay? Told me I could have it for two hundred bucks. Now I don't care what business you're in, you don't let a deal like that go by the wayside."

I take a long, hard look at him. "Let me get this straight. He pulls up with that vehicle. Says he wants two hundred for you to take it off his hands. You agree and he's on his way. Did you even ask about the title? Any paperwork?"

"Well now," Keller says, hesitating. "You gotta understand that the man was in a hurry. And I—"

"Didn't want to ask any questions because you suspected the vehicle was used in a crime," I finish for him. "Answer me this, Keller. Did you pay him, or did he pay *you*?"

"Now wait just a second here, missy, I—"

"You'll what?" I shout. "Sue me for slander? You can't tell me that some rando comes in here with a car in that kind of condition and you don't ask any questions. Unless you are specifically *told* not to. You understand what this means, don't you? I could have your license. I could shut all this down. Today. I might even be able to make a case for bribery here. How do you like orange jumpsuits? What's your size? Large?"

"Okay, just hold on," Keller says, taking a few steps back. "Just… let's take a breath here. I can't afford to be shut down. I got debts to pay."

"Then talk," I say. "All of it. Right now."

"Okay! Jesus," he says. "Lady, I don't know what crawled up your tailpipe, but you need to take a breath or somethin'. You're gonna give yerself an aneurysm."

"Worry about yourself," I say. "Clock's ticking."

"Alright, alright," he says. "Man came in with the Santa Cruz on a trailer. Thing was undrivable. I ain't no idiot, I could tell it had been in a wreck. Head-on collision from the looks of it. Usually we get those vehicles from the tow company after they've been cleared. But he was in a hurry. You can always tell the types. They just want to get in, get out and nary a word passes between ya."

"What did he look like?" I demand.

"Tall. About six-two," he says. "Maybe thirty-five, forty, I dunno. Dark hair, stubble for a beard. Had some kind of tattoo running up his forearms, like a snake or a cobra or an eel or somethin'. I didn't get a good look."

I don't bother informing him cobras *are* snakes. "Keep going."

"He said he needed the car gone. Immediately. Told me if I could make it happen today he'd pay me to take it."

"How much?"

He winces. "Two large."

"What happened?" I ask. "Why didn't you destroy it right then?"

He hooks a finger over his shoulder. "Machine jammed that morning. I told him I could get it cleared and the car would be the first one on the block. But it took longer to clear than I thought. I had Miguel working on it all day. By the time we finally got it working again, your… uh… friend had shown up. She impounded the car before we could crush it."

"You're handing over that two grand," I say. "And I'm placing you under arrest for fraud and conspiracy to cover up a crime. Turn around."

"Wait a second," he says. "I thought you said if I cooperated that—"

"I said nothing of the sort," I tell him. "Now *turn around.*"

"Huh-uh," he says, backing up. "I ain't going to jail. Not for this bullshit."

"Keller," I say. "Don't do anything stupid. My partner is right outside this door."

His eyes flash and I can see him processing the possibilities. We're in a small, confined space. He's bigger than I am and technically I'm injured. He probably thinks he can get past me. "You've got nowhere to go. Don't make this worse than it already is."

"This is bullshit," he yells. "All I did was take a job."

"You knew it was illegal and you did it anyway," I say.

"Now. For the last time. Turn. Around." I put my hand on my firearm but don't draw it yet.

"*Fuck,*" he says as he finally turns his back to me.

"Hands on your head." He complies, cursing me out with every word under the sun. I pull out a zip tie and approach him slowly, wrapping it around one hand and moving that hand to his back. As I reach for the other hand he strikes me in the face with his elbow, causing me to stagger back. Within a second he jumps past me and bolts for the door as I hold my hand to my nose, unsure if it's broken or not.

"Keller!" I yell, heading after him.

He busts through the door into the sunlight with me right on his heels. He looks both ways and takes off towards the yard. I can already see his plan. He's hoping to get lost in the vehicles. I can't let him get that far.

I bolt after him and run him down, adrenaline flooding my body as all the frustration and anger I have about the situation come bleeding out. He's about ten feet from the first stack of vehicles when I launch myself into the air and slam into his back, taking us both to the ground. He wrestles, trying to get me off, but I shove his face into the mud as I strike the middle of his back causing him to cry out and arch his entire body. I yank the hand with the zip tie to his back and pull the other one to meet it, cinching them both together.

Once I'm sure he's secure, I pull him into a sitting position. "Davis Keller, you are under arrest for bribery, conspiracy…and assaulting a federal officer."

"Holy shit," Liam says as he comes running up behind us. "What happened?"

I turn to him, half covered in mud. "He ran. Told him not to. Did it anyway."

"Here," Liam says and I finally get off Keller. Liam reads the man his rights and gets him back over to the porch while I call it in. The entire time I'm gently touching my nose, fearing it's been broken yet again. It's practically gushing blood and I head back into the office to find something to hold against it.

"Here," Liam says once he has Keller secure in our car. "Let me see."

"It's nothing," I say. "He just caught me off guard."

"Emily," he says. "Let me see it."

I sigh and pull the towel away, crimson coating most of it. "I'm *not* going back to the hospital."

He presses gently on the sides of my nose. "Does this hurt?"

"No," I say. He continues probing for a moment until I finally shoo him off.

"It's not broken," he says. "Probably just popped a capillary or something." He puts his hands on his hips. "Did you at least get what you wanted?"

"Yeah, he gave me a description of the guy who dropped it off. Any luck with any cameras?"

"Nothing in the immediate area. I can do a larger canvas though."

I nod. "He said the guy brought it in on a trailer. Maybe if we can find the vehicle pulling that trailer we can trace it back to someone."

Liam pulls out his phone. "Nadia? Yeah. We're here at Keller. Got some info for you." He heads off to give her the details. Maybe she can find something on the surrounding traffic cameras. I go back to Keller's description of the man who came in. Whoever it was, he sounds like a security guard.

That's when it clicks in my brain. The guards watching over me and Zara when we went to see Warden Pearce. If I'm not mistaken, I think I saw some kind of snake tattoo peeking out from beneath the arm of one of their uniforms.

Which one was it? Zara would remember. I pull out my phone and dial her number again, but again it goes straight to voicemail. Where *is* she? I don't like this radio silence all of a sudden. It's not leaving a good feeling in my stomach. Usually

Zara is the one to keep pestering me, not the other way around. That she's been silent this long is not only unusual, it's out of character. She should have at least reported in on her progress, even if she hadn't made any. She's not the kind of person who just goes radio silent for no reason.

"She and Elliott are going to check the area," Liam says as he comes back. "Maybe they'll find something."

I hold up my phone for him. "She's still not answering. Liam, I think something's wrong."

A pained gaze crosses his features. "Okay," he says. "Let's find her."

Chapter Twenty-One

Zara blinks herself awake. Her head is pounding and for a second she can't figure out where she is. But then she looks up and sees the high windows above her and it clicks. She was in the woods, doing surveillance on Lazar. Then someone came up behind her. She didn't see his face, but he ran into her, knocking her down. Then he must have hit her with something because she lost consciousness.

It *has* to be one of Booth's goons. That's the only explanation. And it would explain why all of a sudden she finds herself on the other side of those limestone walls.

As her vision clears, Zara realizes she's strapped to some kind of chair, like a La-Z-Boy. What the hell kind of place straps its patients to *recliners*? Can't they get some quality torture chairs in a place like this?

As she's testing the restraints around her wrists, finding they are quite tight and could cut off circulation if she pulls too hard, the door to the room she's in opens, revealing Nurse Booth with that same stupid smile on her face. Behind her is one of the guards Zara met before when she was here with Emily, and very possibly the *mountain* that ran into her outside.

"Ms. Foley," Booth says. "How's the head?"

"Hurts like a bitch. Kind of reminds me of you," Zara says.

Booth just smiles. "It's so good of you to join us here. And rest assured, we'll be getting you back to what I'm sure is a very exciting home life soon enough. We just have a few procedures we need to follow first."

Zara levels her gaze at the woman. "You realize kidnapping a federal agent is a felony and will result in twenty years in prison. At least. For everyone involved."

"Oh, we didn't kidnap you," Booth says. "We found you outside our facility, unconscious and brought you in for treatment. We tried notifying the proper authorities, but we've been having communication problems lately. I guess that's what you get when you're as isolated as we are. And since the FBI hasn't shown up at our doorstep yet, I'm pretty sure you didn't tell anyone you would be here." She smiles. "Lucky us."

Zara does everything she can not to let her emotions show on her face. She *should* have told someone what she was doing —but she was feeling so damn guilty that she wanted the win first. She wanted to come back the heroine who blew open the whole case so at least she wouldn't feel so bad.

It was a stupid call, and now she's going to pay for it. The team is still working on getting someone in here, but according to Nadia it will be at least a few more days. And there's no telling what they plan on doing in the meantime.

"Do yourself a favor, Booth," Zara says. "End this. Now. And maybe you won't spend the rest of your life behind bars."

Booth only smiles. "The only place I'll be spending the rest of my life is on a beach sipping cocktails with a little plastic umbrella," she says, causing Zara to frown. What the hell is she talking about? Booth leans in closer, so her lips are just beside Zara's ear. "You should have taken the wreck more seriously. When someone warns you, maybe listen next time."

"Guess I'm just too hardheaded for my own good," Zara shoots back.

Booth leans back. "Lucky we found you when we did. The brain swelling wasn't too bad. Looks like you'd had a nasty fall and hit your head. Fortunately, we have something that will help with that. I think in a few days, you'll be right as rain." She turns to the guard who hands her a syringe filled with a clear liquid.

Zara pulls back into the chair.

"Don't like needles? Don't worry, I've done this thousands of times. I can always find a vein."

Shitshitshit. She needs to get out of here *now*. Zara begins pulling against the restraints, but all it does is tighten them, restricting her movement even more. "You can't do this," she says. "It's illegal."

"I can do whatever I want," Booth replies. "Because no one knows you're here, Ms. Foley." She taps on Zara's forearm, getting the blood vessels to show themselves. Before Zara can say anything else, the needle is in her arm and the plunger is depressed, filling her veins with God knows what.

"There," Booth says, wiping the spot of blood after she pulls the needle from Zara's arm. "Not so bad. You're going to take a nice nap and I'll check on you in a little while." She turns to the man behind her. "Armond, keep an eye on her. Make sure she doesn't go into cardiac arrest. If she does, call me."

Zara's vision is already starting to blur. Did she say *cardiac arrest*? What the hell was in that stuff? She tries to speak but finds the words come out slurred, so much that even she can't understand herself. The room tilts to the side and it's like she's plummeting down a spiral, spinning, spinning, spinning.

She can't seem to find her footing.

Zara is nine years old, sitting on the carpet in her room, a game console in front of her as she tries for the fiftieth time to beat the level.

"Still messing around with that crap, huh, squirt?" Zara tries to ignore the voice behind her. He doesn't get it. He says girls aren't supposed to play video games. But her friend Molly two doors down let her borrow hers, just for a little while. *She's a girl.* And Zara has been glued to it since the moment she plugged it in.

"*C'man*," he says with that signature accent of his. "Let's go do something *interesting.*"

"Like what?" Zara asks. Anytime he says he wants to do something interesting it usually means *illegal.* She may be nine, but she isn't stupid. Still, he *is* her big brother. She can't help but look up to him.

"Something *outside.* When was the last time you saw the sun?"

Zara rolls her eyes. She gets to a stopping point and saves the game before turning off the console. Molly said she could have it for the weekend, but needed it back first thing on Monday. Which meant Zara only had a few more hours before she'd have to take it back over to her house.

She turns and looks at her brother. Contrary to most guys his age, his hair is longer, almost down to his shoulders. It needs to be washed. He's got some stubble coming in. More than once Zara's caught him in the bathroom mirror preening himself. "What do you want to do?"

"I thought maybe we could check out that new movie, what is it? Sherk?"

"Shrek?" she asks. That's weird. Sam never wants to go see a movie. At least, not the ones Zara wants to see. Maybe he's just bored because Dad told him to watch Zara for the weekend. But even if that's the case, at least she'll get to see a movie for once. "Okay."

"Great," he says. "My treat. We can take the scooter."

"Dad says that thing is a death trap," Zara replies.

"That's 'cause he's never been on one," her brother says. "Let's move it." He hustles out and down the stairs with Zara close behind. She runs out the back door where Sam is already on the scooter, shoving the starter with his foot to get it going.

"Wait up!" she calls.

"Move your ass, we don't have all day," he replies with a smile. She gets on the back and wraps her arms around him and he takes off. The wind feels good in her hair, blowing it back. She feels free out here, even though she's nervous every time she gets on this thing with him. He weaves in and out of traffic and Zara has to close her eyes just to get through it.

But she trusts him. She always has.

Finally, they reach the theater. "See?" he asks. "Told you it was easy. Lemme grab the tickets." The place is pretty busy for a Sunday afternoon. Parents and kids are running all over the place, getting snacks, playing the arcade games in the corner, trying not to be late to their seats. Zara can't help but look to see if they've gotten any new games in. There's a big one that you sit inside, looks like a shooter based off the most recent Jurassic Park movie. If they have time after, she'll ask Sam if she can borrow some money to play.

"Ready?" he asks, coming up beside her. "Got the matinee price. Just in time too. Starts in like three minutes." He hands her one of the tickets. They rush to get some popcorn before getting into the theater. This is one of those new ones with the stadium seating and they manage to find a pair of seats near the top just as the theater is playing what Zara calls "the rollercoaster" where you fly through the air and look at all the advertisements of food and stuff. That's perfect, it means the movie is just about to start.

"Hey," Sam whispers as the lights go down and the opening credits start. "I forgot to grab something. Be right back."

"What'd you forget?" she asks but he either doesn't hear her or he ignores her. Either way, he's down the stairs and gone in a flash.

Zara sits there, watching the opening of the movie about

an ogre who doesn't want anyone living in his swamp. While the rest of the audience laughs, she keeps glancing at the stairwell, looking for Sam to come back.

But he doesn't.

It's a solid twenty minutes into the movie before Zara gets up, leaving her popcorn behind and goes back out into the lobby, looking for her brother. But he's nowhere to be seen. She doesn't dare go in the boy's bathroom, but she can't imagine he'd be in there *this* long.

It's then an uneasy feeling bubbles up in her stomach. She goes to the front, looking outside only to see his scooter is gone.

He's left her all alone here... with no way back home.

Zara comes to with a start, her heart pounding. She sucks in a breath so deep she thinks for a brief second she may drown in it.

"Oh, good," Booth says. "You didn't code. I wasn't sure there for a few minutes."

"What the hell is in that shit?" Zara mumbles, still trying to catch her breath.

Booth smiles. "Don't you worry about it. The good news is we can go again tomorrow. Unfortunately, you're too weak for another session today." She looks up at Armando, the guard. He approaches and removes Zara's restraints. She tries to lash out at him, to apply some of her martial arts training, but finds she can barely move. He physically picks her up and carries her to an adjacent room, this one with a bed.

"What are you doing to me?" Zara manages to ask as he sets her on the bed before using the attached straps to make sure she doesn't move.

"None of my business," he replies. "I do what I'm told."

"You're not getting away with this... whatever it is," she

says as she feels unconsciousness prickling at the edge of her mind once more. She doesn't want to sleep again. She doesn't want to dream. Especially not of *him*. She's spent a lifetime trying to forget her brother. The last thing she wants to do is reopen old wounds.

But as the guard leaves her alone, she can't help but feel the thoughts invade regardless, and Zara finds herself succumbing to the past once again.

She presses her hands to her head until she can no longer feel it. But it doesn't matter. The memories still come.

Chapter Twenty-Two

Despite repeated knocks, no one answers at Zara's apartment. Her vehicle isn't here either. I check with the neighbors but apparently no one has seen her in a few days. A few of them don't even know who she is, having moved in during our time in New Mexico. Needless to say, Zara isn't close with the people who live near her.

I suppose I can't blame her. As agents we keep strange hours sometimes and it's not like she could go out and chit chat with them about her latest case. This job can be very isolating, which is why we tend to stay as insular as we do.

As I head back to the car where Liam is waiting, I can't help but admonish myself. I haven't been over here a single time since we got back; instead I've left her all on her own to deal with everything… Theo, Janice, the job. All of it.

The pressure on her must have been catastrophic.

"No luck?" Liam asks as I get back in the car. I'm still half covered in mud from my tussle with Keller this morning.

"Something is definitely wrong," I say. "She's not here *or* at the office and she hasn't picked up in almost twenty-four hours. Where could she be?"

"Do you want to inform Pendergast and Vostov?" he asks.

I grit my teeth. As much as I hate to admit it, I don't think we have a choice. Not to mention we're running up against this LEO issue in the case. I had hoped that we could close this one on our own, if for no other reason than to avoid the stares and accusations from Vostov. But Zara doesn't go no-contact like this. Not ever. Unless she's decided to go under-cover for some reason, but she would have told me about that… right?

"We should put a BOLO out on her car," I say. "If for no other reason than to get people looking. It's not like we have to tell anyone who it belongs to. It could just be a vehicle that's connected to a federal case."

"What kind of range are you thinking?" Liam asks, backing out of the parking spot.

"What do you mean?"

"Do you want the BOLO for this area only, or do you want to expand it to the adjacent counties or even across state lines?"

"You're thinking she went somewhere?" I ask.

"I don't know, just examining the possibilities." He seems distracted, but I can't tell why. What could be more important than this?

I catch his Adam's apple bob as he swallows. I think my patience has just about run out. I can't focus on Zara if Liam continues doing… whatever *this* is. I've put up with it long enough and if I don't get it out, I'm going to explode. "Okay, what the hell is going on?" I finally ask. "What do you know that I don't?"

"What do you mean?" he asks but the question itself is enough to give him away. There's a nervous energy about him that isn't normally there. And it's really beginning to worry me.

"I *mean* what is the deal with you lately? You've been moping around the house, distracted all the time. There was that extended conversation between you and Zara the other day, but anytime I mention her you deflect. What's going on with you two?"

"Em—" he begins.

"Liam, I don't have the bandwidth to play games," I say. "I get that all this has been hard on you. That *I'm* hard. That we may never have a normal life together. But I won't sit here and pretend like everything is okay when it's obviously not. If you have something you need to tell me, then tell me."

He's quiet for a few moments and I can see the gears in his head working. It does nothing to calm my anxiety. I'm not sure I can take much more. First we have this case which is proving to be a giant headache, on top of needing this new organization of ours to perform, along with pretty much every single member of my team dealing with some kind of trauma in some way. And now Zara may be missing. If he's going to break up with me, I just need him to get it over with already. To just rip off the Band-Aid. If he doesn't, I think I might scream.

"You're not hard to deal with," he says softly. "That's not what this is about."

"Then what?" I ask. "You've been acting weird ever since we came back from Italy. I know being gone that long couldn't have been easy, but I need you to talk to me. To actually *tell* me stuff. Otherwise, how am I supposed to help?"

Liam gets that look on his face that he always gets when he knows he's been forced into a corner. It happens all the time during game night. I'll outmaneuver him and he goes a little red, like he's embarrassed that he let it happen. It's cute—and it's one of the million things I'm going to miss about him.

I don't know how I'm going to do this alone.

"I didn't want to do this here," he says. "Not with everything going on. I wanted to wait until things calmed down."

I scoff. "I don't think that's ever going to happen."

He pulls the car to the side of the road and puts it in park before turning to me.

Don't cry. Whatever you do, don't you cry. Do not let him know how badly this hurts you.

"This is completely inappropriate timing," he says and I close my eyes, taking a deep breath, waiting for the inevitable. "But I can't lie to you any longer. It's not fair."

I squeeze my fists and my features together as if doing so will somehow protect my heart from being shattered. Like I could somehow shield myself after having been open and vulnerable with this man for almost two years.

What the hell is he waiting for?

I let out my breath and crack one eye, unsure what's going on. It's then when I see it.

Picking up the smallest bit of sunlight and reflecting it right in my eyes, I blink a few times. Liam holds out his hand in front of me, between his fingers a gold ring with a cushion cut diamond embedded in the top.

I exhale.

"So?" he asks, a tremble in his voice. "What do you think? Will you?"

"Will I…" I trail off, my eyes glued to the ring.

"Yeah. Will you marry me?" He clears his throat. "I'd get down on one knee, but we're in the car and kind of in the middle of—"

I turn to him, completely stunned. "I don't understand."

"I've been trying to find the right time to ask," he admits. "But things kept coming up. I was going to do it the night you came back, but then there was the letter from Janice and it seemed in bad taste. And then we got thrown right into the middle of all this and I just… I chickened out. So I asked Zara for her help. I thought maybe she'd have a better idea of how I should propose."

It's like every muscle in my body releases at once. *This* is what he's been worried about? This entire time I thought he was struggling maintaining this relationship. God, Zara must have been ecstatic when he told her. "I bet she was full of ideas." I imagine what she put him through and feel myself grin. Seconds ago I was bracing the for the worst news I could suffer and now I can barely keep the smile from my face.

"She wanted a full-on surprise party," he says. "But only *after* you said yes. She said when I asked, it shouldn't be somewhere public. Just in case you wanted to say no. So you wouldn't feel any extra pressure. I was just… struggling with figuring out how."

I reach out and place my hand on his. "Liam. Are you sure? I can't be a normal spouse. We're not going to have a normal everyday kind of life."

He smiles. "Normal is overrated anyway. Does that mean it's a yes?"

I look at the ring in his hand and all it represents. Security. A partner for life. Something I never thought I'd have again. Not after Matt. I wasn't even sure I ever wanted to get married again. But there's something about being asked that solidifies that decision for you. And you know the answer in your gut.

"It's a yes," I say, feeling the prickle of tears at the corners of my eyes.

He slips the ring on my finger. It's a perfect fit. "How did you know?" I ask.

"Measured your finger in the middle of the night," he replies. "It's not like you wear a lot of jewelry."

"Rings get in the way of gun triggers," I say, smiling back at him. This entire time I thought he was feeling regret at the life we'd made. How could I have been so wrong? I'm an investigator for fuck's sake. I should have been able to figure this out.

But then I remember what one of my old instructors—Mr. Kinger used to say—a case always seems clearest until you're in the middle of it. Emotions have a funny way of obscuring clear judgement. It's why when a case involves an FBI agent personally, that agent is usually barred from working on said case. But I've proven in the past that it's possible to make the tough calls despite being at the center of the storm.

However this… is something different. Maybe it's because I've only ever been proposed to twice in my life. The first time I was probably too young to know any better and had I been a little smarter I might have seen through Matt's disguise.

But this time… this is something else. Something real. I know this man and I know I want to spend the rest of my life with him. For a brief moment all the anxiety and worry I've been feeling these past few days melts away and it's just the two of us.

"It looks good on you," he says, grinning. I hold out my hand, admiring the ring I won't be able to wear for long. Working in the field requires minimal accessories, so a suspect can't gain an advantage by pulling on an earring or necklace. Though, had I been wearing this when I took Keller down, it would have made quite the mark. Still…I'll admire it while I can.

"Thank you," I say before wiping my eyes.

"Thank you for saying yes," he says. "I love you, Emily." He reaches over and presses his lips to mine, the warmth of them filling me up in a way I've desperately needed since getting back.

"I love you too," I say after breaking away from him. I don't want to. I want to stay locked in his embrace forever and just let the world fade away. But I can't do that. My best friend is missing. I need to find her so I can tell her about this. I can only hope she's decided that she just needs a few days by herself, and that's all it is.

"We'll celebrate," I say. "Properly. As soon as all this is over."

"Okay," he finally says, putting the car back into park. "To the office?"

I nod. "Let's find her."

Chapter Twenty-Three

"TELL ME YOU HAVE MORE TO GO ON THAN THIS."

I'm standing in front of Pendergast's desk, still half covered in dried mud, my hair a frizzy mess and a brand new ring on my finger, though I keep my hand in my pocket to hide it. Vostov is perched on her normal bookshelf like a hawk ready to devour her next meal. I'm sure if she saw my hand she'd immediately make something out of it. It's not that I'm ashamed in any way; it's that I don't want Liam and my engagement to become a distraction when what we all need to be focused on right now is finding Zara.

Elliott stands beside me while Nadia is seated in one of the only other chairs in the room, typing away on her laptop.

"All we can confirm is no one has heard from Agent Foley since yesterday morning," Elliott says. "She logged out of her computer at nine-o-six A.M. and left the building. Her phone is either off or destroyed."

I turn to him, incredulous. "Destroyed?"

He gives me a brief sympathetic glance. "I mean… that's a possibility." I swear, sometimes the man is like a robot. If I didn't know better, I'd say Elliott is somewhere on the spectrum. Hell, we probably *all* are. But him more than the rest of us. The man has no problem dealing in facts and figures, but I'd say his emotional side is heavily underdeveloped, at least the emotional side he shows us. If he lets anyone see any emotional vulnerability, it's Nadia.

"There's no indication where she was headed but as Agent Slate suggested, we've put out a BOLO on her vehicle," Nadia says, not looking up from her computer.

Pendergast sighs and puts his hands on either side of his desk, spreading them wide. "This is not what we wanted to hear. You're supposed to be investigating this case, not searching for one of your own team members."

"I know," I say. "And I take full responsibility. But you have to understand, it's not like Zara to leave and not tell anyone what she's doing. I think she's in trouble."

"And yet that's exactly what she chose to do," Pendergast replies. "Look, I get you're concerned for her. But we have a job to do. One that she has apparently put on the back burner. So until we get some sort of communication from Agent Foley, you need to focus your efforts on getting into Lazar. Where are we with the warrant?"

"Judge Connor will be addressing it first thing tomorrow morning," Nadia says. "The clerk promised me again today that it's a number one priority. But given we still don't have solid evidence of wrongdoing—"

"Except for the fact they tried to kill us," I mutter.

"What was that?" Vostov asks.

"Nothing," I say.

"No, please. Enlighten us." She motions with one hand for me to continue in an overly exaggerated wave.

"We don't have a visual ID on the man who dropped off the vehicle that struck us yet," I say. "But based on the description from Keller, I believe it could be one of the guards who works at Lazar."

"Right," Vostov says. "The *tattoo.* Which no one has actually seen."

"Zara and I saw it," I say.

Pendergast lets out a resigned sigh. "Agent Slate—"

"I know," I say, stopping him. "—sir. I realize this probably isn't what you were hoping for when you brought this team together. But I want to assure you we are doing our absolute best. Working with coincidental evidence is…a challenge."

He exchanges a look with Vostov, who only rolls her eyes. I'm really starting to get sick of her attitude. I'd like to see her do better given what we're working with here.

"Tomorrow we should have the warrant and then we'll be able to gain access to the facility—by force if we have to."

"Ah shit," Nadia says, causing all of us to turn and look at her. The woman isn't prone to cussing. Especially not in front of our bosses. She looks up as if realizing what she's done and goes beet red in the face. "I mean… uh…"

"What's the problem, Agent Kane?" Pendergast asks.

"I just got an email from Collins' clerk," she says. "They're pushing the warrant to Friday."

"*What?*" I ask. "Why?"

"He just says it's low priority. Given the circumstances." She gives me an apologetic look.

Every hour that Booth is without oversight is another hour where she could be doing dangerous and probably illegal things to her patients. Especially to the two patients who we know aren't even supposed to be there.

"We need to find another way in. *Right now,*" I say. "I'm tired of waiting for the process to resolve itself. I wouldn't be surprised if Pearce knows someone in the courts who is kicking the can down the road."

"The amount of supposition here is astonishing," Vostov comments.

That's it. I've reached my limit. "Look. If you want results, you don't get to keep your hands clean. Whatever is going on in that place, they obviously don't want anyone finding out. Now, my team and I are going to find our way in there despite whatever snarky comment you want to make."

"Careful, Agent Slate," Vostov says. "Don't forget you're on thin ice here."

"When am I *not* on thin ice?" I ask. "You didn't bring us here because we follow the letter of the law. You did it because we follow the spirit. And maybe that means bending a few rules. The fact is, we're being hamstrung by Pearce, Booth and maybe even Connors. Threatened, delayed and who knows what else. And now we're missing a key member of our team. Despite what you may believe, Zara doesn't do this. Something has happened to her, and I'm not going to rest until I find out what. Pull me from the case if you want. But you're going to have to throw me back in that box you called a cell to get me to stop."

"That won't be necessary," Pendergast says, holding out his hands. "I think we all just need to take a breath. I'm sorry if we didn't properly articulate our concern for Agent Foley. Of course she should be our priority. *If* she's actually missing. But at the same time we're on a clock with Lazar. A clock that keeps getting shorter and shorter." He glances at Nadia.

"We can try talking to the clerk again," she says. "Maybe we can convince him to move it back up on the schedule."

"No," I say. "They could keep jerking us around for a week. We need another way in there."

"What about a *writ of habeas corpus* for the two inmates?" Elliott asks.

"Same problem," I say. "We have to get it signed by a judge."

"But presumably not the *same* judge," he says.

I turn, thinking about it. It could be possible. "The problem is we don't have an incarceration record or transfer orders to show the court. It's like trying to prove a negative. Booth has somehow navigated this thing so expertly that no one even knows they're in there other than their families."

"Could we get the families to testify?" Nadia asks.

"There's no chance the Eatons would talk," I say. "And Andre Sawyer is already skittish enough. I tried to get him on the record and he refused. He knows that if this whole thing is exposed, that he and his family will suffer the consequences."

"It's a masterful plan," Pendergast says. "*If* that's what it really is. But given how many obstacles you're coming across, I tend to believe this isn't just a series of coincidences."

"*Thank you*," I say, finally feeling like we're getting somewhere.

He turns to Vostov. "Any ideas how to get them in there faster?"

She blows out a hard breath. "The problem is without an immediate threat to life they can keep Slate's team wrapped up in red tape for weeks. Maybe months. And if this was all preplanned as you say—" She nods to me, "—then they're right on schedule. They could have an entire exit strategy they're implementing right now so that by the time the inspection teams do gain access, all the victims and guilty parties have conveniently disappeared."

"I just can't believe we can't do something," I say. "This is a federal facility. They answer to *us*."

"They answer to the justice department," Pendergast replies. "But that doesn't mean they can just ignore us. Use whatever means you feel necessary." He exchanges another look with Vostov. "We're giving you some latitude on this, Agent Slate. Don't abuse it."

"I don't plan to," I say. "But thank you for the support." I motion to Elliott and Nadia that we should take the win and head out before they change their minds. Plus I want to see where Liam is with tracking Zara down. I explicitly left him out of this meeting because I suspected it might be less than productive and we don't have time to waste.

"And remind Agent Coll to join us next time," Vostov calls after us as we head out.

"Well, that was fun," Nadia says as we each head back to our respective offices. I need to shower and change clothes. I'm sure I still smell like wet dirt.

"I noticed you refused to remove your left hand from your pocket for the duration of the meeting," Elliott says. "Did you injure your other hand as well?"

What he lacks in emotional range he more than makes up for in his observational skills.

"No, I just… didn't feel like it," I say, trying to move past them.

"That seems like a deflection," he replies, the conversation causing Nadia to stop in her tracks and focus her attention on my hand as well.

"Okay, *fine*," I hiss. "If you must know." I pull out my hand and show them the ring on my finger.

"Oh, Emily," Nadia says. "Congratulations." She pulls me into a hug, despite the fact I'm still filthy.

"I wish you both a long and fruitful life together," Elliott says, giving me a very brief side hug as well, which is probably the most physical contact I've ever had with him. "It was smart not revealing this to Pendergast and Vostov. Please issue my congratulations to Agent Coll as well. I'm sure you'll both be very happy."

"We need to celebrate," Nadia says.

"Not until we find Zara," I say. "That was the other reason. I don't want anything distracting from her. Whatever is going on, it's not normal."

"She has been more subdued lately," Nadia says. "Ever since your trip back from Italy."

"I think the weight of everything finally caught up with her," I say. "It caught up with all of us."

"Ah," Elliott says as Liam comes trotting up. "I can congratulate him myself." He holds out his hand for Liam, though Liam doesn't even glance at it.

"Em," he says.

My eyes go wide. "Did you find her?"

"No," he says. "But I did find something else. And it's not good."

Chapter Twenty-Four

The four of us are crowded around Liam's laptop in his office. The room is as sparse as mine, given I've barely had time to make it my own. But Liam hasn't even opened his boxes from his old office back in D.C.

"I only just happened to look at this," he says as he navigates a series of web pages. "I asked Zara for ring recommendations months ago, before you guys ever went to New Mexico," he says. "She said I'd probably never figure out what looked best on your finger on my own and was *adamant* about sending me a variety of options." He clicks over to a cloud server. "Which meant pictures. A lot of them."

On the screen are literally *hundreds* of images of engagement rings, a variety of sizes, colors and cuts, but all of them with a certain aesthetic in common. I must admit, the girl knows what I like.

"What does this have to do with Agent Foley's location?" Elliott asks, impatience creeping into his voice.

"This is Zara's personal cloud," Liam says. "I didn't realize she'd given me full access. I just happened to check back on it to see if it could offer any clue as to where she'd been the past two days and… well, look for yourself."

He scrolls to the bottom of the page where the last two uploads are both video files. He plays the first.

"This is Special Agent Zara Foley, flight test one," she says even though we can't see her on the camera. It's a shot of nothing but grass and trees. But all of a sudden the image rises about five feet, stays there for a moment and lowers back down to the ground.

"She's set up a remote connection to a drone," Nadia says. "It uploaded the videos directly to her cloud."

Liam clicks on the second video. There's no audio this time, only the slight hum from the blades as the drone lifts high into the air above the tree line. It zooms forward and my stomach drops as soon as I see where it's going. Ahead of the drone is Lazar Correctional.

"Dammit," I say. "She went up there by herself."

"To be fair," Elliott says. "It looks like she positioned herself a good distance from the facility."

"Have you watched all of this?" I ask Liam as the drone circles the facility.

"Not yet," he says. "I wanted to let you know first."

We watch as the drone does a cursory search of the facility, avoiding all the cameras and guard patrols. "She's mapping the facility," Nadia says. "Checking for blind spots so she doesn't get caught." A few moments later she begins checking the individual windows, zooming in on the details inside.

"What's she doing now?" Elliott asks.

"Looking for evidence," I reply. "She wants something concrete to force the judge to examine the warrant."

"Would this even count?" he replies. "Isn't this a violation of the facility's privacy?"

"It is, unless she managed to find something life threatening," I say. "Because when someone's life's in danger it sort of changes the game." As I'm saying it, the camera zooms in on a particular window along the west side of the building.

Inside, clear as day, is Renata Sawyer on a medical bed. She's hooked up to a variety of machines and from the way Zara focuses in on the vitals displayed there, it's not looking good. Her blood pressure is far too low and her respiratory rate is barely above the minimum. It's like she's wasting away before our eyes.

"This is it," I say. "She found it."

"I don't understand," Nadia says.

I turn to them. "That's Renata. Look at what's happening. And why Zara's staying put for so long. She's waiting to see if the depressed vitals trigger some sort of alarm or action from the care staff. And there is none. They're just letting her lay there… dying. It's a clear threat to Renata's life and all we need to push the warrant through." I motion to Liam. "Can you make a copy of this we can deliver to Judge Collins? We can get this thing moved up today."

"Yeah, no problem," he says, getting up to fish out a flash drive from his packed boxes.

"Em, look," Nadia says. The image on the screen indicates the drone is headed back to Zara, flying high over the trees again. As it comes to the clearing where she's operating it, we can clearly see her on the video monitor. But then, like it comes out of nowhere, a dark shape races into the image and slams into her. The drone image tilts back and forth, no doubt a result of Zara losing the control pad.

"No," I whisper. The image goes dark as the drone either dies or docks, but whatever happens, there's nothing more to see.

I sit at the desk and rewind the video, pausing it just as the dark shape comes into view.

"Looks like a person," Elliott says. "A *large* person."

"Like a bouncer," I say. "Or a guard." Even though the image is blurred, it's definitely a person. Someone came up behind her and surprised her. She probably never saw it coming.

"Looked like she was at least half a mile from the facility," Liam says, coming back to the computer to make a copy. "*And* she was in the middle of the woods. How could someone have found her way out there?"

"I don't know," I say. "But now we have a last-known position. Nadia, can you get the BOLO on her car refocused on that area? I want to find it before anyone else does."

"On it," she says and retreats from the room.

"I'll call Collins' clerk," Elliott says. "Tell him we have new evidence in the case."

"But we don't know *what* happened to Zara, just that she was attacked in the woods," Liam says.

"No, he's right," I say. "With the information on that video we can at least get inside Lazar. Maybe in time to save Renata Sawyer." I turn to Elliott. "Do it."

Liam goes about copying the file as Elliott heads out. "Do you recognize the shape on the screen?"

I shake my head. "It's too fast and she wasn't zoomed in close enough. We could try to blow up the video, but without the magnification I doubt we'll be able to see enough detail to matter."

"I'll send it over to you just in case," Liam says.

"Thanks," I reply, though I'm barely listening to him. I'm trying to figure out why Zara thought she needed to try to do this all alone. Why couldn't she tell me what she was doing? Is it because *I've* been too distant lately? I think back to her empty apartment—the people who barely knew who she was despite the fact she's lived there for years.

No, this isn't about me. I think maybe she needed to prove something to herself. I should have been there for her when she was clearly suffering and I couldn't see it because I was wrapped up in my own shit.

"Do you think they took her? Booth and the people at Lazar?"

"I don't know who else would even be out there," Liam

says. "I'm more interested to know how they found her. She was pretty meticulous staying off the radar as she flew that drone."

"Agreed," I say. If Lazar *did* do something with her, she hadn't even been on their property. They have no recourse. But then again, what did I expect from a place that has seemingly abducted two women and paid their families to keep quiet about it?

"Liam," I say, my voice just barely above a whisper. "We need to get in there. Now."

"I know," he says, standing and wrapping me in a hug. "We will. As soon as Elliott talks to the judge we'll break down the gates if we have to."

"What if they've done something to her? Hurt her in some way?" I ask. "I don't think I could ever forgive myself if—"

"Don't do that," he says. "Not yet. Let's figure out what we're dealing with first, okay?"

The ring feels heavy on my finger. Foreign. Probably because I haven't worn one for so long. But it reminds me that he and I are partners and I need to trust him. Liam's right. I can't let myself spiral. I'm no good to anyone if I can't even get out of my own head.

"You're right," I say. "Let's just… make it quick."

"Zara is strong," he says. "She knows how to take care of herself. In the meantime, we'll focus on getting in there before it's too late."

I nod just as Elliott pops his head back into the office. "Did you get the warrant moved up?"

"There's a problem," he says.

I practically erupt with frustration. "What now? Did the courtroom explode?"

He makes a small motion with his head. "Not exactly. But Judge Collins would like to see you in his chambers. Immediately."

Chapter Twenty-Five

Zara shoots up in her bed, her heart pounding. She can be a light sleeper, but has never so quickly gone from a dead sleep to fully awake in seconds. It has to be whatever that shit was that Booth pumped in her. Could be an upper of some kind or it could even be a narcotic for all she knows. One thing is for sure, it isn't good. Nor is it legal. Zara hasn't consented to any medical treatment of any kind. And what was that about coding? Had Booth expected her to die?

Zara glances at the high windows in the room. It's still light outside, but it's beginning to fade, which means she slept most of the day. Again, very unlike her. There used to be a time when Zara was nothing but a night owl, staying up as late as possible and sleeping the days away, but that was a long time ago, before she became a field agent with Emily. She thought she liked the nighttime better, but the days aren't so bad, at least, not when you're not alone all the time.

There has to be a way out of here. She needs to get out and warn Em and the others about what Booth is doing. If only she could have gotten that footage to them, to let them see Renata's situation. Maybe *that* would have persuaded them. It should at least have been enough to get the wheels moving, to get the inspection team in here faster. But given almost a full day has passed and she's still locked in this place, Zara must assume no inspection team has come… or will be coming for the foreseeable future. She can't just sit here and wait for rescue. She has to do *something*.

She gets out of the bed, noting that her clothes are missing and she's now in one of the orange jumpsuits the rest of the inmates wear. Great, that's another phone down the drain, not to mention some of her best work clothes. Of course they'd want her to look like the rest of the population here, that keeps her from standing out. And if Zara tries to tell anyone that she's actually a federal agent… well… this place isn't a mental facility for nothing. She's sure the guards hear fanciful stories all the time from the inmates. Not to mention they're probably all in Booth's pocket anyway. She could try to talk to Warden Pearce, he at least knows *who* she is. But she's not sure she trusts him. He seemed almost *too* helpful the other day when she and Em came back to speak with him. Not to mention he didn't have a problem with Booth's methods then. Hell, if Frey was to be believed, Pearce could be the one behind all of it.

Which means she can only count on herself.

She surveys the room. Her bed is nicer than she would have expected, with cotton sheets. There's a side table and a lamp, but when she tries to move either, she finds they're both bolted into place. She can't even get her fingers around the lightbulb inside the lamp as there's a small metal cage surrounding it. Zara gets up and goes to the door, though there's no handle on this side. Only a small window about head height which she has to stand on her tiptoes to look through. All she can see on the other side is an identical door facing her, with a small keypad beside it. She cranes her neck in each direction, which only reveals more doors in both ways.

She takes a step back and stands on the bed, trying to reach the windows above her. But she's too short. No doubt they are reinforced and locked anyway. In one corner of the room is a small metal toilet and some toilet paper. But no sink. Nowhere to wash her hands or access running water.

It might as well be a padded room.

She examines the ceiling, only to find a small black object in the smallest corner. There's no light that she can see, but there's no mistaking the fact it's a camera. They're keeping a close eye on her so she gives the camera a fake smile before flipping it off.

As expected, there's little she can do in a room like this. They've left her with very few options. Instead she takes a seat back on the bed and tries to do a self-assessment. As far as she can tell, nothing is seriously wrong. She feels a little groggy and her balance is slightly off, but otherwise she seems okay. She pulls up the sleeve of her jumpsuit to reveal where Booth stuck her with that needle. The area around the wound is slightly bruised, but no more than it would have been with any other shot.

What the hell was in that stuff? It sure brought back some weird memories; things she had done her best to try not to think about again—ever. But she supposed she'd opened the door the other day when thinking about Theo's betrayal and she just couldn't help to let the old memories flood back in. But whatever had been in that shot, it seemed to intensify the memories almost so that she was living them over again for the first time. Whatever they're doing here, it isn't good.

Seeing no other option, Zara lays back on the bed again, putting her hands behind her head as she stares up at the sloped ceiling. High above her there's an old water spot—probably due to a leak at some point that was patched. But the ceiling was too high to repaint. It's a weird room and feels very cavernous. Almost like she's in an old church.

A bolt on her door slides and Zara immediately sits up, on full guard.

The same guard from before, Armond, stands before her, a zip tie in his hands. "C'mon," he says. "Time to go."

"Where?" she asks.

He tosses the zip tie to her. "Get moving."

"You're committing a felony here," Zara says. "This is an unlawful imprisonment. And I can guarantee you when you get caught, which you will be, you'll be going away for the rest of your natural life."

Armond flexes his arms, a snake tattoo peeking out from beneath the sleeve of his shirt. She thinks it could be a Black Mamba. Or maybe a King Cobra. "Shut up and put those on."

"And if I don't?" Zara asks.

Alonso pulls a taser from his belt. "Don't make trouble. This can either be easy or hard."

"And what exactly is *this*," Zara asks. "What did she inject me with?"

He flips the taser on.

Clearly this bitch has made his choice. There's nothing Zara can do to change that. But she doesn't have to be a victim either.

An image of Sam flashes in her mind again. Of him telling her to stay out of the way. That if she tried to get involved, she'd get hurt. She doesn't recall what he was referring to, but she's never forgotten those words. Never forgotten how they made her feel.

How they *still* make her feel.

God, she wishes Emily were here right now. She could take this guy down no problem. She stares at the oak tree in front of her and wonders if she could do it. If she could pull a *Slate Special.*

Well, no time like the present.

Instead of taking the zip tie, Zara dashes forward and plows her entire body into the man's midsection. It gives slightly, but she also hits a series of hard abs, though the surprise knocks the man on his ass. He's big, but that size slows him down. As he goes to fire the taser, Zara gets up under his hand and snatches it from him, turning it on the man and letting the little wires fly.

He grits his teeth as ten thousand volts pulse through his body, his entire form shaking and seizing at once.

Zara examines the device and realizes it has a reload function. "Oh man, this is *not* your lucky day," she says as the man continues to convulse on the floor. But he's already starting to move towards her again, despite the shock. She holds the device away from her like it's a live snake and fires again, and again the guard goes into full convulsions, this time foam coming from his mouth.

Zara takes the opportunity to jump over him and bolt down the hall, though her equilibrium is still off and the entire hallway tilts to one side, causing her to crash into the wall. She manages to push herself off the wall and resumes running, albeit a little slower.

She won't have much time, the camera in her room will have picked that up. She needs to find a way out of this place immediately.

A yell from somewhere down the hall startles her, causing her to turn. But there's no one there. Another scream resonates through the hall ahead of her. Is she imagining things or are those real? She can't stop to think about it.

Just get out of here. Deal with everything else later.

She makes her way down the dark corridor, wondering just where the rest of security is. She doesn't recall seeing this part of the prison the last time she and Em were here. Everything is so sterile, so white. It's more like a hospital than a prison.

Turning a corner, Zara comes upon a large ward, full of empty beds. She recognizes this room. It's the same one she saw from the outside where Renata was slowly dying. She rushes to the same bed, but it's empty, the sheets brand new.

And all the equipment is off. Zara checks the other beds, but there's no one in any of them. The place is empty, quiet. Like a tomb. Where is Renata?

Beyond the medical ward is another, smaller room. This one is full of drawers against the wall. Already she knows exactly what it is. She's seen dozens of them in morgues before. Only two are marked as having anyone in them and for a second she's afraid to find out what she already suspects. But she needs to know. If it's true, then she'll need the evidence for when they bring the charges.

Zara opens the first drawer and steps back. Inside is the cold and lifeless body of Matilda Eaton—the other woman they met when they arrived the other day. There's no chart to explain what killed her, just her ID on her toe and nothing more.

She moves to the second drawer, aware that every second she spends in here is costing her time to get away. But she *must* know. "Dammit," she whispers as she gazes upon the body of Renata Sawyer, the occupant of the second drawer. This place killed them both. And Zara has a sneaking suspicion whatever they pumped into her veins was a contributing factor.

There's no denying it now, she has to get this information to Em and the rest of the team. She turns and makes her way back out of the medical ward, but a wave of dizziness comes over her and she nearly collapses on the ground. It's subtle, whatever this stuff is, and it's not moving through her system quickly.

That's when she sees the container under one of the desks in the room. It's marked *biohazard*. Zara pulls it towards her, finding about a dozen vials inside, each labeled with Chinese characters she has no chance of recognizing. But under them is the atomic formula for the drug.

$$C_{24}H_{31}N_3O_5S$$

. . .

Thinking back to some of her chem classes the structure is complex. *Very* complex. Being in the sulfonamide group means whatever it is has lingering effects, which she's still feeling. But it also looks like it may be in the methoxyl group which means it may have something to do with memory.

Whatever this is, it's bad shit. And she doesn't want another drop of it in her system. She grabs a vial and slips it in her sock—she'll need proof once she gets out of here. Judge Collins is going to be in such hot water when he realizes what he's been stalling on here. Maybe they can even get him off the bench.

Zara resumes her way down the hallway in search of an exit. But for some reason her vision is beginning to blur and it's getting harder to walk straight. Whatever this stuff is, it seems to be having a latent effect on her, causing her more difficulty the longer she's upright.

Finally she turns another corner and sees the blessed *EXIT* sign in red and there's not even a gate between them. She tries to run and nearly ends up tripping over her own two feet before falling to her knees, a wave of nausea rising up within her. Zara retches all over the floor, sweat forming across her brow.

"Going somewhere?"

She turns to see Nurse Booth and another guard approaching at a leisurely pace, as if they know there's no chance Zara could get away from them. She doesn't understand what's wrong with her. A few minutes ago she was fine, she took out that mountain of a guard and made it here.

"What did you do to me?" she asks, her strength finally leaving her as she collapses on the ground beside the sick that just came from her stomach.

"Oh dear," Booth says, that mocking concern rising to the surface again. "Looks like she might be ill. We'll need to begin treatment right away. Take her to the medical ward and make sure she can't hurt herself." She reaches into Zara's sock and removes the vial. "And I'll take this."

The guard nods and picks Zara up like she was nothing more than a rag doll.

"Don't worry," Booth adds. "We won't let you suffer."

"You… won't get away with this," Zara manages to say, her vision swimming. But before she can hear the woman's reply, everything goes dark once more.

Chapter Twenty-Six

BECAUSE I CAN'T GO SEE A FEDERAL JUDGE LOOKING LIKE I'VE just come from the farm, I'm forced to go back home, shower and change clothes, all of which takes twice as long as it should due to my injuries. By the time I finally make it downtown to the courtroom, it's nearly five in the afternoon and everyone is already heading home.

Liam and I head through the metal detectors, leaving our weapons with the deputies in charge of security before heading upstairs to Judge Collins' chambers.

"I don't understand what the holdup could be now," I say. "Elliott didn't even get to tell them about the video."

"Don't worry," Liam says, patting his pocket. "I have it. We can play it for him."

I really wish this case had been assigned to another judge. I feel like if we'd gotten just about anyone else we wouldn't be in this position. They would have signed the warrant and we'd have been in that facility within hours. But no. Now we're on day two—three? I can't even remember. It's just delay after delay and people's lives hang in the balance. Including possibly Zara's.

We enter the outer chambers where we find Collins' judicial assistant with an impatient look on her face. Her purse is already out and she's tapping her long nails against the desk as we enter.

"Special Agent Slate to see Judge Collins," I say, straightening my suit jacket. "This is Special Agent Coll."

"They're waiting for you, Agent," she says. "Go on in."

"They?" I ask and she motions to the door. I open the heavy wooden door and head inside to the Judge's chambers —an ornate wooden masterpiece in every direction. Half the walls are filled with law books that are probably older than my parents and the other half are filled with pictures with the judge and a slew of important people through his impressive thirty years on the bench. The man himself sits behind a large mahogany desk, a glass of water in one hand as he looks out the window behind him. He turns as we enter and straightens in his chair, smoothing his dark red tie. His hair is shock white and he holds an impressive jawline which no doubt has contributed to his reputation through the years of not being a judge to trifle with.

"Judge," I say. "Special Agent Slate, as requested. This is Special Agent Coll."

"Come in," he says and motions to the couch where two other people sit who I completely missed as I was so focused on the man himself. They both stand, and the second they do I clock them as corporate lawyers. The five-thousand-dollar suits, the sharp briefcases and absolutely impeccable hair stink of corporate money. "This is Mr. Preston and Ms. Waddington. They represent Lazar Correctional Facility."

I furrow my brow. "But that's a federal facility," I say. "Why are they employing private representation?"

"Mr. Preston and Ms. Waddington are here because they allege you and your team have been badgering their client in what seems to be a personal vendetta," Collins says, folding his hands together on his desk. "Would you care to explain?"

"A vendetta?" I ask. "All we are trying to do is get some

answers. And so far, they have been nothing but uncooperative and have obstructed us at every turn."

Waddington turns to Judge Collins. "That's patently untrue, Judge. Agent Slate and her partner were given full access to our client's facility on two separate occasions. It was only *after* they accused Lazar of misconduct that our client revoked their access." Her voice is high pitched and nasally, annoying enough to grate on my nerves, but not too much to come off as a caricature.

"Agent, are those claims founded?" Collins asks.

"Yes," I say.

"No," the two of them also say at the same time. Waddington takes the lead again. "As you know, Lazar is a Federal Mental Health facility. Which houses dangerous and unpredictable criminals. Security and care are of the highest priority. However, after Agent Slate's first visit, there was an incident at the facility where an inmate almost died. This was explained to Agent Slate and her partner upon their second visit; however they proceeded to assume the rules didn't apply to them and demanded to see Warden Pearce without proper security protocol."

"That's not true," I say. "They were running us through the wringer, making us jump through hoops just because they could. They made us wait two hours for an ID check."

Collins holds up his hand for me to stop before turning his attention back to Waddington.

Waddington doesn't even blink an eye. She's like a robot. "Warden Pearce determined Agent Slate had a personal stake in the facility, given her frankly *insane* theories, which is why he's requested an inspection team *not* associated with her group be assigned before allowing access. Furthermore, we've received information that Agent Slate has been harassing family members of two of Lazar's inmates in an attempt to coerce them into believing whatever story she's decided to come up with."

"This is ridiculous," I say. "The whole reason I'm working this case is because those families made complaints about *your* client's facility, I was—"

"Those complaints were retracted," she says without missing a beat.

"Yeah, because you paid them off," I shout back.

"Okay, enough," Collins says. "Slate, do you have any evidence of a bribe?"

"I'm working on it," I say.

"In other words, that's a no," Waddington replies. "This is what we mean, Judge. How can Lazar expect fair treatment if the Agent assigned to investigate has some kind of personal grudge against our clients?"

Collins is about to open his mouth but I take the drive from Liam, placing it on his desk. "You want proof something illegal is going on in there? Here it is."

"What's this?" he asks, taking the drive.

"Surveillance footage," I say. "Of activities *inside* Lazar. Showing the life-threatening neglect of a patient."

"And would you care to enlighten us about how you obtained this footage?" Waddington asks.

I ignore her and lean on the judge's desk. "We need that warrant signed, Judge. They are hurting people in there and all this obstruction is nothing more than a delay tactic so they can clean up their mess before we get in there."

Collins holds up the drive. "How *did* you obtain this footage, Agent?"

I swallow, looking at Liam. "It was obtained by my colleague. Watch it. You'll see what I'm talking about."

"Did you have a warrant for that footage?" Preston asks.

I ignore him and keep my focus on the judge. "Watch it."

"If there was no warrant then I submit the chain of custody never existed. We don't know what could be on that drive," Preston continues. "Ignoring the fact it was obtained illegally."

"Judge," Waddington says, edging me out of the way. "Our clients are the victims of a coordinated smear campaign from the FBI. Everyone at Lazar is already on edge after what happened to Mr. Frey. He was a valued member of the team and is already greatly missed. We contend the FBI is attempting to use that tragedy to their own advantage in order to circumvent the law."

"I'm not circumventing anything," I say. "I'm trying to save lives."

"Let's save everyone some time here," Preston says. "We already know what's on that drive." Waddington opens her briefcase and removes a series of black and white 8x10 photographs, placing them on the judge's desk. "These photographs show a drone flying at high altitude above our facility late last evening. You can clearly see it here, here and here."

Collins looks up at me, concern on his face.

"We believe the FBI was illegally obtaining video footage that they could then doctor for their own needs," Waddington adds.

"Given the resources of the federal government, they could make those images show whatever they want," Preston adds.

"Judge," I say, feeling like I'm losing control of the situation here. "This hasn't been doctored. The video on here clearly shows a woman *dying* in their custody and no one is doing anything to help."

Collins looks at the device for a moment, then at the photographs again. "How can we be sure of that, Agent Slate? Mr. Preston is right; without a warrant there is no chain of custody. This video could have come from anywhere. You could have had an AI program create something out of thin air for all I know."

"Judge," I protest.

"And frankly, Agent Slate, I've been concerned with this

case from the beginning. You were on shaky ground to start with. *Did* your colleague illegally fly a drone over Lazar?"

"Yes," I'm forced to admit. "But she is now *missing*. We believe Lazar may have her in their custody."

"This is ridiculous," Waddington says, grinning. "She's making our point for us."

"I—"

But before I can protest again, Collins silences me with a look. "Agent Slate, I'm deeply concerned about what I'm seeing here. I'll be recommending to the justice department a full investigation be initiated into your 'special branch' of the FBI—seeing as you're willing to be so cavalier with the law. And you can consider your warrant to be on hold until the results of that investigation are delivered to my desk."

"You can't be serious," I say.

"Watch it, Agent," he replies. "You're already on thin ice. Don't make the situation any worse for yourself."

This is nothing more than a smear campaign and Collins is letting them get away with it. I reach for the drive but Collins keeps it in his hand. "I'll have this examined as well. *After* the investigation. Just to prove I'm not being unfair."

The desire to say something smartass bubbles up in my throat but I manage to swallow it back down. Though it takes all my willpower to do so.

Waddington places another document on Collins' desk. "We'd also like to file a restraining order against Agent Slate and anyone on her team until this matter is resolved," she says. "Given her history, we can't trust that she'll actually follow your orders."

"Noted," he replies. "I'll take it under advisement."

What is this? Shit on Emily day? I spin the engagement ring around my finger inside my pocket. This just keeps going from bad to worse. And we're no closer to finding Zara.

"Agent, please inform your team of what will be happening," Collins says. "And I'd encourage you not to step out of line here. Do we have an understanding?"

I nod because there's literally nothing else I can do. "Yes, judge."

"Good. Ms. Waddington, Mr. Preston, thank you for coming by. I'll be in touch." They both thank him and leave, not bothering to look at me or Liam on their way out.

"Judge," I say, softening my tone. "Don't you find it a bit odd that a federal facility has hired private lawyers to represent them? *After* their primary inspector took his own life? There are a lot of pieces that don't add up here."

"Be that as it may, Agent," he says, standing. "We must allow the law to work. And that takes time."

Unfortunately time is something we just don't have.

Chapter Twenty-Seven

"It's going to be okay," Liam says as we head into work the following morning. I spent most of last evening shuffling between worry, fury and despair at our current situation.

"You keep saying that and yet things keep getting worse," I reply and immediately regret it. I reach over for his hand. "Sorry, I'm just… frustrated."

"Me too," he says. "Collins was way out of line."

"The man is psychotic," I say. "Can't he see what's going on here?" I turn to him. "I mean, I am freaking the eff out about Zara. She's in there. She has to be because it's the only explanation. Otherwise she and her car would have shown up by now." The BOLO on her vehicle has still yielded no results, despite refocusing our efforts on the area around Lazar. I can only assume whoever abducted her took her car too so we couldn't trace her location.

"I think we need to go back out there," I say.

"We can't. You heard what Collins said. You do it and you risk your career."

"I don't care," I inform him. "If it saves Zara's life it'll be worth it. It's the only way. I'm going to let everyone else know this morning and then I'm going." I turn to look at him. "And you're not coming with me."

"Emily—"

"No," I say. "I'm not putting anyone else's career on the line. This is my call."

"That's probably exactly what Zara thought when she went out there alone," he says. "What if what happened to her happens to you?"

"Maybe that's the only way inside," I say.

"You're not doing that," he replies. "I'm not letting you do that."

A rage of indignation burns through me. "Not *letting* me?"

"Yeah," he says, doubling down. "You're my *fiancée* now and I'm not losing you because you decided to go off on your own half-cocked. If we're going up there, we're doing it together and we're going to have a plan."

I set my features and stare out the window. "Do you know you are a very frustrating person sometimes?"

"It's one of my best qualities," he replies, grinning.

As we head into the building my mind is swimming with possibilities. I'd spent half the morning deciding to throw caution to the wind and go search for her myself without really considering what Liam would do. I kind of thought he'd just go along with it, but I guess that was unrealistic. He's right, we're a team and going up there alone probably isn't the best idea.

But on the other hand, I can't have him risk what little he has left for my sake. Even if it is to save Zara. Because the truth is, I don't know that I can. I'm running out of options here and Judge Collins just shut down our last line of defense. Any action we take against Lazar now could be considered an actual crime.

But I *know* they're breaking the law. And hurting people. I can't even say if Renata Sawyer is still alive or not, but I'm not waiting around to find out. No matter what it takes, no matter how dangerous or illegal it is, I am getting inside that facility. Today.

"Em!" Nadia calls out as Liam and I get off the elevator. "Good, I was just about to call you." She comes trotting up. "Elliott found something."

"What?" I ask.

"Something that might help."

"I felt bad about what happened with Judge Collins," Elliott says. "He is clearly following the letter of the law much too closely. So closely that I expect he may have an ulterior motive. But that's neither here nor there."

"El…" Nadia says, gently nudging him with a smile. I can see this is something normal for them and she's used to getting him back on track. If nothing else, I'm glad to see their relationship blossoming.

"Regardless, I went looking in the archives for anything that could help us and maybe change the Judge's mind. Which meant pulling all the information we had on Lazar going back twenty years."

I glance at Liam. "Didn't we already do that? We checked the official records."

"Not the official records," Elliot says. "Everything that's in FBI custody from seizure."

"I don't follow," I say.

He nods as if he expected this response. "We know Lazar is breaking the law. That much is obvious. What we don't have is evidence to prove it. However, we can reasonably assume this is not a recent development, nor that they operate in a vacuum. Which means there could be information out there that relates back to Lazar and their activities but that wouldn't show up in their federal records."

"You mean like a transaction report?" I ask.

He nods. "That's it exactly. I dug into all the financial data we've accumulated over the past five years from every case that the FBI has investigated. And you'll never believe what came up." I exchange a glance with Liam, though I catch a huge grin on Nadia's face. "I found a match."

He hands me a piece of paper which looks to be a shipping manifest. "What's this?"

"It's a manifest for a drug called *Hypoxone*," he says. "It was developed in Asia about three years ago and is an experimental treatment for mental illness. However, it is illegal to use on humans in every country across the globe. And yet I found a series of shipments of this drug being transported from Asia to the Pacific Coast, and then handed off across various intermediaries until it reached a company called *Holston Holdings*. Which I have since discovered is nothing but a shell company. However, the director of the shell company is one Michael Pearce."

"The warden at Lazar," I say.

He nods. "Which leads me to assume that he set up that company so that Lazar could receive the drug for human trials. Because why else go through all the trouble of obtaining it this way? Why not just order it like the rest of their drugs through the normal channels?"

"Because they didn't want a record of it," I say.

"Exactly."

"Okay, so Lazar is ordering an illegal drug and possibly using it on people," I say. "We still don't have a solid connection to *prove* that. At least, nothing that would satisfy Judge Collins."

"This is where it gets interesting," Elliott says. "Who do we know who provided import/export services for illegal operations around the globe… who now sits in federal custody?"

My eyes widen. "No."

He nods. "Yes. Mr. Fletch himself. He brokered this transaction—it's how we found the records. They were in the documents that were seized from his computer."

"You've got to be *shitting* me," I say. "Fletch is behind this?"

"I wouldn't say *behind*," Nadia replies. "More like… adjacent. But we do know he was a major player. He might have known what was going on at Lazar all along."

"Which means he could be a key witness," Elliott says.

"You mean a key obstructor. There's no way he's going to talk for anything other than a full pardon." I can't believe this. Wait, no actually I can. Fletch had his hands in *everything.* It doesn't really surprise me that he was involved in shipping illegal drugs to a mental health facility. "This Hypoxone, what exactly does it do?" I ask.

"It's being marketed as a potential cure for dementia," Elliott says. "But the early animal trials have had a limited success rate."

"So what's the grand plan here? Lazar—and Warden Pearce are using the inmates to test an experimental drug to get it to market faster?" When I met Pearce, he didn't strike me as the kind of man who was very interested in bioscience. His main concern seemed to be the prison. Then again, who knows what's been going on behind those walls.

"I can't say," Elliott replies. "But I do know one person who may be able to answer that question."

Chapter Twenty-Eight

BAD IDEA. THIS IS A BAD, TERRIBLE, STUPID IDEA.

The alarm sounds and the barred gate slides open. The guard to my left indicates I should go first. I set my features and head into the cell block where Fletch sits on his bed, reading one of his books, a leg propped up with one hand behind his head.

I walk slowly into his field of vision but the man doesn't move. Instead he just keeps reading like he doesn't have a care in the world. But I'm not going to talk first. I'm not going to give him the pleasure of watching me come here and beg him for information. This is only going to go one way.

"What happened?" he asks without taking his eyes off the book.

"What?"

"Your finger. What happened?"

I glance down at my finger that held the ring Liam gave me. I took it off before coming in here, not wanting to give him any kind of ammunition about my personal life. But there's no way he could know that. "What?"

"The bandage."

Oh. Right. I was unaware he'd even seen it. How does he seem to have eyes everywhere? "Work injury."

"That's a shame," he replies. "Your fingers are some of your best assets. Long and luxurious. You could have been a hand model in another life."

I blurt out a laugh. "I don't think so."

He puts down his book. "Is this another social visit? Or do we have something more… interesting to discuss this time?"

"We don't have social visits," I say.

He grins at me. The problem with Fletch is he knows how handsome he is, which I'm sure works on all manner of people in his life. But I'm not one of them. "Then you need something."

"I'm looking for information on a certain transaction you performed between Holston Holdings and Jiang Xe Resources Ltd."

"Ah," he says, sitting up. "Hypoxone."

"Glad you remember," I say. "What were the details of that transaction? Who ordered it and for what purpose?"

The grin on his face grows and he *tsks*. "Ms. *Agostini*," he says sarcastically. "Looking into my personal business. Well. It must be important if you came all the way here to ask me."

"Do you know or not?" I ask.

"I remember all my transactions. Especially those that were set up on an ongoing basis."

"Glad to hear it," I say. "What were the details of this particular transaction and relationship?"

He stands, coming close to the bars. "Why don't you tell me why you need the information? Then I can perhaps craft a response that would better suit your needs."

"Or," I say, growing impatient. "You answer my question. I'll determine if it's useful or not."

He pinches his features together. "Not how this works, Ms. Agostini. You can't just waltz in here and demand an answer and not expect me to ask something in return."

"The hell I can't," I say. "And quit calling me Ms. Agostini. You know that's not my name."

"You'll have to forgive me," he says. "I do love how it rolls off the tongue."

"Also, don't forget that you're in federal prison," I say. "And you're not getting back out. It's in your best interest to cooperate."

He picks up the book he was reading and places it back on his shelf. "Oh, trust me, I wouldn't even think about getting back out if I could. Having you come to me for our little visits is far too satisfying."

"How about you cut the shit, Fletch," I say. "What were the details behind the hypoxone?"

"How about," he says, pausing. "We make a deal. I'll give you the information you need. And in exchange, you owe me a favor."

I practically cough on my spit. "I'm sorry?"

He shrugs. "Nothing huge. Just a little favor that I may call on one day."

I glare at him incredulously. "Are you serious? Look around? You're in *prison*. You're not getting out. You have no way of enforcing any *favor* I agree to or not."

"Then there's no harm in agreeing, is there?"

I pause, not liking how confident he sounds about this. What kind of favor could he want? For me to let him out? Fat chance of that ever happening. "Why do you want a favor from me?"

"I don't get many visits, so I feel this is only fair. Call it a form of entertainment. Books," he says, glancing at his shelf, "while wonderful, can't compare to real life."

"What kind of favor?"

"Ah," he says, wiggling his eyebrows. "This is where the fun part comes in. You don't get to know. At least, not yet. But when the time comes and I ask…you'll pay your debt."

"I'm not advocating for you to be released," I say. "That's

off the table. Not to mention it wouldn't matter anyway. With the amount of evidence we have against you—"

He holds up a hand. "The favor won't be related to my incarceration. How's that?"

I shake my head. "No. I don't make deals with criminals. I'm not going to be your informant, your trigger man or anything else your puny brain can come up with. Either give me the information or don't. It's as simple as that."

"Fine," he says, crossing his arms. "Then I don't think we have anything else to talk about."

Dammit. Why does it feel like he's the one in the position of power here? This shouldn't even be an issue. And the clock just keeps ticking. If Fletch knows something about what's going on behind Lazar's walls, I may not have a choice but to agree to his terms. But that doesn't mean I need to stick to them. It's not like he has any honor or integrity to begin with. So why would I fulfill any agreement I make with him?

Of course, there is also the possibility I'll need his help again in the future. He was a well-connected man who knew all the players and had his finger on the pulse of the black market. He may hold information that could be important to other cases.

"Have it your way," I say. "I'll agree to this *favor*. But whatever it is, I won't do anything illegal. And I won't hurt anyone." That is, if I even do it at all.

"Do I have your word on that?" he asks, a slightly more wicked grin on his face.

"Out of the two of us, I'm not the one who lied and cheated my way through life."

He cocks his head. "Eh. I'd say that's open to interpretation. I'd say we should shake on it, but I know the guards told you not to get within striking distance. I guess they're afraid you might get hurt."

"There's nothing you can do that could hurt me," I reply. "But I'm not stupid enough to even give you the chance."

"Fair enough, *Emily*," he replies. "Your word is your bond then?"

I pause just long enough to convince myself not to back out. "Yes."

"Excellent," he says, bringing his hands together. "The man you're looking for is named Ward McIntosh."

"I'm sorry, what?" I ask. "The billionaire? What does he have to do with this?"

"He's the one who made the initial order," Fletch says. "I helped him set up the shell company through Holston Holdings."

"Are you telling me Ward McIntosh is bankrolling a federal mental correctional facility without the government's knowledge?" He gives me a brief nod. "To what end?"

"You'll have to ask him that," Fletch says. "I wasn't privy to those details. I just set up the transaction. Though I can tell you it was a recurring shipment, not a one time. He would bring in a new shipment every three months."

"For how long?" I ask.

"Two years," Fletch says. "At least, that's when he brought me in on it. He may have been doing it before somewhere else, I don't know. But he wanted to use Lazar because he was sure he could get around the inspections easier. For some reason, civil medical facilities have tighter controls than the government. Isn't that funny?"

"Then is McIntosh behind the experimentations?" I ask.

"Again, you'd have to ask him. I know nothing about that."

"And where does Warden Pearce fit in? And Nurse Booth?"

"I'm unaware of Booth," he replies. "But the warden was put in place to keep the transactions running smoothly and to continue to allow the shipments into the facility, via the holding company. I don't know for sure, but I assume he's being well-compensated for his work."

Ward McIntosh. Philanthropist, social do-gooder and one of the few all-around liked billionaires living in this country. Running an illegal human testing program. Though I'm not surprised. People who have that much money tend to think they can get away with anything. And a lot of the time, they're right.

But not this time.

"Okay," I say. "Thanks for the intel."

"Always happy to lend some information," he says and I head back to the gate to notify the guard I'm done. "Oh, and Emily?" he asks, causing me to turn. "I always collect on my debts."

"Bad news," Nadia says, hanging up the phone. "Mr. McIntosh's secretary has informed me his schedule is completely booked and he's leaving the country tomorrow night. He'll be back sometime before June."

"No," I say. "We're not waiting until June. Doesn't he have offices here in DC?"

She nods. "But I don't think he's the kind of person who spends a lot of time at the office."

"Did you tell her we need to speak to him regarding a matter of utmost importance and timing?" I ask, already knowing the answer. Of course Nadia did. She's not an idiot. But at the same time I feel like I'm about to fall off a cliff here. Fletch's mind games have put me on my back foot—I don't like owing anyone anything, especially not a criminal.

"Let me keep working on it," she says. "Maybe I can come up with something."

"Got it," Elliott says, coming into the room. He turns his phone around to show us what looks like a private invitation to some kind of black-tie event.

"What's this?"

"McIntosh is holding a charity gala tonight at his penthouse. Invite only. If we could get access, we could force him to talk."

"You just said it was invite only," I say.

"Yes, but perhaps there is a way we can get you in," he says, winking at Nadia. I don't think I've ever seen Elliott wink the entire time I've known him. Nadia nods and goes to work on her computer.

"What am I missing here?" I ask. "A billionaire, especially a well-known one, is not going to invite the FBI to his private charity gala."

"No," Nadia says, turning her computer around so I can see it. "But certain high-profile people will be there. Maybe I can find a way to wrangle Emily Agostini an invitation."

I back up, my hands in the air. "Oh, no. I'm not getting into that dress again. Those days are done. Over. Off the table."

Nadia glares at me in very much a similar way that Zara would do if she were here and I'm reminded we're still on the clock. Odds of getting a warrant to speak with McIntosh are next to zero at this point, and seeing as he isn't willing to make an opening for us this may be the only way for me to actually interrogate him before he jets off to God-knows-where.

Ugh, but I really can't do this undercover crap anymore. The last time I had to practically drag Fletch's body into his hotel room and halfway undress him. And *then* I had to scale a balcony so his people wouldn't find me, almost costing me my life in the process. "I can't go as Agostini," I say. "Fletch could have let the word out about me. He'll know I'm FBI."

"Then again, Fletch may not have wanted anyone to know he was bested by an FBI agent," Nadia suggests. "Regardless, if you want to talk to McIntosh, I think it's a risk we have to take. The Agostini cover is established. You have a background, it's more believable."

I let out a huff of frustration and stare at the ceiling. I

can't believe I have to do this *again*. "Can you even get me in there?"

She grins. "Zara taught me a few things. I know she could do this in an instant if she were here. Just… give me an hour or so."

Elliott turns to me. "That's enough time for you to get back into character."

I shake my head. "I told you, I'm not getting back in that dress. You are going to have to kill me first."

"What are we doing?" Liam asks, popping his head in. "Did I hear something about a *dress*?"

"No," I say more emphatically than I should. "If I'm doing this, it's going to be a pantsuit or nothing."

"But that doesn't fit the profile you built up as—"

"Look," I say, staring Elliott down. "I have a six-inch gash on my shoulder that is being held together by staples and duct tape. Now if you want to parade all over the place because you insist *Emily Agostini* must appear in a dress, then we'll get you a wig and *you* can wear it. Otherwise, I'll wear whatever I damn well please."

He swallows. "That's… a good idea."

"Thank you," I say, flustered enough that I almost want to smack him but I refrain.

"You know, I'd pay good money to see you in that dress again," Liam says as I head out of Nadia's office and back to my own.

"Don't start," I say. "I've got enough on my plate as it is without having to worry about how I appear at some swanky party I don't even want to attend." I head into my office and throw myself down in my chair, mentally and physically exhausted.

"I caught most of the details. I think it's a good plan," he says. "And the quickest way to get access to Lazar."

"Yeah," I say. "*If* Fletch wasn't lying through his teeth."

"Did you get the impression he was?"

I sigh. "No. He seemed much more interested in whatever this *favor* was. I'm telling you, Liam, the man is playing four-dimensional chess at all times. It's like he's not even behind bars. He looks completely comfortable there."

"He does that because he knows it irks you," Liam says. "I think he has a particular interest in torturing you, probably because you were the first person to best him. So now he's trying to drag it out as long as he possibly can."

"That's what worries me," I say. "What if he *was* lying and all of this is for nothing? We could be wasting valuable time going after McIntosh instead of going straight for Lazar."

"Except Lazar is off-limits, at least for now," he says. "This way you're not sacrificing your entire career."

I shake my head. "I swear, if they've done anything to her in there, if they've hurt her… I will make them pay until the day I die."

He comes over and takes my hand in his. "We're going to get her back. Trust me."

Chapter Twenty-Nine

I step out of the vehicle and approach the ornate lobby. Men in suits on either side of the doors open both for me and I'm greeted by another man just inside.

"Good evening," he says. "Invitation please?"

I show him the QR code on my phone and he scans it, consulting with a small iPad that's set up on a table next to him.

"Ms. Agostini," he says. "How good of you to join us. Please take the elevator to the top floor." He hands me a small rectangular card that seems to be a woodcut. Engraved into the middle of it are the initials W.M.

"Thank you," I say.

"Enjoy your evening," he replies and presses the elevator button for me. The lobby has a bank of six, only one opens for me and I step inside, placing the small card I've received to the reader and pushing the button for the penthouse. The doors close and I slip the card into my pocket.

"Okay," I say. "I'm inside."

"There should be a security check on the top floor," Nadia says in my ear. Take out the earpiece before you go through and slot it into the pocket on the back of your phone."

"Got it," I say.

"Hey, Em," Liam chirps. "You looked pretty good walking in there. I think the pantsuit was the right call."

"Of course it was," I reply. "Going radio silent." I pull the earpiece out and slip it into the back of my phone case where it should be invisible to any scanners McIntosh is using for his party. The only other thing I'm carrying is my ID. I opted not to use a clutch because I'm not exactly sure how this is going to go. I may need to move quickly in there.

Liam is across the street, keeping an eye on the party with a pair of binoculars while Nadia is back at the office walking me through everything, which is normally what Zara would be doing. Thankfully her QR code worked. That's one small obstacle out of the way.

But as the elevator rises, I can't help but feel somewhat claustrophobic even though my outfit is comfortable and flowing. I think it's just because I've gotten so used to not working undercover that every time I do it now I feel a sense of additional pressure. I'd much rather face things head on than try to bluff my way in, but I have to deal with the situation as presented. McIntosh is our key to breaking open Lazar and finally getting our warrant to get inside. I just have to get him to admit he's been part of an illegal drug scheme and I have to record him doing it.

Easy.

I take a breath as the elevator reaches the top floor and I'm greeted by another large man in a suit. "Ms. Agostini," he says. "This way." I follow him down the hall to where they have set up a metal detector before the door to McIntosh's penthouse. "Please remove any metal or jewelry."

I place my phone, my ID and the few bracelets I'm wearing that compliment my ensemble—a good luck charm Zara got me in the habit of doing—into a small tray before walking through the machine. It doesn't go off, though they run my phone and everything else through a small scanner. It comes out the other side and they hand it back to me. "Enjoy the party."

"Thank you."

A woman stands near the doors, opening it for me. "Your invitation please?"

"Oh," I say, handing her the small woodcut.

"Thank you." She indicates I should step inside.

The smell of oud and patchouli is the first thing I notice, followed by the tasteful and sparse décor of the huge penthouse. The ceilings are at least twelve feet high, if not higher, dominated by large, floor to ceiling windows that run half the length of one wall before turning and running down the full length of the other. A large sitting area takes up about a third of the space, but it's probably five times the size of what I'd consider a "normal" sitting area. Large enough that six different circular tables have been set up in place of a couch or other seating, each with four chairs around them. I recognize them immediately and I have to turn and fake a cough to get my earpiece back in my ear.

"You didn't tell me this was a *poker* tournament," I hiss as soon as I've reestablished my connection with Nadia.

"I didn't?" she asks nervously. "I was sure I mentioned that. Well, now you know."

"But I'm *terrible* at poker," I say. "I can't bluff to save my life."

"Good thing you're not there to win money, then," Liam chirps. "Just find a way to get McIntosh alone. Do you see him yet?"

I scan the guests so far. I see a few people I recognize, but no one who knows me as Emily Slate—or at least they shouldn't. A lot of these people I met while we were investigating Fletch, so I became familiar with the players. So far there are about thirty other people here and another couple comes in just after me, giving me a courteous nod.

"Nothing yet," I say.

"Better go mingle," Nadia says.

"I don't want to mingle," I snap. "I want to do my job and get out of here."

"Em," Liam says, and I force myself to take a breath.

"Fine." I make my way into the party, putting on my best bullshitting face and I get to work. It's all a strange sort of dance, each of us shaking hands, meeting new people, chatting about current events or things that happened last year. But I find the more I talk, the more relaxed I become. I keep inquiring about the whereabouts of our host but no one seems to know, all of them baffled as I am. And yet everyone seems to have no hesitations about enjoying the wide spread of food and drinks he's made available.

"Good evening!" An hour in I glance up to see the man himself, Walt McIntosh descending the stairs. He's only in his early fifties, having made his billions investing early in tech and then diversifying into a wide variety of projects. Everyone says most of his money "isn't real" and that it's all in the value of his companies but I know that's bullshit. There's no way he doesn't have a nice little stash for himself somewhere if everything goes to hell.

He wears a casual button up and coat with a trim pair of matching pants and sneakers, a complete antithesis to the formal dress of most of his guests who have come in cocktail dresses and tuxedos.

"Thank you all for coming," he says, clasping his hands together. "I want everyone to have a wonderful time tonight. Enjoy my hospitality and let's see if we can't raise a *lot* of money for some underprivileged kids."

If you want money so bad why don't you just give them some of yours, I think but manage not to say as he comes to each person, taking and shaking their hands. When he reaches me he pauses for a brief moment. "Ms...?"

"Agostini," I say. "Of Thompson Intermodal."

He snaps his fingers. "Yes, of course. Thank you for

coming." He smiles and moves on to the next person with barely a thought. I doubt he even put this guest list together— he probably had one of his hundreds of assistants do it.

"Sounds like you're in," Nadia says.

A set of dealers file in and take their spots at the poker tables and people begin making their way over, the men more than the women. I take a seat next to a large gentleman with a handlebar mustache but I make sure I'm on the edge of the table, as I don't want people on either side of me.

"Wilson Bufort," he says, holding his hand for mine. It's the size of a small car.

"Emily Agostini," I say, shaking it. "What's your business Mr. Bufort?"

"Diamonds," he replies. "Been in it for three generations. Ever since my grandpa came back from South Africa. He didn't know how good he had it back then. Damn market's drying up with all these lab-grown clones they're making these days. Getting harder and harder to make an honest buck, I tell ya."

"I'm sure." No doubt the man is familiar with the term *blood diamonds*. But I have to remember I'm not here to fix the world. I'm here to do a job, get in and get the info so we can rescue Zara. Man, if she could see me now she would be *losing* it. I swore after our last adventure there was no way I was ever doing this again.

I guess never say never.

"The game is Texas hold 'em," the dealer says. "Ten thousand buy in. Blinds will be fifty and a hundred."

I nearly choke on my drink. Did he say *ten thousand?*

"Your credit lines have all been established with your banking organizations," the dealer says. "So no need to worry about carrying a briefcase of cash." This elicits a laugh from the group but all of a sudden I'm sweating. That's a *lot* of money. I want to ask Nadia the *wheres* and *hows* of her pulling this off but it isn't like I can sit here and start talking to myself without giving myself away.

The dealer gives out the correct chips to each player and begins to shuffle the cards, starting the game. My heart feels like it might break through my ribcage; I'm so nervous. But I do everything I can not to show it. Especially to Mr. Big Diamond over here. As he's dealing, I take a second to scan the other tables, finding McIntosh sitting in the middle of the head table, laughing animatedly with the people around him. Getting him by himself is going to be a challenge.

The dealer gives us all two cards and I check mine. An ace and a three. Too bad we're not playing blackjack. At least I know how that game works.

"Ms. Agostini," he says. "Start us off."

I make my bet and he moves to the diamond guy, who also bets. Only one person at our table folds before we're all given another card.

This time it's a ten. Trying my best not to show my hands shaking, I toss another chip onto the pile. Someone down the line raises causing everyone to match it before we get another card.

My next is a deuce. The cards on the table show a king and a six. As best I can tell, I've got nothing so I fold. Only Blood Diamond and the man who raised in the beginning are still in. Finally when they get to the end of the round, the other man shows a pair of kings while Blood Diamond has nothing but a pair of sixes.

"Aww hell," he says, tossing his cards down. From what I can tell he'd bet at least half his hand. Five grand down the toilet in less than two minutes. "At least it all goes to charity, right?" he asks, ribbing me and winking at the same time.

Wait a second. Does it *not* go to charity? "Yeah," I say conspiratorially. "Nice little setup McIntosh has here."

He leans in closer. "This your first game?" I nod. "Don't feel bad if you end up losing your ass. You'll make it all back and more in dividends. A hundred fold." He shoots me another wink and we keep playing.

What kind of scheme is McIntosh running here? Hopefully Nadia is picking this up on her end. But I can't make a move as much as I want to. If I do anything to break cover it puts Zara that much more at risk.

Finally the first few rounds are over and everyone takes a break. I've been playing conservatively, but I'm still down almost two thousand dollars. My only winning hand was a pair of nines when almost everyone else had folded. Gambling has never been my thing, personally. I don't believe in the inherent nature of it. But I seem to be holding my own with the other guests; as far as I can tell no one suspects who I really am. Still… I can't spend the entire night here continuing to lose money. The clock is ticking.

I head back to the massive kitchen to refill my drink—a tonic and lime that makes it look like I'm enjoying a cocktail without anyone else being the wiser. And there stands Ward McIntosh in a rare moment of isolation.

"Mr. McIntosh," I say, jumping on my opportunity. "I wanted to thank you again for the invitation."

He turns, cautious at first but then smiles. "Oh, Ms. Agostini. Yes, my pleasure," he replies. "I hope you're enjoying yourself."

"It's been… educational," I say. "Where's your bartender?"

He gives me a knowing smile. "I never let anyone mix drinks for me. Call it…a peculiar habit. I'm happy to make something for you though."

"Gin and tonic," I say. "Actually I was hoping to get a few moments to speak with you…in private," I add. "I have a proposition for you."

He finishes mixing our drinks and leans back against the counter while another guest comes by to get some hors-d'oeuvres. "What kind of proposition?"

"One that I believe will be mutually beneficial," I say. I lean forward, giving him a better view of what little cleavage I'm showing beneath my stylish jacket. Zara would be proud. "It has to do with a certain drug trial out of Asia that I believe you have a stake in."

He arches an eyebrow. "Interesting," he says. "Normally I don't mix business and pleasure, but in our line of work I find they often overlap," he says and drains his glass. "Let's discuss this somewhere more private." He shoots a quick glance to his other guests.

I steel myself as I follow him into an adjacent room that looks to be nothing more than another living room lined with reflective black floor to ceiling bookcases on three of the walls. The fourth looks out on the city beyond. McIntosh heads to one of the bookcases and removes a book, causing the case to open into a hidden passageway. "No one will bother us in here," he says.

Sizing the man up, I'm confident I could gain the upper hand on him in a physical altercation if I needed to. Not that I think it will come to that, but I remain on guard anyway. There's no telling where he's leading me. And if we're away from the rest of the guests, there won't be any witnesses.

I follow him into the adjacent room which is actually a very stylish office with a massive black desk in the middle of the room. There are screens on the back wall running what look like prediction markets, or some other kind of financial information I don't really understand.

A hand grabs me from nowhere and pulls my arms behind my back and I turn to see a huge man who's been hiding behind the hidden door. A guard of some kind.

"What the hell?" I say. "Let me go."

McIntosh turns and grins at me. "Sorry, we can't do that. Ms. *Slate*."

Chapter Thirty

"Em, remain calm," Nadia says in my ear but I barely hear it from the rushing of blood.

McIntosh knows. He's known since the moment I walked in here. Fletch must have talked… as I had predicted.

"I admit it was a good ruse," McIntosh says. "Unfortunately for you, I have sources everywhere."

"I'm sure," I say. "But you realize that you can't forcibly detain a federal agent. No matter *who* you are."

"Oh," McIntosh says. "We're not detaining you. You'll be escorted off property since you are here without a formal invitation. Unfortunately, this party is private." The guard behind me releases my arms and I shake them out, staring at him. "In fact, I may have to speak with someone down at the justice department about this obvious fishing attempt."

"And I guess I'm just supposed to ignore the fact you're running an illegal gambling operation here."

McIntosh looks at me, his eyes wide in surprise. "I don't know what you're talking about. This is a *charity* event, Ms. Slate. As I said in the beginning."

"Oh, so you don't take the money and invest it in various

ventures before paying dividends back to your *friends* in there?" I ask. "Because they seem to be under that impression." I don't *know* that's what's happening, but given Bufort's reaction out there, I'd guess it's something similar.

"Sorry," he says. "You must have some bad information. You can check my filings with the SEC and the State Commerce Secretary. This is all perfectly legal." He holds up his hands like he's presenting a play. "I think it's time for you to go."

"He's baiting you," Nadia says in my ear. "We can't prove anything. Not on some hearsay from one player."

She's right, but it's frustrating as hell to know something illegal is happening and not be able to do anything about it.

"Thanks for the lovely evening," I say to him through my teeth. "I doubt I'll forget it."

Using his smartwatch, he opens another false door on the other side of the wall. This one leads to a private elevator bank. "I don't think we need to have you going back through the party, do you? Never know what might *accidentally* slip out of your mouth."

"Afraid I'll make your friends nervous?" I ask. "When they learn they've been playing an illegal game with an FBI agent all this time?"

"As I said, Ms. Slate. Everything here is perfectly legal and if you don't believe me, you're free to check my paperwork. But some of my friends are naturally cautious. They may find your presence here disturbing. And I wouldn't want to be a bad host."

"Wouldn't want that," I say, walking past him to the elevator, the guard following me. McIntosh follows and places his watch against the blank metal pad where a button should be.

"Make sure she gets downstairs safely," he tells the guard.

The elevator dings and the second the doors begin to open, I throw my elbow back, catching the guard in the stomach by surprise. He grunts and goes for his weapon but I'm ready for him, grabbing his hand and twisting it back, causing him to yell out. McIntosh tries to get past us but it's a small space and I use the guard's weight against him to throw him into McIntosh, the two of them crashing against each other into the wall.

Before he can recover, I grab the guard's arm again, pulling him to me before driving my fist into his face, my finger screaming in pain as I do. I've probably broken it for real this time. But I can't let that stop me. He's still standing, but dazed, so I deliver another strike to his carotid, dropping him to the floor.

McIntosh stares at me, his eyes wide as I reach into the guard's jacket and remove his weapon. "In." I say, motioning to the elevator.

His chest rises and falls rapidly. "What are you going to do?"

"Now," I say, pointing the weapon at him.

"Okay, okay," he says, his hands in the air.

"Remove the watch."

He unclasps the magnetic strap and tosses it to me; I catch it and place it in one of the convenient pockets in my pants. I'm *dying* to rub it in Liam's face that this outfit was the right call. Thankfully we game planned a backup operation in the event things went sideways, which they definitely have.

Once McIntosh is inside I follow him but before the doors close, I unchamber the round from the weapon, pull the clip and disassemble the slide, tossing them all on the guard's body just as the doors shut.

McIntosh frowns. "What is this?" he asks.

"Your worst nightmare," I say. I slam the emergency stop button and the elevator halts in place.

McIntosh's breathing increases rapidly. "What are you doing?"

I cross my arms and lean back against the doors. "Waiting."

"For what?" But I just stare at him. Sweat is already forming across his brow and his cheeks are beginning to redden. According to Liam's research, Ward McIntosh doesn't have many well-known vulnerabilities, but one that he could find was that this man has a moderate case of claustrophobia. Though seeing him now, I'm beginning to think it's more than just a *moderate* case.

"You—you can't do this," he says.

"Do what?" I ask, my voice innocent. "The elevator is stuck. I'm not doing anything."

He tries to rush past me to the *call* button but I manage to deflect him off it and back to his corner where his breathing continues to shorten. "What do you want?"

"Lazar," I say. "Spill it."

"L—Lazar," he says. "What's that?"

I sneer. "Don't play stupid with me. You're illegally transporting Hypoxone and I want to know why."

McIntosh's eyes dart all over the small space, looking for a way out. But his only option is through me, and that's not happening.

"I—I don't know what you're talking about,"

"Yeah?" I ask. "Because your buddy Fletch gave me all the sordid details. Along with the shipping manifests."

"If you had anything concrete you'd have arrested me," he says, more forcefully, but it's only brief before he winces and looks around the small room again.

"Okay," I say. "I guess we'll just wait this out. I don't have anywhere else to be."

"Someone will notice I'm missing," he says. "They'll come for me."

I shrug. "Maybe. Maybe not. The question is, how long can you last in here?" I pull out my phone. It's only been three minutes and he looks like he's going to pop. "Problem with small spaces?" I cross my arms. "I guess being as rich as you, you have all the space in the world. The biggest hotel rooms, the largest cars, jets, whatever. It must suck to have to see what the rest of us live like for a while, huh?"

He grits his teeth, but large sweat stains have formed at his armpits and he's forced to wipe his face with his sleeve. His hair is beginning to look disheveled too. It's amazing how quickly someone can fall apart when they're no longer in control.

"Okay, look," he says. "I had the shipments brought across because I was trying to fast-track human trials of the drug with the FDA. I wanted there to be plenty on hand so when trials could begin we wouldn't need to wait for the product."

"*Annnnt,* wrong," I say, imitating the sound of a buzzer. "Try again."

He pinches his features together again as he tries to pull himself even further back into the corner. "*Fine!* I set it up so we could begin human trials, okay? I figured testing on pris-oners wouldn't get noticed."

"Why?" I ask.

"My… wife," he says. "She has an advanced case of dementia. I'm trying to find a cure."

I furrow my brow. "You're not married."

"I am," he replies. "But it's not public knowledge. We married young, before I made all my money. But she devel-oped the disease in her late twenties. She doesn't even recog-nize me anymore. I just want to find a cure."

"And you think Hypoxone can do that," I say.

"It's shown to be promising in development," he replies. "Hits all the right receptors. But it's at least five years away from human trials. Shannon may not have that long."

"Nadia," I say. "Did you get all that?"

"I did, we're looking into it now," she says. "So far security hasn't been notified of your situation."

I nod. "Bad news, Ward. No one is coming to get you. So this better be the truth."

"It *is!*" he yells. "I swear it."

"Who else is involved?"

"Just… get me out of here and I'll tell you anything you want to know," he says, practically cowering in the corner.

"Nope," I say. "Information first."

He's all the way down on the floor, looking up at the ceiling like it might collapse in on him. "Pearce… and the head nurse, Booth. They're both on my payroll. I have a few people in Rochester PD watching out for me. And some of the guards at the facility."

That explains a lot. It also explains why Lazar had two high-powered corporate lawyers show up to try and discredit me. I'm actually surprised. I didn't think Fletch's information would come through, but I'm glad it did. Now that we've found the lynchpin to this whole organization, we can begin dismantling it.

"Ward McIntosh," I say. "You're under arrest for bribery, conspiracy and collusion. And if I find out anyone has died from these trials, you'll be going down for murder. You have the right to remain silent. You have the right to an attorney. Do you understand these rights as I've stated them?"

He nods. "Please… just… get me out of here."

I push the cancel button for the stop and the elevator begins moving again to the bottom floor. "Nadia," I say. "Make sure we're ready."

"Already on it," she replies.

"I don't care how much money you have," I tell McIntosh. "You're not getting away with this one. Judge Collins will see to that." Finally we have the witness *and* the evidence we need to get this case moving.

I'm coming, Z.

The doors to the elevator open and McIntosh scrambles forward past me into the hallway, only to be grabbed on either side by Liam and Elliott. They put him into cuffs before escorting him through the back hallways of the building to the loading dock in the back where Elliott's SUV sits.

"Make sure he's comfortable," I tell Elliott as he stuffs McIntosh into the car. "He doesn't like small spaces."

Chapter Thirty-One

By the time we head back to our office it's after midnight. The entire drive back, Liam won't stop fussing over my finger, which is now definitely broken and is swelling badly. But I don't have time to deal with that now, I'll put some ice on it once we get a handle on the situation.

"Make sure you cut any external feeds and I want the building dark when we arrive," I tell Nadia over the phone. "We don't want to give his people a chance to locate him. There's no telling what kind of tech they might be using."

"Got it. We'll be ready."

"You sure about this?" Liam asks. I nod. I have a suspicion and I want to make sure it's right *before* we take action.

"What are you playing at?" McIntosh says from the backseat. "Where are you taking me?"

I exchange a quick glance with Liam, noting the frown on his face. This is tactically dangerous. Especially given our precarious situation. But I'm not about to risk my only hand to play by putting McIntosh into the system prematurely. He would be out of our custody within less than thirty minutes and untouchable.

"I want my phone call," McIntosh says as Elliott pulls up

to the building in front of us. True to her word, Nadia has kept it dark for us. Elliot's car pulls up beside Liam's and they both work to get McIntosh out while I follow, nursing my finger.

We get in the elevator which takes us to our floor, meeting Nadia at the doors. "Conference room?" she asks.

"You're just digging yourself deeper, Agent," McIntosh says. "I have rights." We lead him there while Liam peels off, headed for the kitchen. I sit McIntosh down with his hands still bound behind his back. Liam returns with a bag of ice and some tape for my finger.

"What are you—" I say as he gently takes my swollen finger and "buddy tapes" it to my middle finger, keeping it immobilized. He places the ice pack on top of both of them. It's a small gesture, but sweet. And one I very much appreciate. Already it is feeling better. "Thanks."

"Let's get this done," he says.

I nod and turn back to McIntosh. "You're throwing your career away," he says. "This is unlawful imprisonment."

I shrug, leaning up against the conference room table. "This is a pit stop. Nothing more. We're still going to book you. Just… not yet." I need to be very careful here, while still looking like I'm in control. Because right now I feel the opposite. And I don't want to take a misstep, because we may only have one shot at this.

Nadia comes back into the room, a grim look on her face. "Did you get in touch with Judge Collins?" I ask, my eyes not leaving McIntosh.

"Well," Nadia says, drawing the word out. "We can get him booked. But we won't be able to get him back in front of Collins until Monday. I spoke with his assistant and let me tell you, she was not happy to be disturbed at home on a Friday night." She takes a breath. "Apparently he's out of town for the weekend… golfing."

What a surprise. I cross my arms, staring at McIntosh.

"Pearce and Booth aren't the only ones in your pocket, are they?"

"I don't know what you're talking about," he says.

"All this obstruction, all the delays," I say. "It's all been engineered." I think it became clear to me when I noticed one of his guests at the party was a well-known friend of Collins'. A former judge who now works in the private sector. McIntosh has had his hands on this entire investigation from the beginning.

"You have no idea what you're walking into, Agent," he says.

"I think I'm starting to get an idea," I reply. "You'll do anything you can to keep people out of that place, won't you?"

He sneers at me. "You know, I wasn't sure it was *you* at my party until you introduced yourself. Had I known, I never would have let you in there."

"I guess that's the problem with having your hands in too many cookie jars," I tell him. "It's hard to keep track of who's coming and who's going." I huff, my options now limited. This was *exactly* why I didn't want to take him directly to booking. Once McIntosh is officially in the system, he'll throw up so much red tape we won't be able to untangle it for a solid *year*. And Collins will let him off with a slap on the wrist while casting doubt on our "evidence." We'll never get it to stick to McIntosh.

It was a pipe dream.

I push myself off the table and walk around it, pacing back and forth for a few minutes, thinking. We've been pigeon-holed here and need a new plan. My priority is getting to Zara and I had *hoped* to do it the legal way. But now I see that's impossible. Or at least, impossible to get to her quickly. I'm sure after a week's worth of back and forth with Lazar's "lawyers" we could finally get someone in there. But I'm tired of waiting. This needs to end tonight.

I turn back to McIntosh.

"How well do you know Warden Pearce? I know you said he was on your payroll, but have you ever met the man?"

"Not in person," McIntosh says. "But he obviously knows who I am." He looks around. "You know *none* of this will be admissible right? I'm being held without rights, under duress. My lawyers are going to tear you apart. It doesn't matter what I do or don't say."

Unfortunately, he's right. The recording we have of him could be ruled inadmissible. And yet, it's not entirely useless.

To get what I want… I think I'm going to have to make a deal with the devil.

"Ok, *Ward*," I say. "You win." He draws down his brows at me. "You help us get into Lazar, *tonight*, and this all goes away."

He leans his head back, cackling. "Girl, you think I'm not going to sue your ass for wrongful imprisonment? You'll be lucky if you end up writing parking tickets after this."

I smile. "No one writes parking tickets anymore," I say. "But thanks for reminding me how detached from society you actually are." I take a deep breath. "Here's the thing. I don't really care about what happens to me. What I *do* care about is some people who are at this very moment in danger of losing their lives to your insane experiments."

He chuckles. "Don't you get it? You have *nothing* on me. All you're doing is delaying the inevitable."

"Let me tell you what I get," I say, coming back around the table and taking a seat in front of him. "I get flashing the arrest of one of the world's most *generous* billionaires across the front page of every major American newspaper is going to send the stock price of your many companies plummeting. Your public image is about to be destroyed."

He scoffs. "It won't last, everything will bounce back, especially when I prove this was nothing but an unsanctioned witch hunt."

"Maybe," I say. "But the thing about humans is they love to build people up in their minds, but they love to tear them down even more. You've spent *years* crafting this perfect image people can look up to and you've done a hell of a job staying away from negative press. I imagine something like this will be similar to dropping an atomic bomb on top of your public image."

I see the flash in his eyes that tells me he's afraid of just that. He knows as well as I do that even a *hint* of a misdeed is enough to start the avalanche of bad press. Maybe he gets out from under it and maybe he doesn't. The point is he'll be under a lot more scrutiny.

"It won't matter in the long run. I'll come back. I always do."

"Uh huh," I say. "Meanwhile some of your *investors* might start to get nervous. And I can tell you, this Hypoxone thing won't just 'go away'. Even if you manage to get me fired, *someone* will pick up the slack. And contrary to what you believe, you can't buy off the entire FBI."

McIntosh sneers.

"That's option one," I tell him. "Option two is you cooperate, get us into Lazar. Push the blame for the Hypoxone on Pearce and Booth. You stay clean and out of the media because like you say, your name isn't on any of it."

He narrows his eyes, though I can see he's considering it. "One way or another, though, these experiments end. Tonight."

"No deal. You're not going to just let me go," he says.

"I don't like it anymore than you do," I tell him. "But I can't have it all. I can either go after you and probably fail, or I can take the win. I choose the latter."

"Why?" he asks, appraising me with his gaze.

"Because someone I care about is in trouble," I reply. Not formally arresting and booking McIntosh is the equivalent of kidnapping, which could very well cost me everything. But I've reached the end of my rope here. There's no way I'm letting Zara stay in that place a *second* longer than necessary if I have a way in. McIntosh can do that, at least in the short term. I'll deal with the fallout once I know she's safe. Right now, this is the only way.

"What do you want me to do?" he asks, his voice cautious.

I glance at Liam, who nods.

"Contact Warden Pearce. Tell him there's a problem with the shipments and you need to come in with a team tonight to clear them out. Tell him it's non-negotiable."

"Let me guess, I'm sending you in there."

"Not me," I say. "He knows my face. You'll be sending my colleagues." I motion to Nadia and Elliott standing by the door.

"Why do I even need to be there?" he asks.

"One, to make sure you follow through," I say. "And two so Pearce can't say no. We've already been refused access on multiple occasions."

He looks at each of us in turn before lowering his head and chuckling. "Let me get this straight. You'll drop this whole thing against me. No press. No being booked through the system. And all I need to do is get your people inside Lazar?"

"That's it," I say. "After we're done you'll be free to go."

"How do I know you'll keep your word?" he says. "I don't exactly have any guarantees here."

I get up in his face. "Because believe it or not, I care about something more than you and whatever fucked up program you're running," I say. "Now are you going to help us or do we drive you down to the local field office and book you for drug trafficking?"

"Well," he gives a wan grin. "When you put it like that… where's the phone?"

"Wait here," I tell him, and I motion for Liam to meet me outside the conference room with Nadia and Elliott.

"Are you sure about this?" Liam asks once the door is closed and he can't hear us.

"I'm not leaving her in there, Liam," I reiterate. "This ends tonight. Understand?"

He scrunches his features, looking at his feet a moment before glancing back at Nadia and Elliott.

"Uh, we'll… start making preparations," Nadia says, practically dragging Elliott away. Here I am, putting them both in a precarious position again. I can already feel Nadia's concerns, but right now, my focus is on Zara. Once she's safe, we'll deal with the rest.

Liam speaks, his voice low. "What if things go wrong?" What about us? What about everything?"

I glance at my ring finger on my non-injured hand. I only wore the ring for a few hours before needing to take it off again. I wish I could wear it forever.

Maybe they'll let me have it in jail.

"I know this isn't what we wanted," I say. "But you guys risked everything to get me out of a place that wasn't half as bad as that. I have to do the same. If McIntosh is telling the truth, and they're testing this drug on people in there, Zara could be in much more danger than we initially assumed. I don't care what it costs, we're getting her out."

He must see the determination in my eyes because he softens. "Think we can trust him?" Liam asks.

"Not in the slightest," I say. "But he's our only option. The key is not to leave him alone," I say, and fish in my pocket, pulling out his smartwatch. "And to make sure he doesn't get this back."

Liam smiles. "You're crazy, you know that?"

"It's one of my best qualities," I echo back to him. He pulls me in and presses his lips to mine and I relish in the feeling for a brief moment. If things fall apart in there, this may be the last time I get to kiss him as a free woman. So when he pulls away I find myself longing for him even more.

Through all this, we haven't really had a chance to stop and take a breath. And now, I may be putting our entire future together at risk. I can't imagine what a wedding ceremony in a federal prison would look like, but that may be the future I'm facing if I go through with this.

But what option do I have? Book McIntosh, let him make his call, he gets released and then we have to bring him back in for interrogation and try to build a strong enough case that Judge Collins can't ignore or throw to the wayside? And *then* we get to Zara?

No. It's too much. She's already been in there at least two days, maybe three. All the time Booth and Pearce know the FBI is breathing down their necks. If they're both conducting experiments for McIntosh, we may have inadvertently forced their hand by making them test faster, before an inspection team could arrive. Either that or they've already started moving their entire facility somewhere else.

In any case, we're out of time.

Chapter Thirty-Two

As the van rumbles along the dark road, the first drops of rain begin to splatter the windshield, causing Elliott to turn on the wipers. Nadia is beside him in the passenger seat, both of them clad in black tactical gear we had to procure from a local FBI office. Liam and I sit in the back, him in the same tactical gear, me in a less restrictive outfit, but still utilitarian. My shoulder is burning from all the movement recently and my finger continues to throb but I'm doing my best to ignore it for the time being.

McIntosh sits across from us, his knees up to his chest as he rests on the floor of the van. True to his word, he made the call to Warden Pearce to meet him and his "team" on site, using the excuse the FBI were closing in and he needed to move all the materials if the program was going to survive. It also had the benefit of solving one of Warden Pearce's problems at the same time. He won't want those drugs to be on the premises when the inspection team finally *does* gain access.

"Do you feel bad about it?" I ask McIntosh as the van hits a pothole, causing all of us to bounce a little.

McIntosh looks up, frowning. "What?"

"Jeremiah Frey," I say.

"Who?"

"The primary inspector assigned to Lazar," I add. "He killed himself."

"Oh," McIntosh says. "I hadn't heard."

Why am I not surprised? "Then he wasn't on your payroll?"

He sighs. "An operation like this requires greasing a lot of wheels," he says. "Whatever Pearce earned was more than enough to take care of those issues."

Convenient. He can just pass the buck off to Pearce and keep his hands clean. I don't know what it is about billionaires, but it seems like they've just lost all their humanity. It must be something about having gobs and gobs of money that changes the brain chemistry. He's barely even fazed by the fact someone killed themselves to protect his secret. It's like it doesn't even register for him.

"Em, we're approaching the main gate."

"Showtime," I tell McIntosh. "No games."

"Trust me," he says, getting up and moving to the front between Elliott and Nadia. "I want this all to go away as much as you do."

I push all the way to the back of the dark van, hiding in the shadows. I'm the only face anyone here would know, which means I stay in the van on radio while everyone else gets inside the facility. It's not ideal, but if they see me, the entire operation is ruined. Liam has promised me that Zara is his top priority while Nadia and Elliott will seize all the drugs, documenting everything so that when the arrest warrants finally come for Pearce and Booth, there will be no doubt as to their involvement.

With any luck they'll return to the van with the drugs, Zara and both of our victims in tow. Once I know everyone is safe, we'll skip right over Judge Collins and go straight to the

Attorney General. And if he needs an explanation as to why we were in there, I'll have Zara's video to show exigent circumstances. He won't be able to deny the truth.

Is it stretching the bounds of the law? Yes. But I believe it's still in the spirit. I've been hamstrung and obstructed more than my fair share on this case. It's time for some pushback.

"Yes?" a voice on the intercom answers.

"It's me," McIntosh says. "I called ahead."

"One moment." The gates open and Elliott drives the van through.

"Pull around to the loading dock on the east side," McIntosh orders. "Stay away from the front door."

"Why?" I ask.

"Because pickups and drop-offs don't happen out where everyone can see them," he says as if I'm the dumbest person in the van. I fume at him as Elliott pulls the van around to the east side of the property, following the pavement until we reach a loading dock. "Just park it there," McIntosh says.

"Remember," I tell him. "Stick to the script. One step out of line and the deal's off."

"You don't need to threaten me, Slate," he replies. "I just want this done and over with so I can go back and get some sleep."

I pull Liam close. "Stay safe. Keep me updated as much as you can." I hold up the small radio that's tuned to the same channel as the one that's part of their gear. Liam switches on a small camera mounted on his chest, the image going straight to an app on my phone.

"We're going to get her out of there," he says. "Don't worry. Twenty minutes and we'll be back."

Outside the rain is really picking up, and thunder rolls through the air.

"Check one," I say into the radio.

"Test," Elliott responds.

"Test 2," Nadia says.

"Test 3," Liam adds, smiling. "We're good to go."

"Good hunting," I say as Liam pulls open the sliding door, allowing him and McIntosh to get out. He keeps a sharp eye on McIntosh, though he keeps his weapon holstered. Elliott and Nadia do the same, all three of them "escorting" McIntosh through the rain up the concrete steps to the upper loading dock. There's a large garage door there with a smaller regular-sized door beside it. The regular-sized door opens to reveal one of the security guards for the property who says something low to McIntosh the radios don't catch due to the rain. Still, I watch through the window and on my phone through Liam's video feed as the guard nods and leads them inside the loading dock.

The door closes behind them and I'm left watching though Liam's feed and nothing more. The walk is silent, though another guard passes them by in the opposite direction, paying them no attention. A moment later he emerges from the door out to the loading dock, causing me to duck down in the van again. I peek above the window to see he's just standing there, watching.

What the hell? Is he just guarding the van? Or is something else going on here? I turn my attention back to the feed where the guard has guided the group into an elevator which takes them straight up to the third floor.

Funny how McIntosh doesn't seem to need any special security procedures for the "protection of the inmates." Ugh. I hate that I let that woman get to me.

"Through here," the guard says and I catch it over the open radio this time. He leads the group into the Warden's office where Pearce stands near one of the bookcases that's open to reveal a hidden drink station.

"Ward," he says. "Trying to wake myself up. Want one?" He holds out an amber-colored drink in a clear glass.

"I don't have time for pleasantries," McIntosh says. So far

so good. "The FBI is breathing down your neck and you didn't think to tell me?"

Pearce drains his drink and returns to his desk. "I have it under control."

"The hell you do," McIntosh says. "This puts the entire program at risk. And you're what... just sitting here, waiting for them to come break down your door?"

Pearce holds out his hands. "Everything will be moved before that happens. We're already making preparations. The lawyers bought us plenty of time."

"Let's get one thing straight here, Ward. You work for *me*. Which means you don't make a move regarding *my product* until I say so. Understand?"

McIntosh's tone is fierce and for a second I'm not sure he's acting. He is probably genuinely upset about this, especially if it was all to save his wife. Though... now that I think about it, he hasn't mentioned her again. Strange.

Pearce nods. "Yes, of course. I should have informed you."

McIntosh stands a little straighter. "I'm relieving you of your burden. Tonight. I'm taking all of the product off your hands. And I want both test subjects as well. Everything will need to be moved to a new site."

Pearce gives him an understanding nod. "We can make that happen. Though you won't need to worry about the test subjects. Unfortunately neither of them survived."

The air in the room goes still. "*What?*" McIntosh asks, his voice trembling for the first time.

"I was going to tell you, but we happened to get a third subject in and I wanted to wait to see—"

"Wait," McIntosh says. "*How* did the other subjects die?"

Pearce shrugs. "Bad reaction to the drug, I assume. You'd have to ask Booth. She knows more about it than I do. But as I was saying—"

I don't hear the rest of his sentence because I'm already out of the van, sprinting for the guard at the door. At first he looks confused at seeing another person coming out of the van he's apparently been assigned to guard, but then his eyes go wide as he realizes I'm an actual *threat*. He aims his weapon at me but I'm too quick and I get under it, lifting it up as he fires into the air before delivering a direct blow to his windpipe, causing him to crumple at my feet. I snatch his security badge off his belt and grab his weapon, opening the door with the badge as the general alarm sounds.

I race through the garage beyond as red flashing lights go off all around me. *Both test subjects dead. A third… unknown.* She *is* here. I knew it. But if McIntosh's experimental drug has already killed two women, who is to say it won't take a third? Not to mention McIntosh has to know that this changes everything. He's now on the hook for murder. Before I knew how serious this was I could look the other way, but I can't do that any longer.

As I use the keycard to get through another door, I'm faced with a variety of directions to go, though I'm not sure which way is the right one. Alarms continue to blare overhead and I pull out my phone to check on Liam, but the feed is gone.

"Come in," I say over the radio. "Anyone come in, can you read me?" There's no response other than static, but I can hear people yelling in all directions. Most likely inmates. That coupled with the increasing storm outside makes for a cacophony of chaos to my ears.

But before I can make a decision, something slams into me, sending me skidding back along one hallway, the gun flying from my hands and landing beside me. I look up to see McIntosh, his eyes wild as he struggles to get back up as well.

"Freeze!" I yell, grabbing my weapon and pointing it at him.

He grits his teeth, but raises his hands.

"What happened?" I ask.

"I'm not going down for this, Slate," he says. "It wasn't part of the deal."

"The hell you're not," I reply. "Two women died because of *you*. You're not getting away with it."

He shakes his head and begins backing up down the adjacent hallway. "You're not taking me."

I fire a round but it goes very wide, though he still flinches and ducks down, his hands still in the air. "Don't force me to shoot you," I say. That was supposed to be closer—a warning shot. My injured finger is affecting my aim. "I'm placing you under arrest. Where's the rest of my team?"

"L-look," he says, still trying to control the narrative. "I know you're here for your friend. You want to get to her? She's down that way." He motions behind me with his head. "The medical ward. She's probably being prepped for transport right now. Pearce has his hands full, but if you hurry, you can get to her in time."

"And leave you unguarded," I say, my weapon trained on him. "No chance."

"It's either that, or lose track of her," he says. "I don't know where Pearce will take her. And if you arrest me, I'll have no incentive to help."

I tense, faced with an impossible situation. I can't just let McIntosh go, can I? But I came here for Zara and he's right about one thing: I don't know how much time she has left.

I take a deep breath and lower my weapon. He nods. "I knew you'd do the right thing. Head down that way and take the second corridor on your right. It will lead you to the medical area."

"This isn't over," I say as he continues to back up, his hands still in the air.

"It's been nice knowing you, Agent," he says. He turns and takes off running.

"If anyone can hear me I'm heading to the medical ward," I say into the radio as I take off in the opposite direction. "McIntosh is loose in the building. I repeat, McIntosh is loose in the building."

There's still no response which worries the hell out of me. But Elliott, Nadia and Liam are together and they're armed. Whatever they're dealing with, I have to trust they can handle it. Meanwhile I need to do what I came here to do.

I'm coming, Z. Just hold on a little longer.

Chapter Thirty-Three

THE SOUND OF THE ALARM BREAKS THROUGH ZARA'S SLEEP and causes her eyes to snap open. She recognizes that alarm. It's a security lockdown for the entire building. Does that mean one of the inmates has escaped? Or is something else urgent happening? It's completely dark outside, the rain coating the windows above her with the occasional lightning flash illuminating the sky.

She tries to get up only to find she's been strapped to the bed... that and she's no longer in her "room." She's been transferred to the medical ward she found earlier, the same one where she watched Renata's vitals slowly fade. They mean to kill her here, just like they did Renata. Just like Tilly.

"C'mon kid, you can get out of this," a voice says. It's a voice she hasn't heard in almost fifteen years.

Zara struggles against the restraints, but they are pulled tight. She doesn't even remember how she got here. The last thing she recalls is trying to get out and running into Booth and her goons.

"Don't focus on that right now. Just find a way to get yourself out of here."

"I don't need your... *nngh*... help," she says into the darkness. She really must be losing it. Maybe she belongs in a place like this; a place for people with mental disorders. Zara thrashes one way and then the next, but it's no use. She can't seem to get herself free.

"Any bright ideas?" she asks, but there's no response. *What, now you're not so talkative?*

Above her the lights come to life and she has to shut her eyes for a moment for them to adjust. Booth comes rushing into the room before heading over to one of the supply banks and retrieves a new needle.

"What's going on?" Zara demands.

"We're leaving," Booth says. "I need to prep you to move."

"Leaving for where?" Zara asks.

"That's not your concern," she replies. "But I can't have you fighting me along the way. I need to put you under so we can get you out of here."

Booth fills the needle with a clear substance, but it doesn't look like the same poison she's been injecting into Zara's veins so far. It's probably some sort of anesthesia. But if there's one thing Zara knows, it's that she'll never have a better chance of getting out of here. If they manage to take her to another location, she'll never have any chance of escape. At least right now she knows *where* she is, if little else.

"Now hold still," Booth says as she approaches. "We don't have a lot of time." She tries to pull Zara's sleeve up, but the restraints prevent it. Booth curses under her breath as she's forced to loosen one of the straps to gain access to Zara's arm.

But that's all Zara needs.

With the strap loosened, she manages to pull her arm free and throw her fist directly into Booth's face, causing the woman to stagger back, holding her nose which is now squirting blood. It seems like all those defense classes of Emily's are finally paying dividends.

As Booth struggles to clear her vision and find the needle again, Zara manages to reach under the bed and free a second strap, the one across her chest, which gives her the ability to sit up.

"*No*," Booth yells and charges at Zara, grappling with her to get her back on the bed. Zara fights her off with everything she has, clawing and scratching every exposed inch of Booth's skin until she manages to swipe across the woman's eye, causing her to scream out as she falls to the floor. Zara works quickly to get another strap free, and then a third, until the only one left is the one around her feet.

"You will *not* ruin my future!" Booth yells, having grabbed a wooden crutch from somewhere. Using it as a weapon, she brings it down on Zara who can only try to block it with her arms. There's a crack somewhere and Zara doesn't know if it's her bone or the crutch, but she manages to grab the weapon from Booth and uses the rubber end of it like a pool cue and slams it into the woman's midsection, causing her to lose her breath and fall to the ground.

Her arm throbbing, Zara manages to get the last strap free and jumps off the bed just as Booth scrambles up again, this time with the needle back in her hand. "Go. To. *Sleep!*" She charges Zara with the needle, willing to stick it anywhere it will go. Zara tries to grab the woman's hand but it slips and they get into a tug of war over the needle, pushing it away from each of them until Zara grapples the woman to the ground. They roll over each other multiple times until Booth finally cries out and begins to go limp. Zara pushes off the woman, stepping back only to realize the needle penetrated Booth's upper chest and the plunger is down. Whatever she was about to inject into Zara is now flowing through her bloodstream.

Zara stands over the woman, her chest heaving up and down. "I hope your dreams suck."

"Zara?"

She looks up to see Emily in the doorway, dressed in what looks like tactical gear and a massive bandage around her fingers. She blinks once then again, her mind having already played tricks on her once tonight. "Em?" she can't be here. There's no way. Lightning flashes outside again, throwing shadow on her face.

Emily hurries into the room, a weapon at her side. "Are you… okay?"

Zara reaches out tentatively, and feels the warmth of her friend's hand as she takes it in her own. "You're really here."

Emily pulls her into a hug. "Of course I'm here. I wasn't going to leave you in this God-forsaken place alone."

Zara buries her face in her friend's shoulder. She can't believe this is real. What if it's another hallucination she's just dreaming up? Maybe she's still on that bed in la-la-land, subject to whatever Booth is doing to her.

Emily looks at Booth, who seems to have lost consciousness, a fractured crutch on the ground beside her. "Did you do all this?"

Zara pulls away from her, surveying the damage. "I guess I did."

"I have to say I one hundred percent approve."

"What's going on?" Zara asks. "How are you here?"

"It's too much to explain," Emily says. "But we need to move. I don't know what kind of security response *that* is going to trigger." She points to the blaring alarm at the top of the room, accompanied by the flashing lights.

"Then I'm guessing you never got that warrant."

Emily scoffs. "Far from it. C'mon, I'll explain everything later."

"What about her?" Zara asks, staring at the woman who had become a persistent thorn in their sides.

"She'll pay for what she's done," Emily replies. "But not right now. It's only the four of us here for you. The cavalry hasn't arrived yet. Here." She hands Zara the glock in her hand.

"What about you?"

"I've got my own," she says. "I pulled this off the guard outside." She holds up a keycard. "This is our ticket out of here." She heads through the door and checks the hallway beyond. Other than the sound of the alarm and the yells from inmates, there's no one else in their way.

"Where are all the guards?" Zara asks as she follows Emily down the hallway. But the more steps she takes, the drowsier she gets. *No.* She's not going to let whatever this shit is beat her again. She's going to make it out of this place, no matter what it takes.

"Hell if I know," Emily says, not looking back. "But I'm not about to look a gift horse—Z!" She turns back to see Zara leaning up against the wall, barely holding on to her weapon. "What's wrong? What's going on?"

Zara shakes her head. "It's whatever that crap is they pumped into me. Hy…hy—"

"Hypoxone," Emily finishes for her. "It's a drug for dementia. At least it's supposed to be," she says. "But it has a terrible success rate. There's no telling what it might be doing to you."

"It has a latent effect," Zara says. "The longer I'm up and moving the worse it gets." She wipes her brow, the gun clattering to the floor. "I don't know if it's an unintended side effect or what, but—" Her knees hit the ground, almost followed by the rest of her body were it not for Emily, who manages to keep her propped up.

"Here," Emily says, putting Zara's arm around her shoulder and hoisting her back to her feet. "I'm getting you out of here." She manages to get the gun and stuffs it in one of her many straps before virtually carrying Zara down the hallway.

Zara feels like she's about to pass out, the effects of the Hypoxone taking hold of her and dragging her back down.

"Does anyone read me?" Emily almost yells, Zara realizing

she has a portable radio strapped to her outfit. "Someone *respond*."

"Em," Liam's voice comes through, though there's a lot of static. "Where are you? Elliott is back at the van but says you're not there. We're having comm issues."

"I need help," Emily says. "East wing, medical. Does anyone have eyes on McIntosh?"

"—zzz—ing—posi—zz—" the line buzzes and cracks as another flash of lightning lights up the windows and thunder booms through the facility.

"Dammit," Emily says.

"McIntosh?" Zara asks, barely able to keep her eyes open. She wishes she could walk, so she could help Emily get her out of here, but her entire body has turned to mush.

"Ward McIntosh… the billionaire. He's running an illegal drug testing program," Emily explains. "He's been behind this whole thing. I got the information from Fletch."

"Why?" Zara asks.

Emily readjusts, getting back under Zara again and continues down the hallway. "He said it was for his wife. She apparently has early-onset dementia."

Zara's brain is foggy, but not *that* foggy. She might not be able to walk, but she can still think. "That's not true," she manages to say. "He's not married."

"That's what—ugh—I thought as well, but he said he kept it quiet to keep her disease from getting out." She pauses for a moment to catch her breath.

"No, Em," Zara says, struggling to maintain consciousness. "His wife died six years ago. And not from dementia. She died in an accidental drowning. I know because there was an FBI investigation."

"Wait, what?" Emily asks, setting Zara down so that they're both on the floor.

"There were… suspicious circumstances around her

death. The FBI…" Zara swallows, finding it difficult. "… investigated. Eventually cleared him. He's *not* married."

"Son of a bitch," Emily says. "Of *course* he was lying." She stares down the hallway, Zara barely able to crane her head. There's so much further to go.

"This is Slate to anyone who can hear me," she says. "I need assistance in the east medical wing. *Respond.*"

More static comes through the receiver.

"Just leave me here," Zara mumbles. "I'm… too much of—"

"Don't you say it," Emily replies. "I busted my ass to get in here to get you and I'm not leaving without you. If I have to throw you over my shoulder and *carry* you out I will." But they both know despite the fact Emily is as fit as they come, she doesn't have the raw strength to carry another person her size.

"You! Freeze!" They both turn to see a guard who has appeared at the end of the hall, brandishing a billy club.

"FBI," Emily says, holding up her badge.

"Yeah, I know who you are." Zara recognizes that voice. It's Armond, though her eyes feel so heavy she can barely hold them open. Still, she sees him barreling down the hallway towards them.

"Stop right there," Emily says, drawing her weapon on the man. "This is a federal operation and you will not interfere."

"You got no warrant," Armond says, bearing down on them and takes a swing at Emily with the billy club, which Emily manages to dodge. She squeezes off a round but the shot goes wide, missing him by a mile. Zara manages to train her gaze on Emily's bandaged fingers.

Armond swipes at her again with the club, just barely missing her arm and shoulder. Emily rolls to the side and kicks him in the side of the knee, sending him to the ground in a scream of pain. She uses the opportunity to get his hands behind his back and zip-ties them together with a nylon restraint.

"You're under arrest for assaulting a federal officer," she says.

"And…" Zara tries to say, but she's beginning to lose consciousness.

"Z!" Emily shakes her, but Zara can barely feel it. She's just glad she's here. That's all that matters now. "Stay with me."

But the world fades to black once more.

Chapter Thirty-Four

"Eм!"

I look up to see Liam sprinting down the hallway towards me. "She's unconscious," I tell him. "It's that stuff they pumped into her. She needs a hospital. *Now!*"

Liam surveys the man on the ground, writhing in pain with his arms secured behind his back. "Sorry, we've been trying to break through Pearce's people. He sicced all these guards on us. We got most of them into custody but it's a shit show up there."

"Pearce?" I ask.

"Got him," Liam nods, bending down to check on Zara. "She's still breathing." He gets up under her and lifts her under her knees and her shoulders. "I'll get her back to the van. Nadia is trying to get some backup on the radio but the communication out here is so spotty we don't know if the calls are going through or not."

He begins trotting down the hall and I keep pace with him, leaving the restrained guard behind. We can deal with him later. "What about McIntosh? Do you have eyes on him?"

Liam shakes his head. "He got past us in the confusion upstairs. I have no idea where he went."

I grit my teeth. "Get Zara out of here. I'm going to find him."

"Em," he says. "There's no telling where he could be. He could be running through the middle of the woods for all we know."

"No, he's still here," I say. "He's not going to escape into the dark woods in the middle of a storm without some way to contact someone. He's looking for a phone or something to call his people to come get him."

"We need to wait for backup," Liam says. "I don't know how many more people Pearce has under his thumb." He motions behind us. "Though you obviously took care of one of them yourself."

"And Booth is down too," I say. "Zara saw to that." I try flexing my hand, but of course I can't. The bandage prevents it from moving. It's also hindering my shots. That first shot should have caught the guard in the shoulder and it went wider than I expected. And my "warning" shot to McIntosh shouldn't have been so far off. Thankfully he didn't seem to notice at the time. But I can't count on my accuracy right now, which only makes this more dangerous.

"I already let McIntosh go once," I say. "I won't do it again."

"Once?" Liam asks as we come back to the intersection where I ran into McIntosh the first time.

"Just get her to safety. Leave me if you have to. Do *not* stay for me, understand?" I say. "She needs immediate medical attention."

"I can't let you do this alone," Liam says.

"Yes, you can," I tell him. "Now get moving. Don't make me turn it into an order."

There's clear consternation on his face—a war he's fighting with himself inside. I know that feeling. But right now, Zara needs to be our priority. "I'm coming back for you," he says. "Once she's safe."

I press my hand to one of the arms carrying Zara. "Love you."

"Love you back." He heads back for the garage and the loading dock while I take off down the hallway where McIntosh disappeared. Lightning flashes again, illuminating the dark hallway until I run into a security door. I use the keycard I got from the guard to get through and I find myself in an antechamber for the prison. There's a desk behind glass next to me and another door, but the desk is empty. I try the card on the second door and it opens, allowing me access into what looks like the main gen pop area.

There are four different corridors, each leading to a different common area which then splits into twenty or thirty units surrounding each area. I note the wards: B1-4. And the units: 300-399. There's no telling if McIntosh came this way or not, but if he *is* looking for a communications terminal, it's not here.

I'm about to turn back when I hear an errant scream somewhere down one of the corridors, which causes more commotion among the inmates. It's an eerie sound in a place like this, in the dark with no other noise but the constant blaring alarm and the storm outside. I head down the B2 corridor to the source of the sound, coming to the common area which is behind another security door.

It sounds like cries of pain or anguish coming from somewhere in the unit, I can't tell. But the more one person screams, the more the rest of the inmates do as well. Using the keycard, I open the security door to the ward, taking a cautious step inside.

Another scream from somewhere off to my left catches my attention, only for something hard and solid to hit me on the back, knocking me to the ground, my weapon skidding across the slick floor. I turn to see McIntosh, brandishing one of the guard's billy clubs as he stands over me. His hair is wet and matted and there's a crazed look in his eyes.

"*You*," he says. "This is all *your* fault."

I scoot back out of the way as he brings the club down in my direction again, though it misses and hits the concrete floor instead. Someone in one of the cells behind us screams something god-awful, sending a chill down my spine as McIntosh raises the club up again, the lighting illuminating the features on his face.

"It's not my fault that you were experimenting on innocent women!" I yell and roll out of the way as he misses with the club again. Already the back of my head is throbbing from where he caught me off guard, and I may be bleeding but I don't have time to check. I need to find my weapon. Scrambling across the floor, I search for it, finding it wedged under one of the tables that are bolted to the ground in the common area.

"I only did it because I had to!" he shouts back, practically chasing me down. I manage to get a foot up and drive it into his midsection, causing him to double over for a moment. Taking the opportunity, I scramble and reach for the gun, only for him to grab me by one of my legs and pull me back towards him, driving the club down. I barely get my arm up in time to deflect the blow, but it sends a wave of pain radiating through me that nearly causes me to see white spots in my vision.

"Your wife *died*," I spit at him. "You didn't *have* to do anything." His eyes go wild at the accusation and he yells, raising the club far above his head and aiming for mine, no doubt to bash my face in. Finally, my fingers find purchase on the gun and I swing it forward and pull the trigger at the same time, ignoring the aim. The bullet rips through his hand and the club at once, sending bits of wood and blood all over the floor as McIntosh screams, falling on his back and holding his ruined hand in the other one.

I take a breath and assess, feeling the back of my head. Yep, wet and sticky with my own blood. I'm going to need stitches. And my arm is killing me, but I don't think it's broken. I stand and train the weapon on him.

"Wait, wait," he blubbers, tears falling down his face. "Let's make a deal. I already called my people, they're on the way. Just… just let me go. I'll forget all of this. No one needs to know."

I glance at the bank of phones along one wall. *Of course.* There's something poetic about one of the richest men in the world needing to call collect for rescue. But he's not getting out of this one.

"No deal," I say. "You tried to kill me and you're involved in the deaths of at least two other women. Maybe more. I don't care how much money you have. You're going down."

"I can make it worth your while," he says. "Fletch… he was the one who gave me up, right?" Blood drips from his hand onto the floor as he scoots back away from me.

I eye him carefully. "Fletch provided intelligence about your connection to this operation."

McIntosh nods. "He trades in secrets. It's always been his bread and butter. But what if I could give you something that would give you the truth about him?"

"We already have him in custody," I say.

McIntosh lets out a small laugh, followed by a wince of pain. "He's not in custody because you *have* him," he says. "He's there because he wants to be. Trust me, if Fletch wanted to be out, he'd be out and you'd never be able to find him."

"I highly doubt that," I say.

"I have information," McIntosh adds, still scooting back until he reaches the wall, a bloody trail leading right to him. "Information he can't escape."

"Let me guess," I say. "All I need to do is let you go and you'll give it to me."

"That's right," he says. "Listen… I know what he's claiming he's done. But it's all a smokescreen. To keep you distracted. I have information on the *real* person responsible. Fletch is just taking the fall for them."

I eye him carefully. "What are you talking about?"

For the first time he grins. "You know exactly who I mean," he says. "Solitaire."

"Fletch claims he *is* Solitaire," I say.

"Of course he does, because that's what he's been ordered to do," McIntosh says. "But that's not the truth. If you want to know what's really going on… let me go. I can give you everything you need."

I go still for a moment. Is he offering what I think he's offering? A way past Fletch's lies… to find out who is *really* behind all this? Right now the CIA is convinced Fletch was really behind the bombing and the deaths of those other agents, including Janice. He confessed as much. But I always suspected he was covering for someone else. For this mysterious Solitaire I kept hearing about. This could be the proof I need.

And all I need to do is let a murderer walk.

"C'mon, Agent Slate," McIntosh says. "This is for the greater good. It helps everyone."

"Especially you," I say.

"Trust me, I don't do things *unless* they help me," he says. "So do we have a deal?"

This entire time I've been struggling with what happened to Janice, mostly because it seemed so *unfair*. And I just wanted to find a way to punish the ones responsible. Fletch sitting in a comfy prison cell only spat in the face of where he should really be after what he did. Or claimed to do. The point is, I'm still not sure. And it's been my goal to get to the bottom of it all, if for no reason other than to get Janice the justice she deserves.

But then I think back to this case—to all the obstacles we faced. All the *unfair* judgements and roadblocks thrown in our way when it should have been easy to get in here and I realize that sometimes there is no justice. You can't control the outcome of everything. But you need to keep moving forward regardless, otherwise you'll end up stuck.

If I let McIntosh go, it goes against everything I stand for. And there's no telling if he would keep his word or if the information would be accurate or not. Men like him think they can get away with anything. And maybe I was willing to let him go to save Zara's life. But I won't do it a second time to satisfy whatever personal need within me to find the truth.

"No," I say. "No deal. Ward McIntosh, you are *formally* under arrest for the attempted murder of a federal agent. You have the right to remain silent. You have the right to an attorney. I would say if you can't afford one, one will be appointed to you, but we both know you can. Put your hands behind your back."

He sneers at me. "You're making the biggest mistake of your life, Ms. Slate," he says. "I have powerful friends."

"Yeah, you told me once already," I say. "Parking tickets and all that. Stand up or I shoot you again."

"My hand is *ruined*," he says, holding up mangled fingers that continue to bleed all over the floor.

"Do it. Now," I say. He stands, but instead of turning around, he rushes into me. I try pulling the trigger but my hand is so sore I don't get the shot off before he knocks us both to the ground. He tries to shove his bloody hand into my face as I work to fight him off. Blood peppers my skin and gets into my eyes and mouth as he forces himself on me. I manage to drive my knee into his groin as hard as I can which causes him to cry out and pitch forward, falling on me. As I try to get him off, he's suddenly gone. I look up to find Liam has picked him up and thrown him against the nearby wall, yanking his hands together and cuffing him while he yells and spits obscenities.

Beyond him are Elliott and Nadia, both of whom help Liam take him into custody.

"Are you okay?" Liam asks once they've escorted him from the common area. He wipes my face with his sleeve to get the blood off.

"I need a shower," I say and allow him to help me up.

"Is…any of this blood yours?" he asks.

"Just the back of my head," I say, wiping my face the best I can, but it only smears McIntosh's blood more. "I must look pretty gruesome."

"No, just pretty," he replies. "Let's get some bandages for that wound."

I give him a look under hooded eyes. "Where's Zara?"

"Ambulance," he replies. "On the way to the nearest hospital. The cavalry arrived. We're rounding everyone up now."

"McIntosh's people are on their way," I tell him. "Don't let him out of your sight. We're booking him on attempted murder."

"Don't worry," he says. "We got him. I'm more concerned about you."

"I'll be fine," I reply. "What hospital are they taking Zara to?"

"C'mon," he says, grinning. "I'll drive."

Chapter Thirty-Five

I APPROACH THE DOOR THAT'S BARELY AJAR, NOTING THE ROOM inside is darkened. Not bothering knocking because I don't want to disturb her, I quietly make my way into the room. I'm just here to make a small delivery and then leave her to it. She's been through hell and I doubt she's in any mood for company.

I creep into the room to find Zara on the bed, her eyes closed. The head of the bed is slightly elevated, but as far as I can tell she's asleep. Slowly I make my way across the room and set the pack on the ground beside the only chair in the room.

"Hey."

I turn to see her eyes open and staring at me, but otherwise she hasn't moved. "Hey," I say. "I didn't want to disturb you. I was just coming to leave you something."

She smiles, though it doesn't reach her eyes. "I could use a little disturbance right now. It's so *boring* here."

"Are you sure?" I ask. "The doctors said you'd need at least three days here after the transfusion."

Zara nods. "I'm sure. I'm already feeling better."

I take a seat in the chair. "You sound better."

"Yeah," she says. "Not falling asleep every five minutes is actually a blessing. I still don't know what was in that crap that made me do that."

"I spoke to a specialist at the CDC," I say. "They now have the samples we took from Lazar. Apparently it has something to do with how the chemicals interact with the brain. They're supposed to slow the progress of the disease by interrupting the natural brain functions. It's dangerous shit."

Her mouth turns into a frown. "Did you remove Renata and Tilly's bodies?"

I nod. "And informed their families about what happened. Both families are looking at a class-action against Lazar *and* McIntosh. And that's on top of all the criminal charges we've filed."

"I need some good news," she says. "Lay it on me. The company here has been shit."

I chuckle. "Sorry. I've had everyone working overtime to get this wrapped up. We figured you needed a few days before you wanted a lot of visitors. The good news is we have Pearce and Booth on conspiracy, kidnapping and manslaughter," I say. "Both have admitted to it and are taking a deal to avoid trial." I snap my fingers. "Oh and that guard, Armond. We have him on attempted murder of you and me. He was driving that white truck that slammed into us. On Pearce's order, of course."

She leans her head back, taking in a deep breath. "No wonder I couldn't reason with him. He was part of it."

"As far as we can tell about half the staff was in on the program. They're shutting Lazar down for the time being, transferring all the inmates to different facilities. Pendergast and Vostov have passed the ball on to the Bureau who will be conducting a full and thorough investigation."

She smiles. "Then I guess that means we're not getting shut down."

I shake my head. "We're *not* getting shut down. They're

calling it a success and as soon as you're on your feet again, Pendergast is handing the reins of the program over to you, so *you'll* be able to sift through the data and find the cases we need to work."

"Wait, why me?" she asks. "What's—are you leaving?"

"No," I say. "Of course not. But I'm going to be a little busy and we decided you would be the best person to handle the program from here on out."

She narrows her eyes. "Busy with what?"

I raise my good hand; the one not covered in bandages to show her the ring perched on my finger.

She takes in a deep breath, her eyes going wide. "Oh my God, Em! He did it? Lemme see it." She reaches and grabs my hand before I can react. "That punk. He said he was going to wait."

"I think I kinda… forced him into it," I say. "I've been dealing with a lot of self-doubt lately."

She examines the ring further. "Oh this is nice. Cushion, high karat, looks like he didn't skimp. He kept trying to cheap out on you and I just about had to beat it into him that he needed to get you a *proper* diamond."

"It's actually a lab-grown diamond," I say.

She narrows her eyes. "I guess I can't complain. The less rocks pulled up by underpaid or unpaid people the better off we are, right?"

"Right," I nod, thinking back to my "buddy" at McIntosh's poker game. "In a related topic, this is kinda why I'm here." I pick up the case from the floor and open it.

"My laptop! Oh, you are a *godsend*, Emily Slate." Zara holds out both hands and I hand it over. "You don't know how much I've been missing this. I thought I was going to go crazy in there."

"It turns out McIntosh has been running these 'charity' events for a few years now. But having seen one in person, there's more going on there than I think anyone suspects. I was thinking if you got bored while you were getting better—"

"Say no more. You have just handed a rat a bucket full of cheese balls," she says, typing away. "Give me a day or two and I'll get you some real dirt." She pauses. "Wait, what's the deal with McIntosh? Did you find him?"

"Oh yeah, I found him all right. He tried to kill me before begging for his life—actually, bargaining for his life. He claimed to know who was really behind Fletch—who he's taking orders from."

"Solitaire?" Zara asks.

"Claimed that's who it is. Said he'd trade the info if I let him go. But I couldn't do it. I couldn't let him get off again."

Zara reaches out with one hand, placing it on my bruised arm. "That couldn't have been easy. I know how much getting justice for Janice means to you. Because it means that much to me too."

I nod, grateful for her reassurance. "He's facing murder, attempted murder, manslaughter, conspiracy, trafficking and a host of other charges," I say. "Most will probably get dropped in favor of the murder and attempted murder charges. We'll need to testify. Both of us."

"*More* testifying?" she asks. "We haven't even gotten to Fletch's trial yet."

"I know. But this is a big deal. His companies are falling apart with all the bad press. Looks like he's not everyone's favorite billionaire anymore. And if I have my way, he won't be a billionaire much longer. I plan to speak to the D.A. about breaking up his assets and redistributing them to charity."

"That's… a great idea, actually," she says. "I never did like that guy. His 'squeaky-clean' image was a little too good to be true. Especially for someone with that much money."

"Tell me about it," I say. "We think he had Judge Collins in his pocket, which was why we kept getting delays. But

Collins denies it and has decided to take an early retirement. Purely voluntary, of course."

"Oh, of course," she echoes before frowning. "You were saying something about McIntosh having a wife? Am I remembering that correctly?"

"Yeah," I say. "But you were right. She died years ago; I pulled the files. Something I should have done before taking him at his word, but I didn't know there had been an FBI investigation. How did you know about it?"

"Remember when you were down on St. Solomon? Rafe Connor?"

How could I forget? "Of course."

"Remember he tried to drown his wife? Well, when I was researching that case I came across McIntosh's. Kinda weird… two powerful men in the same business, both their wives 'dying' by accidental drowning."

I sit back, thinking. "Yeah… that *is* weird. You think there's a connection?"

"I don't know. But it might be worth keeping in mind," she says. "You never know."

"Well, regardless. I doubt he'll be signing many more checks. He's actually being treated in this hospital under heavy guard, but he's projected to lose at least one, maybe two fingers from where I shot him."

"Fitting," she says."

I shrug. "He deserved it. For everything he put you and Renata and Tilly through. Not to mention we're still looking for other victims."

Zara goes uncharacteristically quiet for a moment, staring off into the distance. I rub the back of her hand with mine. "Are you doing okay? I can't imagine what it must have been like in there for you."

She smiles. "Fine. I handled it."

"Z," I say. "I'm here. You know that, right? I'm here no matter what you need."

The smile drops a little. "I know. It's just… being in that place, maybe it was the drug, I dunno, but it brought back some uncomfortable memories. Stuff I've tried very hard to forget. And it's not anything I'd rather relive, if that's okay."

"Of course it is," I say, unsure what she's alluding to. As far as I know Zara had a relatively normal childhood, so I'm not sure what kind of memories she could be talking about. Then again, she's never really gone into detail about her past. "But if you ever *need* to talk about it, I'm here. No judgement, okay?"

She opens her laptop, turning her attention to it instead. "You need an engagement party."

I crinkle the edge of my mouth. "Do I? I think *you* need an engagement party."

"Well, whoever needs one, you're getting one," she says. "I'm thinking a week from Friday. Does that work for you? Should be enough time for me to pull all the invitations together, get the details set up, hire the pony and clowns and maybe even a bouncy castle."

"This isn't a birthday party for a six-year-old," I say.

"Hey, *everyone* loves a bouncy castle," she replies. "Plus, how many more times are you gonna get to do it?" She throws up "the horns" as she likes to call them—a hand symbol with her fore finger and pinky extended. "YOLO, am I right?"

I sigh. "Whatever makes you happy."

"This makes me *very* happy, thankyouverymuch. Oh and I'll get right on this McIntosh deal. I wanna see how wide we can throw this net. Maybe we can grab a few more stinky fish while we're at it."

"Knock yourself out," I say. "But don't overdo it. I don't want the nurses yelling at me because you're working yourself to death in here."

"Why not?" she asks, winking at me. "Think they'll give you the business? Like Nurse Booth?"

"If I never hear that woman's name again, it will be too

soon," I say, getting up. "I'll be back to check on you tomorrow. And I'll let the others know they can stop by as well. Nadia is particularly antsy to see that you're all right."

Zara smiles. "She's sweet. Okay, yeah, go, take care of everyone until I get back. But no more cases until I'm back on my feet. Agreed?"

"Agreed," I say. "Hey," I say, holding on to her foot still covered by a blanket. "You sure you're okay?"

"Em," she says in that condescending tone of hers that tells me I'm pushing. "I'm a big girl. I'll be fine."

"Okay," I say. "And hey, now that we're sticking around, we're gonna need that name after all."

Her eyes go wide and her smile goes from ear to ear. "Does that mean what I think it means?"

I sigh, having already resigned myself to this fate. "If you're dead set on Raptor Squad, I'll…back you up."

"Em, you just made me the happiest woman on Earth."

Epilogue

"You're sure you want to do this today?" Liam asks.

"I need to get it out of my system," I tell him. "I don't want to be thinking about this during the party."

"But what will it accomplish?" he asks. "It isn't like he's going to admit to anything."

I take a deep breath. He's probably right and this is a fool's errand. Still… I need to exorcise this from my mind. It's been there ever since I confronted McIntosh in the prison. No, before that. I want to be done with this demon and I think the only way I can do that is to face the devil himself. "Maybe not. But it's necessary."

Liam sighs. "Do you want me to come with you?"

"I won't be long," I say. I reach over and peck a kiss on his cheek, the new ring on my finger glinting in the sunlight. It's weird seeing a ring on my finger again and once I get out of the car, I remove it and place it in the inner pocket of my suit pants for safekeeping. No need to give him additional information.

Five minutes later I'm checked in for my appointment and I've deposited my weapon with security before being escorted down the familiar corridor. My heart thrums in my chest, but

I've been thinking about this moment for a solid week and a half and I'm not going to let it get away from me.

"Don't give the prisoner anything and take nothing from him. Do not engage in physical contact. Do not step past the yellow line. And let me know when you're ready to leave," the guard says.

Like I don't already know the drill.

He opens the outer door and I step inside the room adjacent to the cell. Inside the man looks up, his eyebrows arched in surprise. "Well, didn't expect to see you again so soon."

"Your intel checked out," I tell Fletch. "McIntosh was behind the whole thing. In exchange I've spoken to the DA about providing you additional amenities while you wait for trial. You'll get two more outdoor outings per day."

"That was certainly generous," he says, standing from where he had been on the bed. "Why the change of heart?"

"You gave us something of value, so you receive something of value in return," I tell him.

He draws his brows together before the hint of a smirk forms on his lips. "That wasn't the deal. The deal was the info for a favor. A *personal* favor."

"I've already done you a favor, Fletch," I growl. "McIntosh was ready to expose you for who you really are. Your lies about Solitaire. But it would have meant letting him go so I refused. As far as I'm concerned, your debt is paid. With interest."

"Huh," he says, rubbing his chin. "That's… surprising. I would have thought you'd have taken that deal."

"As much as I'd like to know what's really going on in that head of yours, I'm not willing to sacrifice my principles to do so," I say. "Unlike *some* people. There are some lines I won't cross."

His eyes flash. "Sounds like you did me a solid, then. But of course, I'm *not* lying so there really is no cover up. I *am* Solitaire and have admitted to as much. So regardless of whether you think you helped me or not, I still consider us at an… imbalance."

"Think what you want," I tell him. "But my debt to you is paid."

"Then I certainly hope you never need anything else," he says. "Because next time I won't be so forthcoming."

"The only thing I need from you, is for you to stay behind bars for the rest of your natural life. You want to be a martyr for your boss? That's fine by me. We'll see how you feel in another ten, fifteen years. Maybe I'll come back and check on you then."

He narrows his eyes. "Careful, Agent Slate. You don't want to make an enemy out of me. We were just starting to get along."

"I don't *get along* with criminals and people who kill innocents," I say. "You won't be seeing me again until your trial." I turn to head out, finally feeling good that I've cleared my conscience.

"I will say this," he says just as I get to the door to knock for the guard. "For someone who no longer looks to control the outcome of everything, you seem particularly sure I'll be in here for a long time."

"We have you confessing to the crimes," I say. "At this point, the trial is a formality."

He cocks his head at me. "I guess we'll see."

There's something about the way he says those words that sends a chill down my spine. What could he have cooked up? Whatever it is, I don't like how confident he is.

Stop it. This is what he does. He gets in people's heads. He's just bluffing to try and get me to flinch. But I won't give him the satisfaction. Instead, I call for the guard and leave Fletch standing in his cell, alone.

Over the past few weeks I've questioned whether I made the right call or not, if justice for Janice and the other dead agents was worth McIntosh getting away with literal murder.

And every time I come back to the same conclusion over and over again: *No.* Janice wouldn't have called it justice had that been the case. She would have called it revenge. That's not who I am, and it's not who I want to be. Because then, I'm no better than Fletch—willing to do *anything* to get the outcome I want.

Two women died needlessly. And Zara was almost the third. *Someone* had to be held accountable.

As I head back to the car where Liam sits waiting, I shift my focus and pull the ring back out of my pocket, placing it on my finger again. Things are looking up. The program is a success, which means our jobs are safe. Zara is back home and already close to a hundred percent. And sometime in the near future, I'll be getting married again.

Somehow, I can't believe life could be this good. So I just take it one step at a time.

And enjoy it while I can.

The End

To be continued…

Want to read more about Emily?

In Sable Cove, generosity comes with a deadly price.

Until the bodies of Gareth and Petra Voss are found on the shores of Lake Michigan, the picturesque town looks like a postcard of perfection. But FBI Special Agent Emily Slate knows better. The prettier the surface, the darker the secrets drowning beneath it.

Thrust into a double murder investigation, Emily and her partner Zara quickly realize they aren't just looking for one suspect—they are staring down an entire town with a motive. Navigating a web of long-buried resentments and silent alliances, Emily finds that anyone in Sable Cove could have pulled the trigger.

But the twisting case isn't the only thing threatening to derail them. Zara is battling the lingering ghosts of a recent trauma, and the suffocating pressure of the investigation is pushing her to the breaking point.

As the walls close in, Emily is forced to confront a chilling reality. How do you catch a killer when everyone has a reason to want the victims dead? And what happens when the people you trust are hiding the deadliest secrets of all?

In the nineteenth gripping installment of the Emily Slate series, Amazon bestselling author Alex Sigmore delivers a pulse-pounding thriller about the promises we make, the secrets we keep, and the devastating cost of the truth.

To get your copy of *A Deadly Promise*, CLICK HERE or scan the code below with your phone.

New Series Alert!
A twisted killer lies in wait…

.   .   .

I hope you enjoyed *The Killing Jar*! While you wait for the next installment in Emily's story, I'd like to introduce you to Charlotte and Mona, two amazing detectives who are after a very twisted killer.

When a woman's body is discovered in Oak Creek, local police quickly dismiss it as an accidental drowning from years ago. Brought in from Chicago to help with the case, Detective Charlotte Dawes has worked on more murder investigations than she'd like to remember. An examination of the body tells her what local police refuse to see – somebody moved the victim to this remote location.

After a local artist is found murdered, her body positioned to match one of her final paintings, the sinister truth can't be ignored. More disturbing still, the artist's other works seem to predict who in the small town will be next to die, in increasingly macabre ways.

As fear grips the town, Charlotte discovers a link between the first victim and a local cop, and it's clear the killer has planned their moves meticulously. In a community where everyone guards their secrets, Charlotte must determine who's truly playing on her side, before she becomes the next target…

What readers are saying about *The Darkest Game*:

'This is the start of something special… prepare to fall in love with this new world and its darkly addictive pace.' Reader review,

'I was completely held hostage by my Kindle the whole way til the end.' Reader review,

'Okay, wow! This book was just… whoosh! Mind blown… a masterclass in suspense. Gripping, intelligent, and so compelling, I reread it the moment I finished. I haven't been able to stop thinking about it since.' Reader review,

'I'm kind of fangirling right now. Honestly, I was blown away by how much I enjoyed it.' Reader review,

Interested? CLICK HERE to snag your copy of THE DARKEST GAME!

Now Available

I can't wait for you to read it!

CLICK HERE or scan the code below to get yours now!

Bonus

There's a click of the bolt and the door on the other side of my cell opens. At first I think maybe Slate has had a change of mind and has reconsidered my offer. It was stupid of her to reject me; she'll regret that soon enough. But I go still when I see *him* walk in the room, my eyes going wide.

"Fletch," he says, his deep baritone voice resonating through the cell.

I stand, keeping my voice low. "What are you doing here?"

The man looks back at the guard who has closed the door, leaving them alone. "I just wanted to check on my favorite… son. How are things? They treating you okay in here?"

"Fine," I say, unsure what his *real* reason for being here is. He wouldn't risk exposure unless it was very important.

"I understand you've had a visitor lately. A young woman."

"That's right," I say. Of course he knows. He has eyes everywhere. The whole reason I'm in here is to protect him and he has the *audacity* to show his face? Not that I could ever tell him that.

"And? Is she interested?" he asks.

"Maybe for a short time," I say. "But no longer."

"Mmm." He places his hands in the pockets of his *very* expensive coat. "That's unfortunate. She seems like a nice young woman."

I know exactly what he's getting at, but it seems my attempts to sway Emily Slate have fallen on deaf ears. Then again, she has been here *three* times. Maybe I've done a better job of getting in her head than I initially assumed.

He leans to the side, looking around me. "Been doing some reading?"

"Not much else to do," I say. "When you're cut off from everyone and everything. But hey, good news. I get a few extra outdoor periods until the trial."

His face darkens and somehow his voice deepens. "Do not take that tone with me, *boy*. Don't forget who you're talking to."

I wince and pull it back. "I… apologize. It's… stressful in here."

"You'll sit there and enjoy it if you know what's good for you," he says. "You've caused me enough consternation as it is. You could very easily not wake up tomorrow morning. Do I make myself clear?"

I nod. "Crystal."

"Then do as you're told, sit there and read your silly little books. Since you don't seem to be good for much else these days."

It's as if I've been slapped, but I maintain my composure. "How much… longer will I have to endure this?" I ask. "I have business to attend to."

He leans forward, past the yellow line. "You know the deal. You get your freedom back when you deliver *her*. Until then, get comfortable." He steps back and pretends to survey my space. "Looks like you have everything you need. I'm glad I came by. It's always good to see a friendly face."

I wouldn't call his face anything near *friendly*. In fact, quite the opposite.

"Take care of yourself," he says. "Maybe I'll see you at the trial."

My eyes go wide, which only produces a smile on his face.

"See you around, Fletch."

I watch the man who has single-handedly engineered both my best and worst days on this planet leave as if he doesn't have a care in the world. Somewhere, deep inside, part of me considers coming clean. Of telling the FBI *everything*. But doing that would only put a target on my back.

No, there's only one way out of this.

And that's straight through Emily Slate's beating heart.

The Emily Slate FBI Mystery Series

Free Prequel - Her Last Shot (Emily Slate Bonus Story)

His Perfect Crime - (Emily Slate Series Book One)

The Collection Girls - (Emily Slate Series Book Two)

Smoke and Ashes - (Emily Slate Series Book Three)

Her Final Words - (Emily Slate Series Book Four)

Can't Miss Her - (Emily Slate Series Book Five)

The Lost Daughter - (Emily Slate Series Book Six)

The Secret Seven - (Emily Slate Series Book Seven)

A Liar's Grave - (Emily Slate Series Book Eight)

Oh What Fun - (Emily Slate Holiday Special)

The Girl in the Wall - (Emily Slate Series Book Nine)

His Final Act - (Emily Slate Series Book Ten)

The Vanishing Eyes - (Emily Slate Series Book Eleven)

Edge of the Woods - (Emily Slate Series Book Twelve)

Ties That Bind - (Emily Slate Series Book Thirteen)

The Missing Bones - (Emily Slate Series Book Fourteen)

Blood in the Sand - (Emily Slate Series Book Fifteen)

The Passage - (Emily Slate Series Book Sixteen)

Fire in the Sky - (Emily Slate Series Book Seventeen)

The Killing Jar - (Emily Slate Series Book Eighteen)

A Deadly Promise - (Emily Slate Series Book Nineteen)

No More Chances - (Emily Slate Series Book Twenty)

At All Costs - (Emily Slate Series Book Twenty-One)

The Ivy Bishop Mystery Thriller Series

Free Prequel - Bishop's Edge (Ivy Bishop Bonus Story)

Her Dark Secret - (Ivy Bishop Series Book One)

The Girl Without A Clue - (Ivy Bishop Series Book Two)

The Buried Faces - (Ivy Bishop Series Book Three)

Her Hidden Lies - (Ivy Bishop Series Book Four)

One Dark Night - (Ivy Bishop Series Book Five)

The Oak Creek Thriller Series

The Darkest Game - (Oak Creek Thriller Book One)

Never Strike Twice - (Oak Creek Thriller Book Two)

Standalones

The Forgotten Wife

A Note from Alex

Hi there!

Thanks for joining me on this new journey with Emily and the crew! I have to admit, I was a little scared about releasing this book. *Fire in the Sky* was such a blockbuster that I wasn't sure I could create another book as compelling and interesting.

As authors, we often do that. We'll write something thinking it's the worst thing in the world only to read it again later and think "maybe that wasn't so bad after all". And I think *The Killing Jar* is one of my favorite Emily books yet. It combines all the things I love: creepy castles, sadistic villains, a race against time all under the umbrella of fighting for the truth and finding the good at the end of it all.

I hope you enjoyed reading it as much as I enjoyed writing, because this was hands-down one of my absolute favorite books to write. I love how the group continues to support and be there for each other even in the darkest times. But if you've read the book you already know there is a lot to celebrate too.

Stay tuned, we've got plenty more to come.

Sincerely,

Alex

P.S. If you haven't already, please consider leaving a review or recommending this series to a fellow book lover. Your support is crucial for continuing Emily's adventures. Thank you, as always!

www.ingramcontent.com/pod-product-compliance
Lightning Source LLC
Chambersburg PA
CBHW020919060726
47591CB00004B/1319